# WAIT for LOVE

A BLACK GIRL'S STORY

Also by Wanda D. Hudson

LuvMe

Dating Wanda

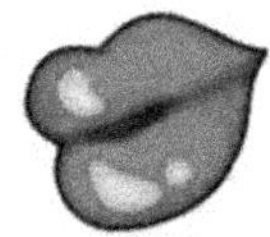

*Miss Luv's Books*

®*Miss Luv's Books*

*Because Everybody Needs A Little Luv!*

Miss Luv's Books
www.wandadhudson.com


First Printing 2008
ISBN 13: 978-0-9815325-1-6
ISBN 10: 0-9815325-1-9
LCCN: 2008901625

Printed In the United States of America

Cover Design: CANDACEK – www.cckwebdev.com

# ACKNOWLEDGEMENTS

Thank you God for the special gifts and talents You have bestowed upon me. The lessons You have taught me my entire life weren't taken to heart. Thank You for continuing to teach me. The Life Exam I've received these last five years was long and hard in its instruction but I will never forget it.

Diana, no matter what you accomplish in this life I will always be proud of you. Never fear the unknown. Reach until you get it. Come to me if you don't. I'm Mommy, I'll always be here for you with love.

Dasia, my sweet little Poopah de Doop. I simply adore you. You came to me when I just didn't know what I needed. You made me breathe when I had no air. I promise you the world is yours. Mommy loves you.

My mother, my father and my brother. Sometimes I wish we were on 22nd Street again. In my memories it was just perfect.

Mrs. Billie Hudson, thank you for your expertise. You did

a wonderful job. Are you ready for novel number two? Miss Sharon Gray of Eve's Literary Services, thank you for your input on part one. Candace, the book cover lady, thank you for your patience and skills. To Michelle, my ATL therapist. Thank you for always listening. Gevell, Keisha, Sheila, Turgenia, Miss Lisa, Jackie, and Linay.
You ladies are always there for me. I truly appreciate all of you. Teresa D, my number one Niagara Falls fan. Jamie, my number one Niagara Falls fan. I love you both.

If I haven't mentioned you I apologize. I truly thank everyone who has ever read a paragraph, a page or a sentence, and encouraged me to write.

If you have ever been in love, or something that was within the classification, this book is for you.

*Wanda D. Hudson*

*For Renee*

*You never had to Wait For Love…you had it all along.*

# Prologue of My Life

## Part One

What else can I possibly do to make him marry me? I don't ask for anything but his love, I've lost weight for him, and if he asks me to get on my knees and beg I will. Maybe he found out about my miscarriage. Is that why he treats me so bad?

"Lynnde! Don't you hear me calling you? Is dinner ready

"I'm coming right now, Otto."

This should do it. He asked for steak, mashed potatoes and peach cobbler for dessert. Through his stomach and into his heart. Yep, this should do it.

## Part Two

"Why don't you move back home with your mama and daddy? I'm trying to get on my feet. If I get a place in my name and I'm late with the rent then what?"

"Don't worry about the rent, Terrance. I'll pay it. I'll pay all the bills."

"Aight. Can you start by paying my car note?"

I should end this right now. I don't love him. Hell, I don't even love myself. *Speak up, Lynnde.*

"Well, are you going to pay it or not?"

"Yes, Terrance. Of course I will."

## Part Three

Thank you, God, for allowing my eyes to see another beautiful day, especially this one, my fortieth birthday. I can't believe I'm forty. Earlier in my life, I thought forty would be the age when you could stick me with a fork and I'd be done.

When I was in my twenties, of course, I knew all there was to know. During those years life was made up of money, love, and sex. Once I hit the big three-zero, I thought I was an expert and wouldn't need any help with the coming years. Now as I look back, I realize what a dumb ass I truly was.

During my early years, the one fact that eluded me was life is a learning process, a never-ending education. The more knowledge you receive, the more fulfilling your life will become. Open your mind. Listen. Don't only hear.

And with that, let the story begin.

WAIT for LOVE
A BLACK GIRL'S STORY

# A Fool Is Born

# I'm A Big Girl Now...

My first venture into the real world was a trip to Florida as a so-called adult. I went to attend a stewardess school, but I blew that opportunity in a major way.

At age eighteen I was pregnant and got rid of my baby by wishing her away. You should know that wishing was one of the things I did best. Wishing my baby away was much more despicable than any man made remedy. I made a mistake by thinking I was an adult and acted like a child when the reality of life confronted me. The saying, "Be careful what you wish for," is oh, so true. I never prayed much, but when I did, it was always something bad to happen. I suffered a miscarriage. God gave me the most beautiful gift He could give, and I wished He would take it away because of my stupidity and ignorance. Death should've come and taken me away for having such hateful thoughts.

My father and I didn't get along very well during my teen years so I blamed him, not the in-your-face fact that being eighteen and ignorant was my fault. If he'd treated me better, I wouldn't have been in such a rush to leave home, and my pregnancy never would've happened.

One day, during my senior year of high school, I saw an advertisement for a stewardess school in Florida. That was it for me, my ticket out of his house. I figured I'd go to the school for the six weeks it required, get the training, and make tons of money as a flight attendant. Then, I'd take care of my mother so well she'd never want to see him again. This had to work. This, I had to do.

The best part of the deal was that the training was free, as long as you signed an agreement to take a job with an airline of the school's choice. That was fine with me, I just wanted out of that house.

Everyday my father spouted lectures on air travel safety and it's history. We never interacted much but got along pretty good during my last weeks at home. Most of his energy towards me was for the fact that he was happy that the school was free. I should've given him free things all along if that's what it took to make him happy. But what could I have given him if my unconditional love wasn't getting the job done?

My parents threw me a big going away party that almost made me change my mind after seeing all the people who came and hearing all the testimonies of love for me. I started to think, "Why should they miss me, I'll just stay here." My long-range goals told me otherwise.

My best friend, Esta, (no, not Esther) was there with her fiancé, Larry. We'd been best friends ever since her family moved down the street from us when we were both eight years old. She was an only child like me, so we became play sisters. Larry became her play boyfriend at age ten, her real boyfriend at age sixteen, and now it seems that they are in it for the long haul.

Many of my relatives were there from my mother's side, and a few of my female friends from school came as well. I usually hung out with Esta and Larry, you know, like a third wheel. They never seemed to mind, and if they did, they never said so.

School and home, at least that's what my father always said, were enough for me. I couldn't wait to leave. Countless people told me I blossomed into a beautiful young woman, and I was in a hurry to show myself to the world.

The looks that I received from the boys at school blew my head up to the size of a watermelon. I felt like one of the Super Friends. Kapow! Blam! Boom! Any woman would die for the breasts, booty, and thighs that I had. It was a shocker because it seemed like I transformed overnight. I still stare at my freshman picture and smile at how shapely I was for a sixteen-year-old girl.

My father wouldn't allow me to date boys and as he put it, "All them boys wanna do is get into your desperate pants. Ain't no man gonna want no woman that's been all over town and got a bunch of raggedy ass kids trailing along behind her."

I was only a teenager and never understood what he meant by calling my pants desperate. The only thing I put in my pants was me. He did allow me to go to my high school prom with a boy of his choice.

What a nerd he was. He was the only guy besides Larry who attended my going away party. All the boys I knew were scared of my father. They thought he was mean and crazy. Hell, I knew he was mean and crazy. They were right. I don't blame them for not coming. My father played racquetball with Willard's father and it was either, "This boy or the TV." Reluctantly I replied, "Thank you, daddy."

Willard Sims. Willard wore black-rimmed glasses, plaid bow ties, and I'd swear his father's leisure suit pants. My father probably didn't think he was the type to try anything like the cool boys would.

Yeah right. Every time he looked at me he drooled. When we were slow dancing, I only danced because I liked the song, he tried to move his hands from my waist to my rump. I gave him an "uh-uh fool, don't try that mess" look, and his hands moved up to my shoulders.

When Willard brought me home he whined for a kiss on my lips.

"Duh-huh, Lynnde. Uh, huh, can I have a kiss? Duh-huh a nice long wet one would be nice. Let's use our tongues, too."

N-A-S-T-Y. I didn't want my first kiss to be with that dork.

"Willard, kissing is special to me. I want my first kiss to be with my husband, okay?"

He still wouldn't give up trying to place his lips on mine. Willard looked at the ground and then circled his head as if he was examining the universe. He startled me when he shuffled his feet like he was about to roll a strike.

"Duh-huh, let's get married then."

Under my breath I muttered the words, "stupid ass," and was quite rude by going into the house and closing the door in his face. I wanted to slam it but my mother would have had a fit. Willard was outside a while because I heard his car start up as I undressed. Before going upstairs to my room, I was busy staring at one of my prom pictures that I took with Esta and Larry and telling my parents about my evening.

Three days after my big shindig, I arrived in Florida. So many emotions were running through my mind and body, but excitement was the one that stood out the most. My mother and I cried at the airport and my father told me to buck up and be a man about it. That statement made me think he wanted a son.

When the plane landed, I felt like I traveled to another country I was supposed to conquer. There were people from the school holding signs letting us know which way to go. I looked like an idiot half walking and running towards them, making sure they weren't going to leave me.

Upon arriving at the school I met my roommates. Eliza Parker was from North Carolina, and Tamara Hunt was from Texas. They were also eighteen, fresh out of high school, and had the same high hopes as me. There were twenty-five of us in the class; sixteen women, and nine men.

Well, we all know I never became a stewardess, and you wouldn't have either if you met him. Who could concentrate on stewardess business after seeing the finest male creature to ever walk the earth? Keep in mind I was a young know-it-all who learned what she thought was correct in less than twenty-four hours.

Lamar, Lamar, Lamar. Uh, uh, uh. Lamar Hilton was twenty-eight, beautiful, and would become my husband. Please stop laughing and let me finish my story. He stood six feet-two inches tall and had smooth sweet butter pecan brown skin.  His eyes were big, sexy and brown, and he had a Rudolph Valentino mixed with Billy Dee Williams flair. His lips were plump, and I would share my first kiss with them. He had muscles, more muscles, and a voice that could soothe any savage beast, so just imagine what it did to me. All he had to do was show his pillar white teeth-inviting smile, and he had me right where he wanted me.

Lamar brought me a rose to class every day and took me to dinner every night. I was going to leave out the part about the roses being fake and the dinners being at a fast food joint, so you wouldn't see how dumb I really was, but if I'm going to tell my story, I might as well tell the truth.

I'm not making excuses for myself, but I was just out of high school, had never been away from home, and didn't know anything about men or being with one. There was no way I was prepared for what was about to happen to me. What was I supposed to do with a grown man I thought I had to have? Nothing. He knew it and I knew it. In this life who ever does the right thing before checking out the wrong one first? Many of us do what's pleasing to us or whatever feels good. It doesn't matter if it's right or wrong.

My problem was I always was in such a hurry. For years my mother said not to rush my life along, that age would come fast enough. I hated to admit it but she was right. She was always right. Some people are smart like that, so don't work against it, just accept it.

I was almost kicked out of the school for being late and missing class. With the instructions I gave, I could've crashed a plane that was still on the ground. I was in love. Uh, that statement didn't call for any laughter so cut me some slack, will you?

Lamar was from Detroit and said he was on a mission to better his life. He didn't volunteer any more information and I didn't ask. Who cared, I was his woman, he was my man, and we'd be married one day. Now I'm laughing. How could I have been so stupid?

After one week of him giving me the beauty queen treatment, he said we should become one. Lamar claimed I was his soul mate and he wanted to show me how much he cared for me. People search their whole lives for their soul mate, and I found mine on my first try. Dumbass. He also said it was going to be beautiful, and he'd be gentle with me, since it was my first time and all.

I told Eliza of my upcoming sexual romp and would've told Tamara but she dropped out of school the first week. She had a nightmare of being killed in a plane crash and that was enough for her.

Since I didn't have much money Eliza and I went shopping for my first time outfit at a store called

Cheap Is Where It's At. I flipped over a two-piece blue short set that was neither made of silk or satin. To this day I don't know what the material was, but I hoped Lamar would love it as much as I did. Fear became my friend shortly after my purchase. I told it to leave because I trusted Lamar totally. Lamar loved me even if he never told me so and would never do anything to hurt me. After we were together physically, he'd tell me he loved me, I was sure.

We arrived at the Roadside Motel at 7:30 that evening. As soon as we walked into the room he began kissing me. He stuck his tongue into my mouth and then licked my face. I thought that was nasty. Who wants someone else's spit all over them? And another tongue in your mouth, too? I didn't know what was coming next and the fear that left me earlier returned with its best friend, terror.

Insecurities crammed my mind as I excused myself from the room.

"Lamar, uh, I have to use the bathroom. I'll be right back."

"Don't take to long. I have a special thing for you," was his sexually vibed response.

I backed away from him and as I bumped into the doorframe I said, "Oh, uh, okay."

In the bathroom I sat on the toilet watching my hands tremble. Lamar asked if I was all right, so I must've been in there a long time. I answered "yes" but should've said no, came out, and told him I wasn't ready for this. Of course I didn't do what was right for me. I put on my seven-dollar outfit, decided it was now or never, and walked out of the bathroom shaking like a stripper at closing time.

Lamar had fallen asleep so I turned to walk back into the bathroom. I planned on asking for some extra courage to come from somewhere to join me. I was unlucky in my attempt. Lamar woke up.

"Hey, lover girl," he mysteriously whispered to me. "Where are you going? Come on over here and let me give you something good."

I didn't say anything as I turned to him with a mild look of fright on my face. He was totally naked.

Lamar smiled and started to rise up off the bed. His body parts rose right up along with him. As he walked towards me I thought, "What in the world is he going to do with that thing and where is he going to put it? Won't it get in the way?"

By then I was petrified and lost my senses. Instead of running or telling him that I was scared, I stood still like a frozen fudgecicle, complete with a stick up my rear end. Lamar reached me, pulled me close to him, and began kissing my face, neck and mouth. He made sounds that I never heard before. The only thing I was paying attention to was that thing down there. It was touching me and I wanted to cry, faint, and throw up.

Lamar hypnotized me with his eyes and growled in a below ground zero voice, "Don't be scared, it's going to be good."

When he picked me up and carried me to the bed I felt like a queen in a romantic movie. My heart started moving up out of my stomach but that feeling didn't last for long. I felt sick all over again when he got on top of me. That thing was on me. It was down there. Nothing has ever been down there.

What was I supposed to do now? I love my mother, but she didn't tell me anything about this. All she said was that sex was beautiful, only have it with your husband, and it was going to hurt. Why didn't she tell me what to do or how I should feel? Too late now.

Lamar told me to relax and that he wouldn't hurt me. That fool didn't know what he was talking about. I do know that he enjoyed himself because he kept saying how good it was, and making some other incoherent noises.

This was supposed to be enjoyable? My entire first experience was traumatizing and the pain was unspeakable. How can you enjoy what felt like a Mack truck trying to enter a cheerio? Picture that for a second will you? Talk about tears. I cried out loud, but he didn't hear me because the louder I cried, the louder he yelled. I was scared his penis was going to come out of my back, or get stuck inside my ribcage.

No, my first experience wasn't enjoyable at all. Where was the gentleness? He rammed that thing inside of me and kept on ramming it. How many times was it supposed to be rammed? Maybe he wanted a prize for a certain number of stabs and jabs. I wasn't ready for sex at all.

Oh, my knees were past my ears and damn near embedded in the pillow. I wasn't a gymnast going for the gold so none of it felt good or natural to me.

Lamar stopped drilling for oil a few hours later. Thank you, Jesus. He asked me if I enjoyed him. Arrogant idiot. I said yes and should've kept my mouth shut because we did it again and again and again. Then he went to sleep.

My first romp with Lamar felt like an attack by some kind of wild beast - a gorilla running wild in the city with the SWAT team, the FBI, and the Secret Service in pursuit. My initial thoughts were that Lamar was fine with all the trimmings, but if this is what sex was like, he'd better find himself a new love.

As I lay next to him in the fetal position afraid to move, I needed my mother. She truly loved me if she did this with my father to get me. Oh, God. I just pictured my parents having sex.

While straightening myself up and walking to the bathroom, my mind was filled with one question. Did all the pain I just felt come from one woman named Eve because she ate an apple?

At some point in my brief lifespan, someone told me Eve is the reason hurricanes are named after women; women talk too much, are so nosey, get beat up, cheated on and are just plain nags. The person that said it was a man. Dummy.

After that night I had officially moved to a town called Fuckville because that's all Lamar wanted to do. No more fake roses and cheap dinners, just a whole lot of sex; mornings, evenings, and everything in between. Most of the time I didn't want to have sex with Lamar, but he was a man, and you know you must please a man.

Eliza said I was crazy and that having sex that much wasn't normal. Still, she high-fived me while ranting and raving, "Thank God for the pill."

Out loud I replied, "Yes, thank God for the pill." But silently I thought, "What's the pill?"

Now look, if I knew nothing about sex and how to do it, what was I supposed to know about protection? The dumb look on my face prompted Eliza to blast me with, "You do know about the pill don't you?" I didn't answer her and was cursed out for the second time in my life. She told me to pray that I wasn't pregnant. Where was my period anyway?

For once I didn't make a wish or say a prayer. Being pregnant wouldn't be so bad. Lamar and I loved each other so a baby would be complete our family. No, he never told me he loved me, but his actions spoke louder than any words. His sexual actions showed me he loved me. A man wouldn't have sex with you if he didn't love you, right? Who just laughed?

Only two weeks of school remained and Lamar and I went into over drive. He acted like he was never going to see me again. He knew he was never going to see me again is the correct statement. During our last night together, I asked Lamar what would he do if I were to get pregnant. He told me all the things he knew I wanted to hear, including how he'd marry me and we'd be the perfect family.

"Why did you ask me that?" He curiously added. "I know you want a career and want to wait to have kids. It's not possible because I know you're on the pill, but I'll be ready and waiting when our time comes."

What's up with the pill anyway? "Yeah, Lamar. You're right. Uh, I was only making conversation." We then started our final love making session and finally stopped, signaling our last time together. I didn't know this at the moment; I thought I'd be married in the coming months and my life would be wonderful.

At the end of the graduation ceremony Lamar and I discussed the possibility of his coming to see me in a week. "Damn, girl. I hope I can make it one week without you. You know how I can't sleep without gettin' some lovin' from you first."

I wanted to ask him to marry me right then and there. I explained my home life to him and we agreed to stay at a hotel when he came to visit. This conversation took place at the airport where we shared a final farewell kiss and went our separate ways.

Three smiling faces and a bundle of balloons greeted me as I exited the plane. I was happy to see my parents and couldn't wait to tell Esta of my first grown up experience. She spent the night at my house and we stayed up all night gabbing. I told my parents how well school went and about the people I met, all the while bragging about how the life of a stewardess was the career for me. Of course I didn't tell them about Lamar. I'd wait until he came to visit, and we'd tell them of our love and impending marriage together. What's so funny?

My life went on even though I thought I wouldn't make it without Lamar. Three days had passed and I hadn't heard from him. Most likely he was busy getting reacquainted with his family and friends.

On the fourth day I decided to call him. Instead of hearing his sexy voice, all I heard was a recording saying the number had been disconnected. Figuring I misdialed, I dialed again, and stopped pounding the keypad twenty times later after finally accepting that it was the wrong number.

The period that never came kept me in the bathroom checking myself. Esta suggested that I go to the free clinic to take a pregnancy test. My naivety showed and I blew it off as a time zone thing.

Esta let me have it then. "Lynnde, New York and Florida have the same time! What's wrong with you?"

Knowing it was my fright and my stupidity working against me I fought back. I listened to Esta, knowing she'd never harm me, and went to the clinic. Once the nurse told me I was pregnant, I started to cry like an innocent man in the electric chair. Esta said I should tell my mother, but I decided to tell Lamar first. Once he arrived we'd tell my parents together. Please let him call tonight.

He didn't. The next day I called information and was given a number that wasn't even close to the one Lamar gave me. That was probably just a mistake. Lots of people forget their phone numbers, right? Maybe he did try to call. We didn't have call waiting so every time someone was on the phone I behaved like a drug fiend. When no one was on I kept picking it up, so I was a wreck either way. All those feelings were behind me now. I had his number and I couldn't wait to tell him of our joyous news. I'd have to put my career on hold but I didn't care. Lamar loved me. I'd have a good husband and a baby, that's all I needed.

My heart jumped championship double-dutch as I dialed his number. When he answered four rings later, my stomach did the jitterbug.

I heard aggravation and sleepiness along with his, "Hello."

"Hi, Lamar," came from me in a short excited breath. "How are you? I haven't heard from you and I miss you. I hope everything's all right."

"How did you get this number?" was his abrupt response. No "hey baby," or "I miss you too," or anything else a man would say to the woman he loved.

"I called information because I wrote your number down wrong. I miss you, Lamar."

Instead of receiving the same affectionate phrase in return, I heard one that stung worse than two full beehive attacks.

"I didn't give you the wrong number. I gave you the number I wanted you to have. What is it you want anyway?"

Damn. What happened to all the sweet talk I was getting down in Florida? I needed to hear some of that right now. Tears swelled my eyes as I lost all sense of control and blurted out my joyous news.

"Lamar, I'm pregnant. I'm sorry. I love you." I sounded like a jerk, but all I wanted to hear was how he loved me and everything would be fine. He didn't say anything. "Lamar, baby, did you hear me?

"Yeah." After a heated pause he exhaled heavily and then said the last words he ever spoke to me. I still hear them. The frostbitten hateful tone, that he must have wanted to direct towards someone else, sprayed all over my body. This was a mistake. He loved me. He couldn't mean what he was saying.

"Your getting pregnant is your problem. My wife and I are expecting a baby and I can't, and won't, do a thing to help you. You're on your own. What did you think was going to happen? Did you think I would marry you or something? Well, if you did, you thought wrong. You're not my type. You're just a kid. Next time you want to play a grown up do yourself a favor and play by the rules. Protect yourself. Don't be so stupid and think someone like me is going to be with someone like you. And don't ever call here again because I'll deny knowing you." The line went dead as I responded.

"Hello? Hello? Lamar are you still there?" A dial tone was the only thing that answered me. My heart went underground and my brain followed. And then came the tears, so many tears. I thought my head was going to explode. What did I do to make him speak to me that way?

Did I hear him say he had a wife? When did he get married? What about us? Didn't he love me anymore? Did he ever love me? What about his baby? Doesn't he even want his baby?

After my last thought, I began slapping myself. This was a nightmare; this wasn't real. Maybe that wasn't Lamar on the phone. Maybe I called the wrong one? That's it. I called the wrong man. My Lamar would never speak to me that way.

Why didn't anybody tell me that man didn't love or care about me? He probably didn't even like me. They should've told me I was just being used for my super friend body. Who are they? Oh don't give me that. You know who they are. The people that don't have a name or a face but are always in your business.

That's when I felt pain all over my body, especially in my stomach. You stupid baby! If it weren't for you, Lamar would want me. This thing has to get out of me. All I have to do is get rid of it. I'll call Lamar back and everything would return to the way it was. He wasn't really married; he just said that because he was scared. He loved me; he had shown me how much. You only have sex with someone you love. Yeah right. I'm so damn dumb. Where is death when you need it?

Crazy thoughts rambled through my head and out of my mouth.

"Oh, I know what I'll do. I'll drink a glass of bleach and get rid of it that way." I pulled myself together and went to the laundry room to get the bleach. After I retrieved the gallon jug, I thought I'd need all of it, I went into the kitchen, got a glass, and went back upstairs to my room.

Talking out loud made things seem rational so once again in a voice that sounded like mine I heard, "The sooner I drink this bleach and get rid of this problem, the sooner I can call Lamar back and tell him I made a mistake. He'll want me back then."

I poured myself an eight-ounce glass of bleach and turned the glass slowly towards my mouth. As soon as it touched my lips it burned and I dropped the glass on the floor. My parents never redid my room and the blue carpet in there still has a white spot in the center of it.

Once I stopped gagging I had another brilliant thought. I'd fall down the stairs. Dumb idea. All I did was twist my ankle. Why did I let this happen? Lamar was so fine. I was too stupid, always in a hurry. Just go away, baby. Please, just go away.

I was miserable. I called Esta and asked her to come over. When she walked in the door I started crying, which was the only thing I could do right, and told her what a fool I'd been.

"Oh, Esta! Lamar rejected his baby and me! I don't know what to do!"

"Lynnde, calm down. I'm here for you, but you have to tell your mother."

"Esta, I can't tell. It will hurt her." Thinking of my father's reaction of killing me, she seconded the motion of not telling.

Trying to sound sensible, Esta said, "Why don't you call Lamar again? He was probably surprised by the news and didn't know how to react."

"I can't call Lamar until this baby is gone!" is the passion that blared from every pore of my body. "Why couldn't this happen to someone else?" We then heard the front door open and my mother calling my name.

"What are we going to do now? We have to do something," were Esta's panicked filled words. Her eyes were about to lift up and out of her head. At that moment I realized how much I loved her for wanting to help me. She was just as scared as I was, and I hated myself for putting her through this.

A disgusting mood took over me. Thinking I could wash it off I started towards the bathroom. Esta looked at me as if she were waiting on an order. "Grab my shades off the dresser. I need to use the bathroom." She obeyed and I ran into a temporary safe haven. The disgust I felt changed to a clammy feeling on my body. It made me want to jump out of the window to escape my life.

I called to my mother, "I'll be right down," and thought how glad I was that it wasn't my father. We went downstairs and told my mother we were going for ice cream, and I'd be back in time for dinner.

"Okay, baby. Be careful and don't eat too much. I don't want you to spoil your dinner."

Mother, I love you. These words came from the sweetest woman on earth. No way was she going to find out what I had done.

Esta and I walked to the park and sat there for a while. She seemed to think somehow my parents would understand, and they would love to be grandparents. I couldn't see what she saw. All I could see was my mother crying and my father yelling at me for the entire world to hear. I'm sure he'd say he wished I were a boy because boys don't do stupid things like this. Who would he think did this to me? It wasn't a boy at all. It was a grown man.

Why didn't I know about the pill? Why didn't Lamar tell me? I should never have had sex with him in the first place; I didn't know what I was doing anyway. This is all my father's fault. Everything is his fault. If my mother had taken us away from him none of this would be happening. I swear I'm going to make it my first priority to kill him as soon as this baby is gone.

As we sat in silence I thought about the one positive force in my life. What did I do to deserve Esta? Right now, I wish I were her. She has a good father, a boyfriend that wants to be married to her, and most importantly, no unwanted baby ruining her life. She isn't stupid like me. Nobody is stupid like me.

My walk home was an episode from Lost In Space. I felt as if it were my first time traveling a route I'd taken so many times. I wanted to ask myself where I was and who I was. Once I saw my house, my starring role in a show that will never air made all my who's, what's, and where's disappear.

The only good thing about arriving home was that I got there before my father did. My mother was glad also; she wanted to talk to me. Please don't let her know. She can't know.

"Lynnde, I'm so proud of you for having the courage to leave home and take on the world. Whew, I'll never be as strong or as smart as you, and in no way would I be able to be a stewardess so high up in the sky."

My mother who sometimes didn't think her heart could hold all the love she had for me, and even though she'd miss me, was so glad I wanted to take a chance in life.

"Lynnde, baby. You get out into this big ole world and show it what my baby is made of. Don't let anything or anybody hold you down. If you ever get scared don't be ashamed, no there's nothing to be ashamed of. Just come on home to your mama because I'll make sure you're safe and always have so much love."

We were standing up facing each other while holding hands. After hearing what she had to say, I fell to my knees and burst out crying.

"Oh, baby. Don't cry. I don't want to see my baby cry. Everything's going to be all right, you'll see. Now stop all this fussing, you hear me? I don't want you to mess up that pretty face of yours."

She held me close and rubbed my face, head, and back and it felt so good. I wasn't able to speak. I wanted to tell her how much I loved her and would never do anything to hurt her. This baby had to go now. This would devastate my mother. She wanted so much for me, and I couldn't let her down. I'll take an oath if I have to. I'll never let you down, Mother.

"Baby, remember when you were sixteen and I told you I never graduated from high school because I became pregnant with you? To this very day I've never regretted my decision of getting married and having you. I wouldn't change a thing if I could."

I can't hurt her. I can't. This baby has to go.

We heard my father pulling up in the driveway, and I got up with my mother's help.

"Go and fix yourself up, baby. I don't want your father asking questions because this is between me and you."

She watched me walk up the stairs with a look of pride on her face that I never noticed before. This baby has to go.

After dinner I turned in early, telling my parents I had a busy day tomorrow. I was scheduled to go back to Florida in nine days and said I wanted to go and see a few people. This time when I walked up the stairs, they both watched me. I felt sick to my stomach. The thought of committing suicide turned on the light bulb in my pea brain. The grief stricken vision of my mother's face quickly turned it off.

As I lay in bed, I saw Lamar and the nights we spent together. What kind of man would keep having sex with you especially if he knew you didn't like it? I never actually told him I didn't like it but he knew.

Every time he was finished with me I wanted to talk. He would always say, "We have to get back to the school now. I'll talk to you tomorrow." Why was I so stupid? I should've asked him if he was married or if he had any kids. Maybe I should have waited two weeks instead of one before having sex with him. Maybe he would still want me.

The only thing I could think of next was asking God to take this baby out of me. I got up out of bed, got down on my knees and started asking Him to do just that. I can't say that I was praying. You're not supposed to pray for bad things to happen. I'd say I was wishing. Wishing for this not to be happening. Wishing for this to go away so I could start over again. Wishing for Lamar to come and see me and tell me he wanted us to be a family. I wished all night long during my interrupted sleep. Wishing that I still wouldn't be stupid, dumb, retarded, shoot, all of the above, in the morning. Wishing for a solution to the confusion I'd made.

My wish came true. I woke up at 5:30 in the morning with the nastiest cramps I ever had in my life. I smothered myself with my pillow to stop from screaming out loud. What in the world was happening to me? I begged for the cramping to stop but it didn't. It got worse. I wasn't the smartest person on earth but maybe I was having the baby. It wasn't time yet, was it?

Aloud I silently asked God to please let the hurting stop. I tried to get up and go to the bathroom, but the pain wouldn't let me move. Then I felt something wet between my legs. I'm thought I was dying.

The agony that took over my body prevented me from opening my mouth and calling out for my mother. The pain was worse than Lamar. I promised myself right then and there that I would never have sex again. Damn, I was dumb.

Dialing 9-1-1 was my next thought, but the noise would wake up my parents. Oh, God, let this pain stop. I need to get to the bathroom, get some towels and go boil hot water. Isn't that what you're supposed to do when you're having a baby?

When the cramps began to ease, I stood up. The heavy feeling and the wetness between my legs was enough to make me vomit. I walked slowly towards the light switch and hoped the baby didn't cry out too much. If my parents heard it, I'd be busted. Flipping the switch and seeing my bed made me muffle a scream. The blood, there was so much blood. My thighs down to my toes were covered in it. The sheets were blue when I put them on the bed. They resembled dark wet spinach green. The light smell of ignorance combined with freshly rotting fish attacked my senses. I wanted to disappear. Why don't I know what just happened, and where is that baby?

Hating the way the blood felt on me made me walk with my legs apart. It was thick and discolored and slimy. When I reached my bed, I stood and stared at it like it wasn't mine. There was no way all that could have come from me. I moved the covers back thinking the baby was under them, but it wasn't. Where did it go? After the pain I just felt, I know that baby came out.

Painstakingly, I managed to pull off my pajamas and put on my robe. If that baby was still inside of me I was going to get it out. I went to the bathroom, sat on the toilet, and began to push. The feeling was excruciating and I didn't know what I was doing, but I kept on pushing.

More blood came out but still no baby. Taking a shower would make me feel better and maybe, with enough scrubbing and water pressure, I could wash that baby out of me.

After my shower I went downstairs to get some garbage bags for my sheets, there was no way they were going to come clean. I put on some underwear and a Kotex pad, and kept checking it for confirmation of what just happened to me. While stripping my bed down, I still felt cramps, but strangely, there was no trace of blood and no baby.

My mother kept aspirin in the medicine cabinet and I took a few to subside the aching throb. There was nothing in there to help my brain shove out smart thoughts, though. The garbage bag containing my sheets and pajamas were hid in my closet. I'd wait until no one was home and throw it in the dumpster in the alley where it wouldn't be thought about again.

It was 6:34 a.m., and at 7:30 every one would be gone. I'd call Esta and tell her I had that baby, but I didn't know where it was. She'd know what to do; she'd help me find it.

I didn't know anything at age eighteen. If I told my parents, I wouldn't have had to endure the coming years of unnecessary heartache I put myself through. Even after I called Esta, and told her what happened, and even after we came back from the free clinic and the doctor explained to me that I did indeed have a miscarriage, I would've handled it better.

I thought I wished my baby away, thought God didn't think I was good enough to have a child. My losing that baby made me think I wasn't good enough for anyone, and that it was my fault. I didn't realize it was something I had no control over. Instead of hating myself for years, and thinking I was unworthy of any good happening to me, I could've been loving me and meeting people who would be a positive force in my life.

Wishing my baby away made me turn to food to comfort me. I thought if I ate enough, and felt full all the time, my body would feel complete, whole, like a baby was actually inside me. The only problem with that was I never felt full enough. I just kept eating and eating and only felt like I was extremely overweight.

From the day of my miscarriage, until the nine days later when I was supposed to leave, I gained a total of twenty-six pounds. After my airport episode, which I'll fill you in on in the next chapter, my weight doubled. Within six months of my miscarriage, I put on another forty-three pounds. Of course now I realize I should have told someone. I needed help. Depression consumed me and I relinquished everything but the air I breathed.

There was my mother who never said anything to me about my weight besides, "Lynnde, baby don't worry about your weight. Most men like a woman with a little meat on them."

My father was the total opposite. I disgusted him. He paid for me a year's membership to a health club because he thought he was going to die watching me go up and down the stairs.

"Damn! Looking at your fat ass is going to give me a heart attack you fat-pig-hog girl! Ha, ha, ha!" I'm glad my mother wasn't home to hear him say that or to see my reaction. I did what I did best; you got it, burst out crying. As I walked up to my room crying, all my father said was, "Shit, I hope you hurry up the stairs, I'm sick of hearing your voice." Yeah, he loved me all right.

Esta knew I wasn't happy but she did her best to try and cheer me up. She wanted to be a fashion designer and used me as a model, which kept me in style for the fat girl that I'd become. As long as I looked nice why should I worry about losing weight? Being two hundred and ten pounds was all right with me. Never mind the fact that I had once been one hundred and twenty five, that didn't matter. I had gotten rid of my baby, and anything bad that happened in my life was deserving of me.

Of course there will always be the whys. Why didn't I just tell someone? Why wasn't I smarter? Why was I even born?

I never thought about Lamar after my miscarriage. He didn't care about me so my baby and my life were none of his business. I didn't even want him anymore; he wasn't fine enough to make my life miserable. No man was for that matter. One day I'd learn that looks weren't everything.

My first life lesson was about trust and ignorance, and never having the two meet at the same time. This is a lesson I didn't learn until much later. Once I accepted it as the truth, nothing seemed like a burden anymore. Eventually, I learned to be responsible for me, and that no one will take care of you better than you can. No one will care for you if you don't care for yourself.

# What Am I Doing?

When I allow my mind to wander, I think of my younger days. I'm always reminded of the small beliefs I had, like the one of when I reached the age of forty; my life would be half over. I figured if I were going to live until the ripe old age of sixty, forty would be the start of my down slope. Time would be running out, so I'd better hurry up and do something meaningful.

At some point I opened my mind and realize life doesn‘t start ending as a person grows older, and every life has meaning. Life is measured in time, but at any age, a goal can be accomplished. A sixty year-old person can take a trip around the world the same as a twenty year-old person. The difference will most likely be the capacity in which they view what they see. When I was younger, I viewed ten thousand dollars as a colossal amount of money. Age made me view it as money, but not a colossal amount.

For the next two years following my miscarriage my life went into a rut. I earned ten thousand dollars a year and still lived at home.

"Your rent is one hundred dollars a month but it ought to be at least one thousand with all the food you eat."

My father made me sick with all of his hurtful comments but he was right. I hated myself after I weighed in at two hundred and forty eight pounds. He always added, "You're the fattest twenty-year-old person I know." Silently I would always answer with, "Why don't you die and you won't know me anymore." I had to get out of his house.

The only reason I hadn't moved was because my mother didn't want me to leave just yet. She'd say, "Don't pay your father no mind, baby. He's just talking out of his head." I hated him.

I took a computer class three nights a week because my father said, "High tech is where it's at." My reason was because the class was right next to a donut shop. I really wasn't into the class, but the donuts kept me going. Usually, by the time I got home my father would be asleep, so I didn't have to see his face.

At the age of twenty-one I purchased my first car. It was a two door black Ford Escort. Esta and I wanted to celebrate and decided to go to what was called a Scorpio party. Every year, a large group of people who had birthdays in October and November got together and threw a bash. We heard the party last year was a fashion, food and people extravaganza. There was no way I would miss the one this year.

As excited as I was, you'd think the party was for me. It cost eight dollars to get in and all the food and drinks were included. I planned to eat a big meal before going so I wouldn't look like all I wanted to do was eat. One of my coworkers told me they always ran out of liquor. Actually, it was kept in the back for the people who were celebrating a birthday. That piece of information didn't bother me because I wasn't a big drinker, but there had better be plenty of food. Wow, that was quick. A millisecond barely passed and I changed my mind about the food. I said I'd eat a large meal so I wouldn't overeat when I got there. Oh well.

Esta wasn't a big drinker either. The first time she tasted an alcoholic beverage was at Larry's going away gathering the week before he left for the Marines. She had a bit too much champagne, and I don't know what happened afterwards, but she decided to only drink it with him. Every time she thinks about that night, she has the slyest grin on her face. Esta said since it was our first Scorpio party, she'd have a few glasses if they had any. I hope they do. She's been missing Larry lately so hopefully the party, along with a little bubbly, will help to cheer her up.

Thank goodness for small miracles, which in this case would be the large pantsuit Esta made for me. I had a hard time finding something decent to wear and went into the maternity section looking for something cute, but ended up looking like a hungry baby elephant in a flower garden instead.

Mentally, I decided to step up my exercise routine a few notches but was only physically walking once a day in the park. Every time I finished my slow stroll, I went and had a rather large meal to reward myself. I've accepted the fact that my slim days are long gone at the tender age of twenty-one, so I make sure I never miss any meals that I'm supposed to, or not supposed to have.

Regardless of my size, I really hope I meet someone special tonight. I haven't had sex in over a year, and sometimes I feel like if I got it more I wouldn't eat as much. Me not eating? That would be a catastrophic sight don't you think? Huh? Sex? Oh, you caught me. You're thinking the only time I had sex was when I was eighteen. That should've been it but I experimented again. When would I ever learn? I'm quite embarrassed to talk about it but the story goes as follows.

The transaction took place with a man named Roger Pitkins. He worked with me at the shoe store, and I thought he was the ugliest man alive. So why did I have sex with him? He talked to me, which translated into he liked me. Besides my father's put downs no man even bothered to speak to me. I thought I was onto something and felt a tinge of self-esteem. It's too bad my momentary uppity attitude made me see Roger as someone who was purple blue-black black with a tainted shine.

Is there something wrong with a dark person? No. He was just an ugly one, which was brought on by my attitude. His eyes were so big they reached you before he did and one wandered around. Every time I witnessed his eyeball roll, I wanted to slap him on the side of his head. He was overly knock-kneed; malnutrition type skinny, and his teeth were the color of burnt yellow butter. And his use of the English language was something no animal alive could understand. He usually worked in the stock room, so he didn't interact with any customers.

I don't quite know how I let our working relationship become a physical one. Why did I allow myself to be used by him? He told me he thought big healthy women were sexy, and I was the prettiest girl he'd ever seen. Roger always asked me to go out and I always said no.

When he kept asking it was as close to begging as I ever had. With that, I thought he liked me and figured he didn't look that bad after all. Any brand of toothpaste and a few speech lessons were all he needed.

We decided on dinner and a movie the coming Saturday. When I told my parents I was going on a date, my mother was thrilled. She wanted to help me with my hair and offered to take me shopping for the perfect outfit. I told her that would be Esta's job, but I needed her for support. My father's reply was, "Something must be wrong with that boy if he wants a big ass girl like you." He asked was he handicapped, and what kind of car was he going to haul me around in. Then he walked out of the room. I wished he would plummet, I mean hit the ground so hard that his head popped off and died, but I heard him in the kitchen on the phone. I guess I didn't wish hard enough.

Roger and I made plans on a Thursday and it seemed like Saturday would never get here. I was excited because I figured we'd get to be friends, and then I'd help him step up his style. Never mind what I looked like; he wanted me just the way I was. Finally, my life would be complete.

Saturday arrived and Esta came over to make me gorgeous, or at least make me look presentable. She pressed out my shoulder length hair and pulled it up into a bun with cascading curls. With an artistic eye she applied my makeup to rival that of a beauty queen. My outfit consisted of a long blue skirt with a small split and a matching blue shirt. I said I looked like walrus bait and was glad my father wasn't there because he would've said, "Well, they gotta eat, too."

My mother folded her arms and with the loving look she always had on her face said, "Baby, you're still beautiful whether you think you're fat or not. Now stop talking crazy and have a good time." She then began picking imaginary lint balls off of my clothes. We all walked downstairs and as I thanked her I silently hoped the night would be amazing. My thoughts halted when I saw my father sitting on the couch.

"Lynnde, you look better than you did earlier. Enjoy yourself tonight."

I stood stunned for a moment and then thanked him. I still wanted him dead, but coming from him the comment was nice.

Prince Roger, the man of my dreams, picked me up at seven o'clock. He came to the door with one red rose in his hand. I introduced him and the smiles on their faces told my secret of never going out on dates. That part of my life was over now I thought.

Roger actually looked fine. He wore a brown silk shirt and black dress pants. His hair was cut in a low top fade and his teeth looked a normal shade of yellow. Maybe I was only seeing what I wanted, but I thought he looked a little different. His car was a green Chevette and was spotless. I imagined us riding in a horse drawn carriage. Talk about a fairytale imagination.

Once Roger and I were in his car, he asked if I wouldn't mind going for a drive and talking. He said he wanted me to himself and wanted to get to know me a little better. Delighted, I almost exclaimed yes but nodded instead. After fifteen minutes of compliments, we ended up in a motel parking lot. I asked what we were doing there, and his answer was he thought he was in love with me. Roger said I was so beautiful, he had to have me and added the many fantasies he had about me. That's all it took for me. He was never late for work and that had to count for something, didn't it?

His yellow teeth clacked when he asked to borrow twenty dollars. He then went to the front office to get a room. As I wondered if he'd ask me to pay for dinner, my first sexual experience appeared. It couldn't be like that because I knew what to expect. I wanted to have sex because that's what he wanted and he wanted me. When he came back to the car he opened my door, and led me to our first and last encounter.

We entered the room and before the door was halfway closed, Roger was naked. He was black skeleton skinny without any clothes on. Maybe I shouldn't do this? Maybe I should tell him we should wait? We didn't even have dinner yet and I was hungry.

I stood in the middle of the room half afraid to open my mouth. When I finally decided to say something, Roger hopped into bed.

"Wha is you waitin' fo? An inbitaton? Yet's git fuckin."

Translation: What are you waiting for? An invitation? Let's get fucking. How romantic. I asked did he mind if I turned off the light and he said, "goed." Translation: Go ahead.

After the lights were off, I started taking off my clothes. Is this how it's supposed to be? I thought he was supposed to kiss me or something?

Even with the lights off I could see him staring at me. All I wanted to do was tell him to take me home. I didn't though. I took off all of my clothes and got into the bed next to his eye. He still didn't kiss me, and all the nice compliments he'd given me earlier were never heard again.

Roger pounced on top of me and started humping like a dog in a humping hell. He didn't know it, but he was humping my thigh. I thought he was ugly all over again. He realized his mistake because he spread my legs and jammed his pet dog dick into me. Off he went, changing his form to equal that of a greyhound losing a race. I felt so stupid and misused then. My breasts were flopping around all over my chest. I had some big ones so he was moving pretty fast. He stopped five minutes later. I know because I looked at the clock on the nightstand at the start.

He never looked at my face, but I couldn't stop looking at his. His yellow teeth were clenched, and his eyes were so far out of his head I think they actually touched me a few times. He looked like a dead catfish mixed with a gargoyle. Yes, he was back to being ugly.

In the car ride he'd been doing okay with his English. He talked at a moderate pace so he didn't sound too bad. After I let him use me, he went back to normal. He rolled over off of me, and the words he spoke came from a one hundred percent fool.

"Dat wah dom goo' dicah wahet?" Translation: That was some good dick wasn't it? I felt like pure white, black, Spanish, Russian, you name it trash then. Just nasty. How could I let myself do this? Ugh. He got up, started putting his clothes on, and told me to hurry up; he didn't want to be late for his reservation. At least he's going to feed me is what I thought. After tonight, I'd tell him we should take it slow and start out as friends. I planned to tell him how to make love to me; there's no way I was doing that again. I didn't like him, so why that thought was on my mind, I'll never know.

Our ride to the restaurant (at least that's what I thought) was a quiet one. Nothing was said by either of us while he drove ten miles over the speed limit. I didn't care;

I just wanted to get out of his car and into anywhere. Maybe I'd forget about what just happened.

I noticed he was driving in the direction of my house, and I asked what restaurant we were going to. Roger transformed into a cool collected asshole but sounded illiterate in his reply.

"I'm going to a restaurant and you're going home,"

I looked at him like a dumb mannequin.

"Stop looking so retarded. I know you don't think I want to be with your fat ass. It's a disgrace to be seen with you. The only reason I fucked you is because my friends bet me I couldn't. As your fat ass can see, I won the bet and I'm going to meet them for dinner. Now shut up. I'm tired of talking to you."

He then tried hard to focus his eye on the road and said nothing more. He didn't say any of that clearly but that's too much stupid shit to write down. I mumbled for him to stop and let me out now. The car came to a screeching halt and before I got out, I asked would I see him at work tomorrow. No, I didn't defend myself or give him a piece of my mind. I asked would I see him in the morning. He told me he never wanted to see me again, said he quit, and then sped off.

I was close to home but I couldn't return this early. It was only 8:10 and I told my parents I'd be home at twelve. I walked to the park and decided to sit there until 11:30. While sitting on a bench, my brain spun thoughts I had no control over. The first was what just happened and why? I don't think it was rape because I was willing even though I knew I shouldn't have. Would it qualify as an out of body experience? He did look like an all points bulletin from a Government list of unidentified objects. Then my true thoughts came plowing through. Roger Pitkins did not want me for his girl. He didn't think I was beautiful or special. He even quit his job because the sight of me disgusted him. He won a bet by going on a whale ride. Why was I so easy, so naive, so, so... Oh hell, here come the tears. *Stop acting like a baby, Lynnde. Did one bad experience turn you into a "Take whatever you can get girl?" Stop it, Lynnde. Stop crying. You made a mistake. Bad judgment, that's all.*

What if I'm pregnant? He didn't use a condom. Oh, God, what if I have a disease? Why am I so ignorant? No one will ever want an idiot like me. I might as well face the fact that I'm fat, useless, and worthless. There's no way I can be pregnant because God wouldn't make a baby suffer with a fool like me. Did Lamar make me so stupid or was it my father? One person can't have that much ignorance in their head, it's not allowed. My fat nasty ass deserves every evil thing that can happen in a person's life. Who am I to think a man, ugly or not, would want me? I don't even want someone like me. Yeah, go ahead and cry fat girl. Just keep crying. You always give up easy, anyway. Maybe I'll lose what the world calls water weight. That's at least a half a pound. Come on 11:30. I'll tell my mother a good story about my evening, then go up to bed and get my goodies. To hell with Roger Pitkins and Lamar Hilton. I don't need them or any other man for that matter. I hope there's some food left over from dinner. My mother was going to cook a pot roast, and right now, that's all I need. Hurry up 11:30.

My mother was sitting in the den with a smile on her face. I couldn't bear to tell her what I let happen. Lying felt better than the truth, so I made up what she needed to hear, said I was tired, and probably wouldn't be down for breakfast. She kissed me goodnight saying, "As long as my baby's happy, I'm happy." After she floated up the stairs my tears returned.

Leftovers summoned me into the kitchen, and I polished off the remaining half of the pot roast, potatoes, and rolls. In my room, I had a dessert of four king-sized chocolate bars, a family size bag of chips, and an assorted bag of cookies. I thought I felt better and took a bath. While soaking the events of the evening away, I remembered the half-gallon of chocolate chip ice cream in the freezer. I might as well not let my date with food end with my stash. I'll eat what was meant for me and everyone else. Maybe I'll feel whole and fulfilled for at least one day.

When I was eighteen, I had a nice shape and was dumped. Now I'm fat and no one in their right mind wants a fat girl. If this is what my life is going to be like, I'll make sure I commit suicide in the morning. With my luck, morning will never come.

Esta called the next day and I told my first lie to her. I said Roger Pitkins really wasn't my type and I dumped him. She knew I was lying but didn't tell me until three years later. At the time all she said was, "Don't worry, girl. You'll find someone special. Just wait for love."

My face formed an ass's smile that I was glad she couldn't see. I added, "I hope you're right," but thought I'd be dead before love would want me. When I left for work, I went straight to the store and replenished my stash. The only love I need comes from eating, and I'll make sure I never have to wait for that.

Okay, I told you of my sexual episode. It's nothing to repeat so I'll continue. The night of the Scorpio party was finally here. I called Esta to say I'd pick her up at ten o'clock on the dot. None of that fashionably late stuff for us. We wanted to be the first ones to arrive and the last ones to leave. I thought I could exit without my father reminding me of his lecture. Wrong.

"Now, Lynnde. Don't act a fool. Drinking and driving is for idiots and even you ain't no idiot." Why is he still breathing?

Esta lived a few houses down the block and was standing on the porch when I pulled up. Her parents were in the doorway waving like we were taking off on a seven forty-seven. I couldn't believe my eyes; Esta didn't have her long brown dog that she took everywhere. When she got in the car I asked where the wiener was. She responded as if a serious exclamation mark had spoken.

"Girl! Do you think they'll let me take him in? I feel kind of bad leaving him at home. I don't want him to feel left out."

"Hell no, that dog can't go," I rudely answered.

"You don't have to be so nasty, Lynnde. What's up with your attitude lately anyway? Are your hormones out of sync or something?"

Esta always had questions to ask or a point to make.

"Look. Just because Larry serves you up on a regular basis doesn't qualify you as a woman's bodily function expert. I guess I'm just thrilled about this evening and I hope I meet someone tonight. It's been a few months, weeks, days, and minutes since a man has shown me any attention. My luck is bound to change sooner or later."

"Lynnde, girl are you going on a ho stroll?"

That's what Esta said a single woman was doing when she went out looking for a piece of man, ho strolling. I guess that term fits because it's definitely the case tonight. Who am I kidding? It's not like I can handle a one-night stand. My last experience was, well, I still don't know what that was, and I'm not out looking for any type of trouble. I'll just be looking. Wait for love, the right man will come along. Yeah right. Just having him come will suffice for now.

I know I need to change my way of thinking, so don't waste your breath and say it. This is going to be the last time disaster rules me. I just need one more chance. I'll never make a mistake again. Hey, I'm not lying to you, just myself.

Esta snapped me out of my mini self pep talk. "Well...are you going to answer me? Are you going on a ho stroll or what?"

"Answer you? Why should I? All you're going to say is wait, girl, wait. Waiting is what's wrong with me now."

Sucking her teeth with an attitude she replied, "All right. I won't tell you what you already know. I'll just sit here and say it to myself out loud."

Esta has never lied to me, and boy is she blabbing on and on about waiting. I love her. I hope she has a good time. Her words are true, but I'm going to cross my fingers every now and then and pray a man asks me for my phone number.

As we entered the packed lot we scanned the cars to see if any of them looked familiar, positive we'd have a good time. Esta asked if I was ready when we were walking to the door. I answered rather loudly with, "More than you'll ever know." For some reason we burst out laughing. I guess that's one of the silly things best friends do.

We waited in line about ten minutes talking to other partygoers who'd waited on this night just like us. Finally, it was our turn to enter into party heaven. The security guard at the door asked if he could see my ID. He didn't ask for Esta's. When he handed it back to me, he said my name in a low hush that only my ears heard.

"Lynnette Lee, hmmm. Will you give me the joyous pleasure of a dance?"

I would've answered him, but my dumb meter went over board so silence was my reply. He leaned in close to give me hint of his glorious cologne.

"Enjoy yourself, pretty lady, and I'll catch up with you later."

"Okay." I'm so damn dumb.

When we were a few feet away Esta blurted out,

"Lynnde! Who was that big hunk of man? Girl, have you been holding out on me? No wonder you had to get here on time."

My face damn near cracked with the smile the guard placed on it and my body tingled all over.

"I don't know, but I'm going to find out or this night will not end."

"Calm down, Lynnde girl. I'm sure he's interested in you. You don't have to rush." This is one reason she's my best friend. She's always concerned about me.

"Yeah, Esta. You're probably right. I'll take my time." I may have said those words out loud, but I was going on a special secret agent mission to find out who he was. Right now, listening to someone else's advice was not an option. I knew it would only benefit me, but my ears remained closed. I know, slow down girl. Slow down.

Esta and I found an empty table after searching for twenty minutes. A waitress quickly approached and took our drink orders. The food was set up buffet style, and I couldn't believe there was something else on my mind besides it. The security guard's face was the only vision I saw. Who was he, where was he, and would he be mine? I know I'm rushing, but a man was all I needed.

Esta talked about our surroundings, and I nodded to show her I was listening. She didn't have my total attention; the security guard had ninety-five percent of it. I spotted Larry's brother, Wayne, as he walked towards our table. I'm sure he'd ask Esta to dance, and I wanted her to accept. It's not that I don't want to talk to her, I just want to scope out the room for that big hunk of man who'd make my life complete.

"This must be the fine lady table. How are my favorite sister-in-law and her best friend doing?" Wayne could never stay still and bee bopped in place.

"Hey, brother-in-law. Long time no see. Come over here and give me a hug."

Esta and Wayne hugged and I wanted them to hurry up. They were blocking my view. Wayne looked around the room as if a hit man was after him.

"Esta, you'd better get in a dance with me now before all the other ladies get a hold of me. You know how they love me."

Throwing her hands up in amusement Esta said, "Oh, Wayne. The only lady that wants you is your momma. I'm surprised she let you out, you big mama's boy."

"Girl, don't say that too loud. She might hear you. I told her I was going to get a loaf of bread. Now hurry up and dance with me so I can get back home undetected."

Wayne's answer made us laugh, and it brought me out of my security guard daze for a moment. He is a momma's boy and he probably did sneak out the house.

"Maybe next time, Wayne," Esta replied. "We just got here, and I want to sit with my girl for a little while."

I thwarted my eyes around the room quickly before answering.

"Go ahead, Esta. I'll be fine. There are plenty of things in here to keep me occupied."

Esta stood reluctantly and gave me a behave yourself look, and off they went. I watched them dance for a few minutes and realized how beautiful Esta was. She wore a studded blue jean outfit and had a million Shirley Temple curls in her hair. I never saw her dance like that. That girl was working out.

As I sat and admired Esta's moves, I felt someone walk up behind me. My body temperature rose as they sat beside me. Please let it be him. "So, Lynnette. Are you having a good time?" Those words came from the man I was going to marry. His voice was low, deep and sexy. "Yes." was my reply. I wish I had something a little more intriguing to say.

"Do you mind if I join you?"

"No, I don't mind." As soon as I get home I'm reading the dictionary; my vocabulary needs help.

He sat and said, "Do you work at the mall? I know I've seen your pretty face before."

I'm getting married. "Yes I do. I'm a clerk at Just Shoes. Do you work there, also?"

"No. I work at my father's detailing shop over on One Hundred Seventh and Park. I shop sometimes and I've seen you there. Have you ever heard of Otto's Autos?"

"No, but the name is catchy. Are you named after your father?" He hung his head and laughed a bit before he spoke.

"Unfortunately, yes. But I've learned to deal with it."

"I'm sorry, I didn't mean to offend you. I just wanted to know your name."

"No harm done, pretty lady. Otto Parker. Hey, how about you bring your car in for a free wash and wax? A pretty lady needs to be seen in a clean car."

I wanted to dive into his arms but we'd both probably end up on the floor. "I've only had my car three weeks and haven't had it cleaned yet. It would be my pleasure to have it done by a professional."

"Well, it would be my pleasure to clean it up for you and make sure it's running smooth. Uh, before this conversation goes any further, can I ask you a semi-personal question?"

Elated I said, "Yes, go right ahead. I don't mind."

"I'd like to know if a beautiful lady like you is taken? I don't want to say anything to embarrass myself. So tell me, are you spoken for?"

I know I had a stunned look on my face. Did he just ask me if I had a man? Does he have some kind of vision problem? Can't he see how big I am? Who would want me, and why? I glanced the room quickly to see if Roger Pitkins was in view and was glad he wasn't. I was able to finally say, "No, I'm not spoken for," and wanted him to say let's get married.

"Good. Your answer is music to my ears. In that case, umm...do you mind giving me your phone number?"

Heatwave's Groove Line was rocking the crowd and Otto's groove owned mine. I didn't answer him. I wrote my number down and told him to call me at his earliest convenience.

"Thank you, Lynnette. These seven digits have made my night. I'll give you a call tomorrow evening if that's okay with you?" Words don't fail me now.

"That's okay." I'm stupid.

"I'd better get back to my door duty. I'm doing this as a favor for a friend, and I don't want to disappoint him. I'll be back for my dance, though."

"I'll wait right here." My life has just begun. He winked his eye and walked away. I must be easy because that's all it took for me to fall hard. He was a sexy something. He looked football player hard. I'd say he was at least six-feet-four and a solid two hundred and seventy-five pounds, not jello-ish like me. His head was shaved bald and his skin color was that of milk chocolate. Otto's eyes were set deep in his face and were piercingly sexy. I'm sure they were dark brown but they looked black. He was going to be the one. He had to be. *All right, Lynnde. Slow down. Don't rush it. Don't mess things up before they get started.* Where is Esta? I have to tell someone what just happened to me. Before my last thought was completely out of my mind Esta came barreling towards the table.

"Lynnde! Who was that? Do you know him? What's going on? Hurry up and tell me everything."

"Wait a minute, wait a minute. Sit down and catch your breath, Miss Solid Gold Dancer.

"Ha, ha, ha, very funny. Just start talking."

Water from the big gulp Esta took spilled over her lips as she watched my mouth. I bought her up to speed on our conversation and when I finished, we turned and looked at the door. Otto was looking at us. We all smiled and I noticed how appetizing his mouth was. A man that looked delicious, could wear a uniform well, and was interested in me? That could only mean one thing. That man would be mine. Totally.

I didn't think this at the time, but my problem was I rushed into life too quickly. Especially where a man was concerned. I gave into any and everything a man wanted. My life's mission was to have one and make him happy even if I wasn't. Otto Parker would halfway teach me how to take care of myself. He didn't know that's what he was doing and I didn't know it either, but after him and the relationships that followed, my eyes opened and I saw life more clear.

Otto and I didn't get to dance that night, and it really didn't matter. I was on cloud nine the entire evening as it was. He occupied my mind as I danced with a few friends from work, and paid no mind to the buffet table. A giddy schoolgirl ran inside of me as I looked at the door several times. My head surely looked like a sun-powered plant. I radiated light from the rays he turned on inside of me. The doofus thing was that Otto wasn't even at the door all the time but I smiled anyway.

Our first Scorpio party evening came to an end at three a.m. I didn't want to go home alone, but didn't dare say this to Esta. Taking a few deep breaths before I walked out of the door helped me keep my mouth shut and my composure. When I reached Otto he pulled me to the side. Oh God, help me.

"Don't forget, I'm going to call you tomorrow, pretty lady."

I wanted to tell him he could call me tonight, or do anything else on his mind, but I didn't want him to think of me for what I was at that moment, a ho.

"I won't forget. I hope you make it home safely." Damn I sound like a dunce.

"Thinking of you will get me anywhere safe. Umm... pretty lady, would you grant me the pleasure of giving you a kiss on your beautiful cheek?"

Once again I didn't reply. I just leaned forward and accepted the first of what would be many kisses from Otto. His lips were soft and moist and so was I. See, that's my problem, everything has to come down to sex. I'm going to do things right this time. This, I promise myself. You have to give me some credit; at least I didn't end up in a motel flat backing it and feeling used.

Floating, I told Otto I'd be waiting for his call, and Esta and I ran to the car. We yakked all the way home about our very eventful night, but no matter what we talked about, all I could see was Otto's godly face. Did I mention that he had a goatee? He's fine.

Esta turned towards me as I pulled up in front of her house. Her face was full of concern and love as she gave me words of wisdom.

"Lynnde. Girl, don't rush this. Take your time and do yourself right. You're a beautiful person. If he's the one for you, he'll be a perfect fit." She gave me a hug and I watched her walk inside.

While driving home, I thought about Esta's short speech. The part about him being a perfect fit. She gave me a speech before about men and women fitting together like puzzle pieces. What she was saying is if I didn't feel happy, safe and secure in this relationship, it wasn't the one for me. This was advice I planned to follow.

Surprisingly, my father was sitting up watching television. I asked him was he okay, since it was 3:35 in the morning. My father was always in bed by ten.

"Baby girl, did you have a good time?" he said rather cheerfully. I stood perplexed for a few seconds before repeating part of his question. "Baby girl?"

"That's what I said. Did you have a good time?" His face exuded love but there was some sort of desperation in it, also.

The moment was strange but I hadn't felt this relaxed with my father in a long time, and I called him something I hadn't said in years.

"Daddy, I had a wonderful time."

"Now that's what I wanted to hear my Lynnde-hop say. Babygirl. Don't worry about a thing. You're all right."

He smiled and patted me on my shoulder as he walked upstairs to bed. Lynnde-hop? He hadn't called me that in years. He didn't seem to be drunk, so this definitely was a exceptional night. I'd met someone whose first impression told me he was special, and my father treated me like I was his daughter. My luck was about to change. No food for comfort tonight. Humph, don't need it. Love is on the way.

# Who Does He Love?

I didn't have to go to work until twelve in the afternoon on Sundays, so I slept like I hadn't been able to do for months. It was strange that I didn't dream about Otto, but he was the last thing on my mind before I went to sleep and still there when I woke up.

Happiness feels so good. Shoot, I hadn't been this happy since, well, I don't think I've ever been this happy. Why didn't I know I could be happy just being with me? Of course, it's always a pleasure when you meet someone, but I should've known I was somebody all by myself.

Love songs were on my mind as I turned the radio on to hear Peabo Bryson singing, I'm So Into You. That song confirmed I met the man of my dreams. This would be our song. He was into me or else he wouldn't have wanted my number. Let's not forget the kiss on the cheek.

Half skipping and half lumbering to the shower, I sang along with Peabo. Before I began my washing process, I caught a glimpse of something in the mirror. For a second I thought, "What the..." Then I realized what it was. It was me. The full-length mirror that I never look in irritated me. What's the use, fat is fat, but boy was I shocked by what I saw.

Tears came to my eyes as I studied my naked body. Where was my waistline? I'm positive I have a gut. My face is wide and round, and someone else's chin is attached to mine. No more sexy onion booty. I have a rutabaga. I never did like that vegetable much. That's it. No more weight gaining for me. My exercise plan is going into overdrive. I don't care if I have to starve myself. This weight is coming off. The problem with that was I wasn't doing it for myself, but for someone else. I didn't understand that people liked me for me. Not the way I looked, or the size I was. If I wanted to lose weight, I should do it because I wanted to. Not to make a man, who I knew nothing about want me.

The warm shower gave me a new attitude, and I went through my workday with added pep in my step. The day went by smoothly but not as quickly as I wanted it to. I couldn't wait to get home and talk to Otto, wishing all day that he would come into the store and sweep me off my feet, like a York Peppermint Pattie moment.

Most of the day I wondered if he was thinking of me and was he really going to call. Maybe he was intoxicated last night. Maybe when he woke up, he realized how big I really was. Maybe he changed his mind. Please don't let that be the case. 5:30 must get here sooner than it's planning to. It has to understand I have a date with a man who's the man of my dreams.

I can't believe I haven't eaten anything all day. My stomach is very upset with me, asking how can I treat her this way. I'll make her understand the results will all be for the better. We must go through a little pain for a lifetime of love. When I get home, I'll tell my mother about my evening and maybe my father, too, if he's still in a good mood. Then I'll slip into something comfortable and talk to the man who'll make my future materialize.

Upon arriving home, I ran slowly into the house to see my father sitting in his TV chair, and my mother sitting at the kitchen table reading the newspaper.

"Hi, baby. How was your day?" She asked in her Girl Scout friendly voice.

"Good, Ma. Everything went very well today. Did anybody call?"

Softly switching to nosey mama she replied, "No. Are you expecting a call, baby?"

"No, I just asked."

"Uh-huh. Okay, baby. Well, your plate is in the oven. I cooked pork chops, and if I do say so myself, they're the best I've ever made. They're so thick and juicy."

I hadn't eaten a thing all day and my stomach was cursing me out. Hmm, one pork chop wouldn't hurt. But my diet, I must stick to my diet.

"Maybe later, Ma. I'm not really hungry right now." Did I just turn down food? I'll have to write this down on the calendar. No better yet, get it engraved in stone because I've never turned down food. My father even looked away from the television to ogle me. My mother's smile showed she knew something was going on.

"Baby, you're feeling all right aren't you? You didn't catch a cold or something last night, did you?"

"I'm fine. I want to take a bath now, that's all. I'll eat later."

Quite comfortably she said, "Okay, baby. Do you feel like telling me about your big night?"

"Anything for you, Ma." I gave her a short version of our evening, and she seemed satisfied for the moment. There'd be more questions later, and I'd gladly answer them after Otto called.

" I'm going to lie down after my bath. I'm a little tired."

"All right, baby. I'll check on you later and wake you if anybody calls." She knew a man was my reason for declining dinner and asking about phone calls. I gave her a kiss on the cheek and she squeezed my hand as I walked away. Yeah, she knew all right.

When I walked past my father, I said hi to him. He didn't answer so I said it again. He turned away from the TV and mumbled something incoherent. I figured he was back to his old self and decided right then to find myself an apartment first thing in the morning.

As I walked up the stairs, the phone rang. My heart began beating itself out of my chest. My mother answered and kept talking. I stood at attention until I noticed my father watching me. I gave him a nippy smile and continued my climb. We finally had two-way calling so I wasn't worried about missing Otto's call, but I wished my mother would get off the phone so I could hear it ring.

Since I hadn't eaten anything all day I must've lost a few pounds and headed straight for the full-length mirror in the bathroom. The mirror showed me I was mistaken.

"It'll probably show tomorrow," I concluded. I took a nice long bath, slipped into my comfy-don't-want-a-man-to-see-you-in, but they're perfect- for-talking-on-the-phone-pajamas, and waited for my so very important phone call.

Three hours later I was still waiting. I'd given in to my stomach's pleas for food and had eaten my mother's pork chop dinner. I waited this long to start a diet, one more day wasn't going to hurt.

At ten o'clock I heard my parent's going into their room for bed. My mother tapped on my door and asked was I still awake. I didn't respond because I didn't feel like answering the questions I knew she had. She said goodnight and, "I'll see you in the morning, baby." I wish I would've answered her.

At one a.m. I dozed off but woke myself up with my snoring. He hadn't called. I should've known he wouldn't. No one wants me and no one ever will. Routinely, my arm reached under my bed and grabbed my stash of comfort. Come here chocolate bars, I need something and you'll do just fine.

The alarm clock went off the next day on time and on time every morning for the next three weeks. No Otto. His number was listed in the phone book so I figured there'd be no harm in me calling him. When I called, a woman answered and I hung up. Esta said I should've asked for him anyway; it could've been a relative or a friend. What I didn't tell her was the time I called, which was six o'clock in the morning. I kind of figured it wasn't a relative.

Something inside me told me not to push the Otto issue. My life hadn't changed for the better since meeting him. I still worked, slept, and overate. If anything, he brought a few inches of stress into my world. Was he ever going to call and if he wasn't, why did he bother talking to me in the first place? Didn't he know I wanted a man? Did he understand I just had to have one?

It was during the fourth week of his no call no show treatment that I looked up the address for Otto's Autos. I couldn't take it anymore. *So what, Lynnde. You met a man at a party who showed you two minutes of attention? Evidently, it wasn't meant to go any further than that. Open your eyes and mind. Don't just look at the picture, understand it.* Look, I need a better reason than that. I'll find Otto and let him know there will be no turning me on and off at the same time. I'll let him know that I'll be so good and so right for him and to him. He'll have to give me a chance once he hears what I plan to bring into this relationship. *Goodness, Lynnde. Get a grip. It was only a kiss on the cheek.* I'm trying to get a grip, but you don't seem to understand that the cheek was my round chubby one. These cheeks haven't been kissed since my father kissed them when I was a little girl. I miss that feeling of tenderness. If he is the man to make me feel it once again, I have to have him.

I couldn't get past that thought as I drove to Otto's Autos. My brain didn't belong to me anymore. Not thinking clear should've been the only sign I needed. I was beyond the point of listening to common sense and at the point of common idiot. Many of you've been there before and know exactly what I'm talking about. You get up, get bathed and dressed everyday, and go through your life in the normal process you're supposed to. Then when this man comes into the picture, you lose all sense and sight of what is right or wrong. You only want what you think is good for you. You haven't gotten to the point where your work or other relationships suffer. Hell, you don't even know you've arrived there until you've passed it. Listening to sensible solutions are not an option. If I was starting out like this, I was in for nothing but heartache. Good Morning Heartache was once a popular song. Remixes are in now, and besides, humming it will give me something to go along with my morning coffee.

I arrived at the detailing shop forty-five minutes later after my mind took me inside and back out of sanity. Pulling into the parking lot reminded me of the movie Car Wash. There were seven men wearing blue jumpsuits, and the one who approached me had the biggest Afro since nineteen-seventy. He had to use a blow out kit to obtain that effect. I thought he looked kind of funny at first, because no one really wore Afros anymore. But then I thought, "Hey, he's doing his own thing, he's being himself." I should apply that way of thinking to my life.

"How can I help you, Miss?" said Superfly in his best come on voice.

"Hi. Umm, I'm looking for, Otto. Is he here?" I tried to sound cute but it came out hoarse.

"Which one? Senior or junior?"

"Junior."

"Follow me."

Superfly opened my car door and took my hand. Chivalry is not dead.

"I'll have your car nice and clean when you return. Take your time." He licked his lips after saying that. I hope he doesn't think it turned me on.

Superfly led me into a well kept heated building and down a long corridor with an office at the end of it. He knocked on the door and I started to sweat to the point where my hair edges began napping up. An authoritive voice asked, "Who is it?" from the other side.

"Hey, man. It's me, Jethro. There's a nice lady out here for you."

I thought of leaving at that point but made no attempt to move my feet. What was I doing here anyway? What was I going to say? Who did I think I was coming on this man's territory and demanding his time? What if he gave me a few choice words and threw, no, rolled me out of the building? Should I start running down the hallway? Wait, New York doesn't have earthquakes. I'm going on a diet first thing in the morning. The door opened and he appeared. Okay, maybe that's a bit much. No, no it's not.

"Hey, pretty lady. Come on in." Umm, he is sexy.

My steps through the door took the form of a child starting her first day of school. Otto came in behind me and I felt tight all over. He looked better than I remembered. I'll starve myself for him. He'll be my chocolate bar, potato chips, and pork chops. Otto Parker will be my life-sustaining source. These words came from my twenty-one year old mouth.

We looked into each other's eyes for a minute and a devious smile appeared on his face. I stood with my mouth partway open probably looking like a dork. I can't think. Please let some decent words come out of my mouth.

"Hi, Otto. Remember me?" I am so damn dumb. Remember me? Brains please don't fail me now.

"Yes, I do. Lynnette Lee. I could never forget a face as beautiful as yours. I'm glad you finally came looking for me. I feel like a fool for losing your number, and not knowing how to get in contact with you."

Now, he just told me he wasn't interested. Our number is in the phone book. If he was really interested in me why didn't he just look it up? Sure, there are a million Lee's in the book, but if he were truly interested, he would've kept calling until he found me. That wasn't my reply though.

"Oh, that's okay. I figured you probably lost my number."

Otto eye's focused on my lips. I didn't want to lick them and look hungry, so I kept my mouth shut and prayed that they weren't chapped.

"I'm sorry, pretty lady. We've been really busy with the holiday season coming up. Snow and salt aren't good for cars and many people want to get and give detail packages as gifts. Please forgive me.

"Oh, that's okay. I understand." I think I have to go to the bathroom. Oh, not now, please, not now.

Otto explained the car care process to me as we stood in the middle of the room. He circled me as he spoke. If he touches me I'm going to faint. Why am I so fat?

He continued to circle me and stopped behind me. When he reached my front his arms were crossed on his chest like a commanding genie. "I should've given you my number. That way, you wouldn't have had to bring your pretty self out into the cold to find me. You're prettier than I remembered. May I have a kiss?"

Oh, somebody help me. This fine hunk of man wants to kiss me on my lips. He bent to kiss my lips but stopped at my forehead. I'll take whatever I can get. I didn't say a word or move because I couldn't. I'm going to marry him.

Otto stood within inches of me and asked, "So, Miss Lee. How about a dinner date?"

I could taste his breath. "Yes." My response put a smile on his face because I answered without hesitation. I was coming un-glued.

"Do you like Mexican?"

Look at me? Can't you tell I like everything?

"Yes. Mexican is fine."

"All right then, pretty lady. It's settled. Mexican it is. How about this Saturday at five o'clock? I've already wasted enough of your time. I don't want to prolong getting to know you any longer."

"I'll see you Saturday at five."

We exchanged all the pertinent information, and I wanted to include wedding plans. Leave me alone, will you?

"Well, pretty lady. As much as I'm enjoying you right now, we're going to have to cut this short. I have an appointment that I can't reschedule. You understand don't you?"

My fat ass was so excited I didn't think to doubt anything he said. "I came here unannounced, so I'm glad you were able to give me this much time."

He walked me to the door and kissed my chubby round cheek. "One day I'm going to kiss those beautiful lips, Miss Lee. One day soon."

Kiss my lips? I couldn't believe what I just heard! If I weren't so heavy, I would've pirouetted around the room.

I stood mesmerized outside his office a few seconds with my hand touching the nameplate on the door. It read, Otto Parker, Assistant. Manager. I was gone. It only took a kiss on the cheek and I was gone. Not only did my brain not belong to me anymore, it left my body. I had a date. I'd found the man of my dreams and made a date with him.

Maybe he did want me. He said he'd lost my number and had been very busy. I had to give us a chance. We would work.

Esta will flip when I tell her what happened. While walking down the hallway I wanted to do a cartwheel, but quickly changed my mind when a vision of a wrestling rhino flashed before my eyes. I couldn't believe it; for once I'd have a date during the holidays with a man. I never get excited around the holidays. I always have family and friends, but I still feel lonely. All those feelings were about to leave now. I have someone to share my world with. Otto will be a part of my hopes and dreams, my success and failures. We'd take from, and give each other exactly what we needed. *Damn! You haven't even made it to your car yet, let alone gone on the date. Slow down, Lynnde. Don't give yourself up so fast.* I promise myself I won't make any mistakes this time. I love this man. Slow down, girl. At least until you get home to the phone and Esta.

No one was home as I told Esta about my adventure. With the way I screamed on the phone, my parents would be sure to hear the whole story.

"Oh, Lynnde. Girl, I'm so excited for you. You know I'll be at your house Saturday at noon to start your beautifying process. I won't have much to do because you're already a sexy lady."

"Thanks, Esta. You always make me feel so special. But what about Larry? Won't you miss him?"

"Lynnde, Larry is an enhancement of my life. I won't stop breathing if we're not in the same room."

"Thanks, Esta. What would I do without you?"

"Girl, we'll never have to find out. See you Saturday."

"See ya. Give Larry my love."

I hung up and thought about the word enhancement. A man won't enhance me. He'll complete me and make me feel whole. I want him to be my everything. Our lives would revolve around each other.

That's what I wanted my love to be all about. Love was about to teach me the hard way. I was someone who had to physically feel what was said instead of hearing it. Trust me, feeling is much worse.

In the three days before my big date I was filled with triple the life I previously had. During my daydreams I planned trips for Otto and I, exotic places I never thought of before. Tropical islands, Spain, France, anywhere our love would take us. Of course we'll be in love. I'll make sure he'll be in love with me.

Saturday arrived and I planned to be the perfect girl on the perfect first date. I wouldn't order a lot, probably a salad and definitely no dessert. My eating habits changed since I last saw Otto and I think I lost a few pounds. Esta came over at twelve and I was really feeling myself. She said her first duty was to style my hair and whipped up a French roll with a short bang. My mother was even in on the action. I had to tell her about my date when she commented on my new attitude two days ago. She wanted me to wear a long gown with a shawl.

"Ma, I'm not going to a ball, just dinner."

"Excuse me for caring. I thought you'd look extra special and nice in it, that's all. What do you plan to wear anyway?" was my mother's sassy reply.

"Don't worry, Mrs. Lee. I made her a nice burgundy pantsuit. Our girl always looks good."

I loved to hear them debate over my looks, so to prolong it I added, "I don't know about all that, Esta. But I love the outfit."

"Stop it, baby. Esta's right. You always look good."

I smiled realizing my comment worked and figured no matter what I said, they'd never agree with me. My pantsuit didn't look like work or fat girl attire and I loved it. A crisp white blouse and a pair of black pumps would help to complete it. Esta even picked out my matching jewelry. When I gave myself a once over before going downstairs, I thought there was hope for me.

My father showed a little enthusiasm. He was sitting on the couch waiting to see the finished product. Why did it have to be a big deal every time I went out the house on a date? I know I didn't go out a lot, but when I did, it always seems to turn into a Lynnde production. I'll stop complaining because this would be the last time I'd leave this house on a first date. Otto would make sure of that.

It was 4:50 p.m., and I was more than ready. Everyone kept looking at each other and smiling at me. I felt I'd just won a beauty contest. My mother placed a straight back chair by the door for me to sit in. She said she didn't want me sitting on the couch because I'd get all wrinkled up.

We heard a car pull up, and all our eyes met at once. They secretly thought he wasn't going to show up. I had the same thought and unfortunately it came true. At seven o'clock, everyone knew he wasn't coming.

"Lynnde, I have to go. I made dinner plans with Larry's family, but you know it'll be no problem to cancel them."

"No, Esta. Go ahead. I'm fine. He probably got tied up, that's all. I'm sure he'll be here."

With a quick shoulder rub Esta replied, "Call me if you need anything, okay?"

"I'll call you tomorrow with all the juicy details."

We kissed goodbye knowing he wasn't coming. My father said people don't like their cars rushed and not to worry, he'd be here soon enough. Huh?

My mother took over Esta's duties of applying pressed powder to my face when I started to sweat. At 8:30 my father suggested that I call him. I did, but got no answer. I called the detail shop, also, and didn't get an answer there either. Then I went back to sitting in the chair by the door, looking like a dog waiting on her owner. Why didn't I just embrace my TKO and face the fact that he wasn't coming?

At eleven I decided to give up hope. Yes, I sat in the chair the entire time. Ten o'clock passed with my father still up watching me go nowhere. My parents looked so sad. Pitiful would best describe their expressions. My father tried not to look at me, but my mother stared hard. She must've been looking for the tears that I wouldn't let fall until I reached the pillow on my bed. This was the final straw for me. I'd get an apartment the first of the year. I wasn't going to put them through this again. *Sure, you're old enough to handle your own disappointments.*

"Something important must've come up. He'll call tomorrow and explain. I'm sure everything's fine." I tried to sound collected and reassuring.

Offering as much support as she could my mother perked up and said, "Baby, I'm positive that's what happened. Do you want me to fix you something to eat?"

"No, Ma. I'm not hungry. I'm going to turn in. Goodnight." I couldn't wait to remove my sorry self from their sight. I don't believe it; I declined food for the second time in my life. Actually, the first time doesn't count because I ate the food later on anyway. I barely made it to my room before tears white water rafted down my face. My steps morphed into a pathetic walk before plopping down at my vanity and staring myself into a headache. I closed my eyes and wished for a gun. One squeeze on the trigger would stop my dejection and crying.

There has to be a reason for his no show. Maybe I'll go to his job on Monday and make sure he's all right. Actually, I want to go to his apartment, but I know I'll see something I don't need to see. *When you talk to yourself do you ever listen to what you're saying?*

A seemingly burst of sense filled my mind, and I did something I hadn't done in years. I got down on my knees and prayed that Otto hadn't been in an accident, that he was safe and sound, and begged God to please take care of him. I didn't pray for people who I knew loved me, would never hurt me or stand me up. I prayed for a man who never called and never showed up.

When my headache or tears wouldn't subside two hours later, I took six aspirin and asked sleep to hurry up and come greet me. The morning has got to be better than this.

Morning came. And then three weeks of mornings came. Three weeks of waiting to fall asleep at night came right along with those mornings. Why was I still waiting on that man? Calling his apartment was a waste because I never received an answer. I called his job and was told he was on vacation. He could've at least given me the courtesy of one phone call. Sometimes I wished he were in an accident or in a coma somewhere. That's the only reason that would take away my embarrassment. Remembering what happened the last time I wished for something to happen made me decide to forget about Otto. I felt aggravation for a man I didn't even know yet. If I did get to know him, would things get worse?

A new year was approaching and I wasn't going to rely on Otto to make my year any better than the last. I'd lost twelve pounds, knowing I had a long way to go, and felt I was well on my way to my weight loss success. I resolved not to make any more mistakes and was going to try hard to see that resolution through. 1981 was going to be a great year for me. It would be the year my life began as brand new. I'd think everything through, and there'd be no more hasty decisions.

Moving into my own apartment was at the top of my list. I finally found one that was twenty minutes away from my parent's house, and my main concern was making my mother understand. What am I saying? She'll understand. She always does.

As I dressed for the evening and thought of my future plans, I still couldn't get Otto out of my mind. Hearing my mother's sweet mischievous voice gave me a quick reprieve.

"Lynnde. Baby, get the phone."

"Okay, Ma," I answered. "I got it."

Thinking it was Esta; I spoke in my girlfriend tone. "Esta, girl what's up? I hope you get here early so we can start on those mimosa's you keep talking about."

The response I received didn't come from Esta. The voice was deeper and very masculine.

"Hey, sexy." I didn't say anything. The short phrase was repeated.

"Hey, sexy. Are you still there?"

Dementia took over as I began half stuttering and talking.

"Hhhhello, um, yes. I'm still here. Uh... who is this?"

"What man's been calling my beautiful lady sexy? Don't let me find out who he is."

I lost all sense of control then. To hell with my new life plans, he called me sexy and beautiful. Who cares where he's been and no I don't want an explanation. I want him.

"Hi, Otto. How have you been? Is everything okay? I mean, I haven't heard from you in quite some time."

"I know, baby. I'm sorry. I had to go out of town to visit my grandmother. I'm her baby and she wanted me there with her. I just returned home today and you were the only woman on my mind. I couldn't wait to call you. Do you have any plans for this evening?"

Lynnette Donna Lee's senses have just left the building and the entire universe for that matter.

"We're having some friends over for a celebration. You're more than welcome to come." Please let this man come be with me tonight. Please oh, God, please. If he were in my sight, I'd get down on my knees and beg him. *Damn, Lynnde.*

"Do you think your family will mind? I can bring a dish or something if you like. Or even a bottle of the bubbly if it's okay?"

I wanted to scream yes, yes, yes it was okay; just show your sexy self up. "Oh, Otto. No, they wouldn't mind. The more the merrier."

"Alright, pretty lady. What time do you want me there? I know I disappointed you before, but it won't happen tonight or any other night."

Yes you disappointed me, made me look like a fool in front of my family, and didn't give another thought about me. Hell no I didn't say that. Are you stupid?

"We usually get started around nine but anytime you come is fine. Do you need my address?"

"No, pretty lady. I have it right in front of me. I can't wait to see you."

That did it for me. I gave him my address anyway. Better to be safe than alone tonight.

We said goodbye, and as soon as I hung the phone up, my mother knocked on the door. She and her smile came in and I explained that we were just friends, and I asked him to stop by tonight. I added that he might not be able to because he has a large family, and I hope she didn't mind.

"Oh, baby, of course not. Any decent friend you have is welcome in this house. And if he can't make it tonight, you just invite him some other time, okay?"

"Oh, Ma. Thank you."

"Anything for you, baby. You know that. Now you finish getting prettier than you already are. I'll see you downstairs."

When my mother walked out of my room, I realized I'd told her the first of many lies I would tell about Otto. I didn't know if he had a large family or not. Who cares! He called me beautiful, sexy and wants to be with me on New Years Eve. He had a good reason for not showing up, and it turns out he was thinking about me just as much as I was about him. Here I was ready to give up on him and he still wants me. *Slow down, Lynnde. Slow down.* I was satisfied with his explanation and if he didn't show, we had an entire year to get things right between us.

To start things off on a perfect note, I had to wear the right outfit. I planned on wearing a pair of blue jeans and a blouse. That won't be dressy enough for my third encounter with Otto. The pantsuit I had on the night of our first date that never happened came to mind next. Maybe that outfit is cursed. *Come on, Lynnde. Get it together. Don't fall apart now.* Oh, Otto. Please show up. The second time for us has to be the charm. My heart won't let you fail me again. Please, show up.

Our guests began arriving at 8:15. The first person through the door was my father's best friend, John. I'd bet money he was drunk. With a jolly swig on his brown bagged bottle he dribbled, "Guhurl, pwease, I still gots a long way to go!"

A tad bit of something similar to slob or drool flew at me but I moved to the side and it missed. I saw him sleeping on our couch tonight. My mother's two sisters and three of my cousins came next. They looked a little glassy eyed themselves. Everyone was excited about the upcoming year, and I'd join in on the festivities. Even if

Otto didn't come by, I knew what my plan was for him. Esta and her parents arrived and the mimosa party began.

Even though a new year was approaching, my father pulled out his dusty albums from the fifties and sixties. He was well on his way to a drunken stupor, and I'm sure he'd be bunking with John on the couch.

There was plenty of food, music and drink. A few people were playing cards and one of my cousins thought she was Aretha Franklin. She wasn't, and I wanted her to shut up yesterday. Liquor is not everyone's friend.

At 11:25 my mother pulled me to the side and attempted to make my depression she saw coming go away.

"Don't fret none about that fella, baby. If he doesn't show up, I want you to have a good time anyway. You hear me, baby? I want you to have a good time, you hear?"

"Yes, Maaaaa... I hear you." She had a few too many glasses of wine. My mother never talked loud, and she swayed from side to side holding my hands for balance. I wanted to say nothing was going to spoil this night for me but decided to show her instead. Larry had to return to Marine duty, but he called for Esta and said he wasn't hanging up until the New Year arrived.

Watching her happiness made me feel relaxed and mellow like I never had before. Maybe for one night I realized that I was loved for being the person I was. No one expected anything from me or made any requests either. Lynnette Lee was feeling no pain. Then, the doorbell rang. I know I went into mild cardiac arrest, but I can't prove it.

My chest hurt and I began sweating. It was him. Otto had shown up. Esta's father answered the door. Thank God, he beat my father to it. He was beyond talking with any sense.

"Come in here, young fella."

"Thank you, Sir."

I walked towards him with my mouth open and smiling at the same time. He held a bouquet of flowers and a bottle of champagne. Otto was here for me. I looked around and found Esta's face. We gave each other an approving look, and she turned back to the phone no doubt to tell Larry what was going on. My mother and father walked up and before I could make the introductions, my father's drinks spoke.

"Hi, boy! Do you want a drink? We got some powaful shit here for yo ass!" He then burst out laughing. I looked at Otto with an, "I'm sorry for my father," expression and he returned a, "That's okay, baby. I understand," look.

"You must be Lynnde's friend. It's so nice to meet you. Come in and make yourself at home, and don't mind my husband. He's had a little bit too much to drink."

Thank God for my mother. She must've slowed down her wine affair. She took Otto's hand and led him to the women's table as my aunts and cousins looked him up and down, while looking at me at the same time. They all wondered how did I get him to come over. I'm glad no one asked because I didn't know either.

Otto wore a two-piece tan suit and looked like my husband should. He stood taller, maybe six-feet six-inches, and prouder, too. I looked at his straight white teeth and had a vision of our first child looking exactly like him. My evening was perfect now. We danced and I felt like Cinderella without the pumpkin or glass slipper mishap. At twelve o'clock, he kissed me on my lips and my life began.

"Lynnette, this is the best New Years I've ever had. Lord knows I don't want to leave you now. I don't want to offend anyone, so a gentleman I must be. One night, hopefully soon, we can celebrate this evening again...all night."

Thank you, Jesus. "I wish we had all night, too, Otto. I'll be moving into my own place soon, and you will always be welcome over there."

"Oh, really? Am I special enough to get a key?" We had been holding hands and he gave mine a gentle squeeze.

"You can get anything you want from me." I felt semi sluttish after I said that, but I didn't care. This man would be mine by any means necessary. We kissed a moist goodbye on the lips and he promised to call as soon as he woke up. I'm in love. Uh oh, I see a sunbeam coming, and it's bringing my mother with it.

"Baby, if he's what you want, then I want him, too. Anytime you want him to come over, he'll be more than welcome."

Smiling replaced my voice. I couldn't bring myself to tell her about my new place and decided to wait a few days. I had a new man to love and make love to. There was no way I could do it in the room across the hall from my parents. How nasty would that be?

My mother and I cleaned up everything but my father and John. Before turning in, I hugged her for a few minutes and felt good I was the reason for her happiness, promising myself I wouldn't disappoint her this time. I won't let her see me hurt or depressed. Otto was the one, and I would only let her see me happy. I promise you, mother, no matter what the situation, only happiness.

# He Doesn't Love Me

It was hard sometimes putting a smile on my face when I was in so much despair. Many times I wished I never met Otto. I don't know why he even bothered getting to know me. We went through a dating charade for three years. Three years of his lying, cheating and walking over me like cracked cement. I asked him to marry me three times as an extra anniversary present and three times he gave me a resounding, "Hell no! Are you crazy woman? That's the furthest thing from my mind."

Pleading I'd say, "Would you just think about it? I love you."

"If you love me, you'll stop asking. I don't need this kind of pressure," was his frustration filled reply. If he were near a table or wall he'd usually hit it.

"I'm sorry, Otto. I'll never ask again."

"Good. That's just what I wanted to hear. I'm hungry. Would you hook a brotha' up?"

"Sure, anything for you." I never asked again after the last time, but wanted to badly. Otto did any and everything he wanted. He knew I didn't like his actions, but my wants didn't matter. I don't know what I did wrong or if it was even me that was the problem. Turning gray haired would happen before he'd change and just love me.

When I asked him to try living together, he answered "hell no" to that, also. He did ask for a key to my place and

I gladly obliged. He came and did as he pleased and I let him. When I asked for a key to his apartment he didn't answer me. Wrong question I guess. I never got a key.

He finally said I didn't need one because he was always at my place. Actually, he wasn't. He wasn't there the nights his out of town flame came and stayed with him. I didn't find any of this out until our second year together. I just happened to be in his neighborhood and...*Oh, Lynnde, don't lie!* All right. I was checking up on him. Don't you say a word, because many women do it in their busted relationships.

The weeks leading up to my sleuthing Otto had been acting stranger than usual. He told me he couldn't spend the night with me because he had appointments. Half crazed I'd ask, "Otto, since when do you have appointments at night?"

With a disgusted frown he'd turned to me, sigh, and say, "Lynnde, mind your business."

"You are my business. What appointments do you have and how long are they going to last?"

"If I'm your business, it's closed for the night. That's all you need to know."

Usually, he'd walk out or hang up on me. Sometimes he was busy at work and probably had a lot on his mind so I never pushed the issue. I didn't want him to be upset with me. After one of our phone confrontations, I prepared a meal of roasted duck and rice pilaf. Surprising him with it would make him feel better, or at least that's what I thought. Please, I was the one who was surprised and didn't feel better at all. I knocked on his door and the, other woman, wearing a pair of red thongs and nothing else, opened it. Surprise. Surprise.

"Baby, did you order any food because a delivery person is here with some?"

"Baby, did you order any food? Who are you calling baby? And hell no, bitch. I'm not the delivery person. I'm his woman. Who are you?"

She didn't answer my question, but she did tell me she wasn't a bitch. Before I could get another word out, Otto showed his face. He took the food and began closing the door. Frantic I screamed, "Otto, what's going on? Who is she and what the fuck is she doing here?"

Every silent signal he gave off read get outta my face, beeyatch. I'd never seen him so hard.

"Lynnde, wait in the car. I'll be out in a minute."

Dummy see, dummy do. Somewhere I saw a woman begging a man. I was on the verge of a tantrum before I remembered it didn't work for her either.

"Otto, I'm your girl. Make her leave. You love me."

That's when he slammed the door in my face. And what did I do? I went and sat in the car. He said he'd be out in a minute and I wasn't leaving before that minute was up. Five hours worth of minutes passed and he never came out.

Why did I sit there so long? Why didn't I go back and demand to know what was going on? I mirrored his signals that's why. I was scared Otto would get mad at me and chose to wait for an explanation that he felt I didn't deserve.

While driving home crying, I thought about him being with another woman and her eating the dinner I made for him. He didn't call until two days later. Four days after that I received an explanation.

"She's just a friend. I used to date her, but I don't like her like that anymore," was the nonchalant reason he gave.

"Well, what do you like her like?"

"Just drop it, will you. You're making something out of nothing, and you wouldn't understand it anyway."

"Otto, please, make me understand." The dead line I heard sounded nothing like Otto's voice. I hate the sound of a dial tone.

Once, I saw him going into a hotel room with a woman. I'm positive I saw him; a blind bat with contact lenses and bifocals would've seen him. It was broad daylight and he was less than twenty feet away from me. I wouldn't let him do this in my face and called his name as he hurried inside. He slammed the door as I ran towards him. For ten minutes straight I pounded and banged on the door. I know he heard me. Everybody heard me.

Hoping I could get inside though a back entrance, I walked around to see. I was entering psycho-ville and didn't care. There was a window cracked open with thorn bushes in front of it and no flowers in sight. Carefully, I weaved my body through the bushes, but I became entangled in the blood prickling spikes. As my pants ripped, I fell in mud. Picture that, my round ass busting out of my pants and falling in mud. Although I was down to one hundred and ninety-two pounds, I probably looked like a hungry hippo.

On my way out of the mud pile, I ripped my shirt and stepped in what I thought was more mud. It was dog shit. I burst out crying then. That's when a woman opened her window and told me to go home. She knew exactly what I was feeling and going about it this way was degrading to me.

"Just go home, lady. Just go home."

I took her advice and just went home. I was in some other world but went through the motions of cleaning myself up and eating everything that I made come face to face with me. When I was choking down a half frozen box of chicken, it was taking to long to cook in the microwave; I heard keys in the front door. I jumped up and began screaming, feeling the same as a wronged psychiatric patient.

"Otto, what are you doing to me! Don't you love me anymore?"

Thinking I was going to take a swing at him he threw his hands up as a defense move. "Girl, what the fuck is wrong with you! I'm getting sick of you and your crazy ass mood swings! What is your problem this time?"

Did he say sick of me and my mood swings? He was the one that had a few personalities.

"Don't try and make me look stupid or crazy! I saw you! I saw you with my own eyes! No one told me anything this time!" Over the course of my dealings with Otto, I received many anonymous phone calls and letters. They were sent to either help or embarrass me, and told of the dirty deeds he did. I'd throw them away and never say a word about them to him. I knew they were true. I just kept hoping one day he'd change, we'd be married, and all of his games would stop.

"You saw me where and what was I supposed to be doing this time, Lynnde? What is it now?"

Enraged I said, "I saw you going into a hotel room with one of your garbage bag hos! I saw your car! And I know you heard me knocking on the door, because everyone else did! Don't lie to me, Otto! I can't take it anymore!"

"Lynnde, you couldn't have seen me at any hotel because I've been at work all day. If you don't believe me, call and check. But if you do, it will be the last call you make about me. Calling will let me know you don't trust me. If you don't trust me, I'm leaving and never coming back."

We both knew the truth, but I started thinking maybe it wasn't him after all. Everyone has a twin. Maybe I saw Otto's. Stranger things in life have happened. So what did I do? I told him I was sorry and probably mistaken. Even though I knew it was Otto, I didn't want to be alone. I had to have a man regardless of the way he treated me.

I stood stupefied as he gave me a pitiful peck on the cheek and said he was hungry. Where had all my self-respect gone?

"Would you mind fixing me something to eat? I'm going to take a shower." His voice was sneaky, but I obliged him as usual. When I heard the water running, I began wailing. I saw him; he'd just been with another woman and was washing off the evidence in my bathroom that I'd have to clean. I had to get myself together and get out of this chaos. Otto didn't love me and never would. I knew this but hung on thinking things would change. They never did. Things only got worse.

He exited the shower looking guilt free. It was four in the morning so I prepared breakfast for him. Who in the world cleaned cars until four a.m.? Otto then smacked and slurped up his food without saying a word, and went to bed. I am so sick of his shit.

We rarely had sex anymore, and when we did it was nasty. One of Otto's sexy points was that he was very well endowed. When we first started making love it was beautiful. I couldn't get enough of him. He made me feel like it was the first time we were together every time. Then two months into our relationship, things changed. He could never maintain an erection and wanted me to orally work on him the entire time. I still didn't get any results. He'd damn near drown himself with gin and that didn't help either. I know for a fact that the gin rumor is definitely not true.

What were these other women getting is what I wanted to know? Maybe when my turn came around he was too tired. We never used condoms, and although I was afraid of getting a disease, I never said anything to him about it. There were times when we were a good five minutes into physical activity when he did manage to obtain an erection and he'd go limp. He'd shrivel up to the size of a miniature raisin that had been soaked in rum overnight. One time he was drunk when it happened and he garbled, "You not suckin' it right! You only get an honorable mention! Go for the gold!" Then he farted. I thought I didn't turn him on anymore.

When we began dating, I weighed two hundred and forty-four pounds. Within three months I was down to two hundred. I said I was going to starve myself for him and I was. He never commented or complained about my size, so I don't know where his problems with me were coming from.

After my next Otto episode, my weight dropped drastically. I went from one hundred and ninety-two pounds, to one hundred and thirty-eight pounds within two months. Esta and my mother suggested that I see a doctor. They thought something was wrong with me. My father told me he knew I could lose that weight, and it was about time I did.

"Lynnde, I was starting to get embarrassed telling people that fat girl is my daughter." When is he going to die?

"Thanks for the compliments," was always my reply when any made a positive comment about me. "I'm on a new revolutionary diet that's doctor approved. Don't worry about me, I'm healthy and every things fine."

Liar. I didn't tell them of the problems I had in my personal life. The official title of my diet was The-Otto-Stress-Panic-Attack-Feel-Like-An-Idiot-All-The-Time-Knots-In-Your-Stomach-So-You-Can't-Eat-Weight-Loss-Plan. I looked like a newfound crack addict who couldn't get enough.

I spent less time in my apartment, and more time in my car traveling the city wasting time looking for a man who didn't want to be found. Trying to spare my feelings stopped me from going to Otto's' house or calling. If I went, I knew I'd be hurt every time. Rock bottom and suicide contemplation was my next phase when something came to my door looking for him. I told her he wasn't there, but he was. Things had been running smooth between us for a week and I didn't want anything to break our streak.

We were six hours into a peaceful day when the devil's bitch showed up. I had turned all the ringers off on my phones and had soothing candles lit. My world was perfect, or at least my version of wonderful camouflaged my senses.

"Shit, I know the mothafucka in there! I saw his truck," it said.

I blasted this thing using the bile from the bowels of my intestines. "Leave! Just leave! He's not here and I don't need to hear what you have to say!"

"Oh yes the fuck you do! My name is Andrea and I am two months pregnant with Otto's baby."

The bitch's neck was rolling hard at that point. An ashy wrinkled finger damn near poked me in my eye.

"You better tell that mothafucka I'm taking him to court for child support. Sorry to bust up your happy home, but Otto is avoiding me and I'm sick of his game playin'."

"Whaaaa?" I couldn't conjure up any magical words around such an evil human spell. She leaned past me and screeched loud enough for the entire city to hear.

"Mothafucka, I know you in there and you hear me! You can't run forever! Don't come by my house either, tryin' to get none! I ain't fuckin' wit' you no more!"

I stood like some sort of flagpole ruler combination and watched it walk away. When it was no longer in sight I closed the door and turned to Otto. I knew it wasn't lying, but he was about to. He was lounging on the couch and heard the words come from its mouth the same as I did. I walked towards him, stood in front of the couch, and waited to at least hear him breathe, because the truth I wouldn't get. Otto sat up, looked at me, and the game continued.

"That girl has been bothering me for months. She has three other kids and is looking for a free ride. She probably doesn't even know who the father is if she even is pregnant."

"Just tell me the truth will you. Have you been with her?"

"I'm sick of your ass, Lynnde. You're always believing other people and I'm tired of it." When he started getting up to leave, the top of my head hit the ceiling.

"My ass! My ass! I'm not the one who fucks everything that moves and has women coming to his so called lady's house to tell them of an upcoming child birth!"

"You have a woman? Damn, baby. You've been holding out on me."

"Shut your fucking mouth, Otto! I'm the one who is sick of you! When your sorry ass gets up to leave, leave. Leave my keys and don't bring your nasty ass, or your dirty trashy ASPCA rejects here again. I hate what you've done to me and I'm on the verge of hating you. Get out!"

I don't know where those words came from, but they couldn't have come at a better time. He looked at me like I was a different person. After his minute gape of me, he laid my keys on the counter and left without saying a word.

For once I didn't cry. I ran to the refrigerator and started with the food on the top shelf and didn't stop until I reached the bottom. Then I ran into the bathroom looking for something to commit suicide with, falling to my knees crying when I couldn't find anything to relieve me of the pain I felt. As I crawled out of the bathroom, the phone rang. I prayed it was Otto. It wasn't. It was my mother.

"Baby, you don't sound very well. You want me to come over? I haven't been over in awhile and I miss you."

"No, Ma. My stomach is upset that's all. I'm going to lie down. I'll be fine."

"You sure, baby? I don't mind taking care of my baby."

"I'll be fine. How's my father?"

"He's fine, baby. Well, since you don't want your poor old mama, I'll let you go."

"Maaa...."

"I'm just funning, baby. I'll call you later, okay?"

"Okay."

"Tell Otto I said hi, and to take care of my baby. Bye, bye."

She knew. I heard it in her voice. She knew I wasn't happy and was waiting for me to tell her. I couldn't. My father would think I was a failure, and I didn't want my mother to worry about me. I was an adult and I wasn't going to run to mommy and daddy every time something in my life was out of place. So what I needed someone to talk to? So what everyone needs help sometimes. I will not allow them to look at me with revulsion in their eyes. That's not an option.

My thoughts then turned to Otto. Why had I spoken to him that way? I had to get him back. He had to understand I was upset and didn't mean anything I said.

Why was I so stupid? He could've been telling the truth for the first time. It's not his fault I didn't believe him. His family does have a successful business and there are many women after him. That's it, that's all it is. She wanted money. She couldn't be pregnant. Otto wouldn't do that to me. I was the woman who would have his babies. The first one, the last one, and all the ones in between.

There's no way my man would be with something that looks like that. And if he was, she must've drugged him with some of her horse face maintenance pills. That girl was ugly. Her mother conceived her with a farm animal that was part horse and part goat. I saw a small trace of sea monkey in her, also. Oh, and the bumps on her face. I can't forget the bumps. If I connected those things I know I'd be looking at an ass. Ugly. I should've asked her what was she pretending to be.

I must've really upset him. He couldn't have meant to say he was sick of me. We've been together for two years and with all the lying and cheating he's done, I'm still not sick of him. I love him. He'll change. I can't give up on him just yet. He's twenty-six and hasn't gotten certain desires out of his system yet. I'll let him cool off for a few days and go and apologize. He'll see the love I have for him and understand. We're in love; I can't let him go through this Andrea dilemma alone. *Love? Is that what this is?*

Otto is mine even if he does choose to stray a bit. What do you mean what does he do for me? He does everything for me. No, he doesn't pay any of my bills, or buy any thing for my household, but he's mine. No, I don't remember the last time he told me he loved me, but I know he does. Does he take me out to public functions? Well, no, but that's only because he's so busy with other things like work. Look, I don't want to hear any negative talk about Otto anymore. You don't know him like I do. I have to have him. I'll show him how much I love him and things will work out for us. I'll go to my grave as Mrs. Otto Parker, and I won't make that trip for years to come.

My life went on as usual, and work was going well. I'd been promoted to the position of assistant manager at Just Shoes eleven months ago, and heard through the shoehorn (that's what we called gossip at the store) that I was up for a store manager's position. The personal problems I had never interfered with my job. At work I guess I tried harder to put up a front. I didn't want my co-workers to know that I had the same problems as everyone else. Someone should have told me that everyone knew who Otto was and knew of his animalistic ways. Everyone talked about me behind my back. They wondered who I thought I was, and what kind of mind problems I had to stay with a man that put me through some form of hell on earth. They didn't understand he loved me and it was going to take a little extra effort, and time, for it to show.

I planned to wait a week before I went to Otto and apologized for the way I'd spoken to him. I lasted two days.

Leave me alone, okay? I thought I'd die on the first, and the second day was spent willing the clock to move.

The last words I said to Otto should've been the last words. After making reservations at a restaurant to make my apology complete, I left work early to pick out a card and some flowers, and made it to his house luckily without receiving a speeding ticket. When I saw his car in the parking lot my soul ran to his door before my physical frame even moved. All of me belonged to him and he never even asked for what I had to offer. I knocked on the door. It answered. Andrea Litten was its name. My composure was outright embarrassed by me and left as I started crying right in front of Otto's pet. What was happening to me?

She didn't say a word and called for Otto to come to the door. I was still crying when he got there. Otto leaned on the doorframe, as if to block my entrance, and let me down hard.

"What do you want now?" I was crushed.

"Well, answer me? What do you want?"

That's when I really lost control. "I want you, I want you, and I love you, and please marry me, and I don't care if the baby is yours, we can raise it together, and I love you, and I didn't mean what I said, and come back to me, and here are your keys!" More tears followed my hysterical outburst. I fell into his chest and a fool was born.

Otto didn't hug me or tell me things would be okay. He told me to go home and he'd be there in a little while.

It began cursing and told him he wasn't going anywhere, adding that it was over, that there never was anything between him and me, and I better accept that as the law.

He didn't respond to it and I viewed him with disbelief. He didn't tell it to shut up or say anything in my defense. He took the keys, stepped back into his place, and closed the door.

Will someone please tell me what's going on? Why didn't he ask me to come in and what is it doing there? Why didn't he tell it to shut its mouth and just exactly who were its comments directed at? I need help if I'm going to willingly deal with this. Breaking down for a half human, half animal to see was not part of my plan.

For a few minutes I stood bent with my head damn near through the door trying to hear some form of support on my side from Otto. All I heard was the beginning sounds of lovemaking. That's what my dumb ass gets. If one reader out there has a gun please use it now. Take me out of this misery because I seem to be unable to do it myself.

Picking the card, flowers, and my face up off the floor slowly didn't make Otto open the door, so I feebly walked to my car. The woman across the hall saw the event unfold and walked behind me in the same direction. I thought she was coming to make sure I was all right, but instead, she stopped at the first apartment in the building and knocked on the door. Her voice was fairly loud and I heard her telling the people inside that they wouldn't believe what just happened.

Once I reached my car, I turned towards the building and saw her pointing at me. She stood there with two other women, and they all gawked at me. I felt so ashamed to be alive. One of the girls looked familiar and during my drive home I kept seeing her face. When I remembered where I'd seen her, I felt the king size version of a dunce complete with a tailor made cap and all, sit on my lap.

Three months ago, I went to Otto's job to take him lunch. He said he was very busy and didn't have time to go out. I went earlier than planned because I didn't want him to feel any hunger pains. Now I wish he would've choked on the meal of burgers and fries. When I turned the doorknob to his office it didn't move, the door was locked. I thought it strange because Otto never had his door locked in the past. I knocked and called out letting him know it was I, and that I had his lunch. Five minutes later the door opened and the girl I just saw emerged. She looked like they were engaged in something they had no business doing. When I entered his office, she rushed past me before any proper introductions could be made. The smell of hot sweat with a trace of funk in it made me turn my nose. It wouldn't have bothered me if the smell were mine, but smelling someone else's ass, when the smell was created with your man, oh hell no.

"Otto, who was that and why does this room smell like tail?" Our game of slay and tackle was about to begin. He caught the ball I tossed him and took a defensive stance.

"Oh, here we go again. She's my cousin."

"Your cousin? What's her name and why did she leave so fast?"

"Look, I don't have time for this right now. Where's my food? I'm hungry."

My voice started to wobble and raised a few octaves but I wanted answers.

"Why can't you answer my questions? Why does this room stink and who was she?"

Not bothering to look at me he sat down. Then he picked up the phone and began dialing. "Give me my damn food and leave now."

I stood tough for a second and then placed the food on his desk. In anger I turned to leave but felt bad. Leaving without trying to apologize was wrong.

"Otto, will I see you later?"

He barely stopped his conversation to answer me. "I'll let you know. Close the door with you on the other side."

I closed the door, lowered my head, and began to cry silently. What did you think I was going to do? Say something that made sense? Please.

While crying needless tears on the way home all I did was think about Otto. Esta was sitting outside my apartment when I pulled up and she helped me get out and up the stairs. Once we were inside, we sat on the couch, and she listened to me try to talk through tears and sobs.

"Esta, Otto doesn't love me! Why?" I, the blubbering idiot, said.

With love and comfort Esta calmed me by saying, "Lynnde, you don't need his kind of love. Look, I know that man isn't doing you right, and I'm tired of waiting for an explanation. You're better than a sister to me, and I've been hurting right along with you. Don't you know I love you and will do anything to help you? Leave his sorry ass alone. You're a beautiful woman and will make any good man happy. Let him go. You don't need this."

Esta always knew what was right. Otto wasn't the one for me, but I hated the feeling of loneliness. He wasn't with me always, but at some point I knew he was going to show up. How could I make Esta understand my feelings? Even though Larry was miles, away she still had him. That's how I wanted to feel. If I ended things with Otto, there'd be no one showing up, ever. I wasn't ready to feel alone yet.

The next morning I called Esta to say I felt much better. We made lunch plans to meet at a Chinese restaurant. For the first time in weeks, I had something to look forward to. Usually, my days were filled with thoughts of Otto and what trash he was going to dump on me. My morning was going decent until the self-imposed impulse to call Otto came over me. I dialed his number and it answered. Fright slapped me as I spoke.

"Hello, uhmm... may I speak to, Otto?"

"He's asleep. Who is this?" I received nothing but skank ho-tude.

"Would you tell him to call, Lynnette?"

"If this ain't about a car, I would appreciate it if you never called our house again. Otto is my man now and we expecting a baby. We getting married next week so leave us alone."

Startled I asked, "Getting married? Otto will never marry you. He loves me."

"Bitch, you wish. Give him up and go eat something, it's over."

Mr. Dial Tone became my conversational partner. A tiny bit of sense told me to let him go. We didn't have a good relationship and never would. That baby was his and there'd be more. He stood me up too many times to count and lied like it belonged in the English language. I had to get over him.

My life was fine after I stopped seeing Otto. I started going by my parent's house regularly, and my mother couldn't have been happier. Of course, they asked what happened and it felt good to explain that Otto and I had grown apart and didn't want the same things out of life anymore.

Esta was going to be married in a month, so I started going back to the gym. I had to look my best as the maid of honor. She'd gone out to California to set up their new home, and I missed her more than I let on. If anyone asked about her or her wedding, I became depressed. I was very happy for her, of course, but knew once she was married, she'd be gone. I didn't want to think about her moving away until it actually happened.

My professional life still moved along at a steady pace. I was promoted to the position of manager and would be working at a store outside the mall while I received extended training. The change of scenery and my new attitude excited me. I began believing I was a normal person who just had a few bad experiences and looked forward to my new position and the responsibility that came along with it.

It had been four months since I called Otto's house, and I haven't had the desire to call back. The super changed the locks at my apartment and my life was finally feeling like I belonged in it. I thought I had a tight grip on the reins until I backslid almost to the point of no return.

With Esta gone I was always at home if I wasn't working or at my parent's house. It was a Friday night and I stayed up late watching movies. The phone rang at two a.m. My parents were usually in bed by ten, so I figured it was Esta calling from California to talk about her new home and Larry. I answered the phone and heard Confunkshun singing Love's Train. That man knows I love that song. I'm so sorry and weak.

"Lynnde, baby I'm sorry. Please give me another chance? Please?"

I didn't respond vocally but my lustful thoughts said, "yes."

"I'll never treat you wrong again. I'll take a blood test to prove that baby isn't mine. You're the only woman I want and it's killing me that we're not together."

Why didn't I hang up and let him talk to Mr. Dial Tone? Well, I did hang up, but not until I told him he could come over. *Goodness, get a grip.* You don't honestly believe that after I've told you how much I love him, I don't have any feelings left for him do you? One more rendezvous isn't going to hurt. Besides, this time I'll be in charge. He said he missed me and even offered to submit to a blood test. He wants me.

Humph, so much for my leadership role. My little rendezvous turned into a nondezvous. Otto was too drunk to do anything but fall asleep on the bedroom floor. If it didn't work when he was sober, I knew I was out of luck when I saw him. When I opened the door, he was leaning to the side, just waiting for that extra shove to push him over. He saw me, slurred he loved me, walked past me to the bedroom and lie on the floor. Maybe he fell, I don't know.

I walked into the room and listened to him snore while watching slob come out of his mouth. I hated myself. He should be out of my house and out of my life for good. Staring at him made me see him in a different light. I didn't love him anymore and hadn't felt love for him in a long time. Shaking him with my foot to wake him and make him get up and leave didn't help any. He was drunk and deader than a brick. He wasn't moving until he decided to.

Then a feeling of mischief came over me. I dialed his number, it answered, and I put the phone to Otto's mouth. It heard him snore, all right; I won't take my frustrations out on it. I'll address her properly from now on. She knew it was him and cursed like an animal. Sorry. And this was going to be the mother of his child? I laughed, hung up, and went and slept on the couch.

When morning came I'd tell Otto that I felt sorry for him. He needed to hear that we were over, and he wasn't welcome here anymore. I'd tell him there was someone so good waiting in the world for me, and he wouldn't stop me from getting to him. I'd let him know my amusement park ticket expired and I'd take no more rides with him. I'd tell him the hang up calls and the anonymous letters would no longer be received at this address. I'd tell him that I would no longer be stood up, hurt, or brought to tears by him. I'd tell him not to come here, call here, or let my name come from his lips ever again. I'd tell him to find another fool; this one is way over her allowed limit.

Yes, I'd tell him these things and much more. As soon as he woke up, he was going to hear the strong Lynnde, the one who wouldn't be used anymore. The one who people would no longer talk about behind her back in a negative way. It was over and I'd tell him this as soon as my eyes met his.

Otto woke up at 2:55 in the afternoon but the person I was going to tell everything to didn't. I never said one word I wanted to say to him. Seeing him reminded me of how fine he was, and the previous strength I displayed and was so proud to feel, left my body without a trace. I was the one who was right, the one who possessed the power. With one look, I let him take it away. I'd be okay without Otto and would get much better if I allowed myself to. I felt like a car stuck in a muddy ditch that knew it was capable of getting out but needed a little extra push or traction for it's spinning wheels. My problem was that I didn't know my extra push was inside of me.

I stood over Otto before he woke talking to myself, planning what I would say to rid him of my world. *Okay, Lynnde, tell him now. Tell him before he speaks one word of lies to you. Hurry, tell him.*

"Lynnde, baby. I'm sorry." *Too late.* "I'm sorry for hurting you these last few months."

Last few months? How about the last two years? Why wasn't I able to open my mouth and tell my thoughts to him? I wanted him that's why. I wanted him to say things would be perfect between us, that there'd be no more mistakes, and that the baby wasn't his. I wanted to hear that he'd love me and only me, and that we'd be married. *Well, change the channel stupid. This is the Otto network, not Lynnde's version of the Dating Game. The saga continues.*

"Baby, please give me another chance. I miss you and need you. I'll do whatever it takes to please you. I'll take a blood test. Andrea means nothing to me. I was only seeing her because you put me out, and I didn't have anything else to do."

What did that fool just say to me? Did he say he only saw her because I put him out, and he had nothing else to do? I know I repeated it word for word but you know that's part of the upset routine. We all know the first part was a lie and if he were so into me, he wouldn't have worried about having nothing else to do. Exactly what level of fool has Otto risen to and will he continue to climb higher?

"I'll give you time to think things over and I'll be home waiting on your call. If I don't hear from you, I'll understand. I won't bother you again."

This was my chance to exit this scene right here. I should let him leave and never have to worry about him again. I didn't. Don't start yelling at me dear reader; I think I'm in love with this man, remember? I don't want to be alone, I can't.

"Otto, you don't have to leave if you don't want to. I love you. We can make it work, we just have to try harder that's all."

"Thank you, Lynnde. Thank you. You won't regret this. I promise."

He then kissed me on the cheek and said he was hungry. He asked did I mind preparing one of my perfect breakfast meals that he loved so much. He was going to take a shower. Rewind. Didn't I play the part of a shark attack victim already? *You must've enjoyed it because you're about to play it again.* His treatment of me was the same as being devoured by a great white, and then him spitting out the bits of your body he didn't enjoy. I knew things with Otto would never work out, but I'd been on the ground so long it was starting to feel comfortable. I was too lazy to get up.

Once Otto re-entered my life, the feelings of insecurity and the second guessing games returned, also. I couldn't sleep with him near me and couldn't sleep when he was away.

My parents found out I was seeing Otto when they stopped by for an unannounced visit. I felt very awkward and ashamed. Everyone was cordial in a fake kind of way, and they never mentioned Otto to me afterwards. That made me feel dirty, you know, like I was doing something unlawful or unnatural. It's because I was. There's an unwritten law that says a broken heart is illegal when it's obtained in a malicious manner.

Whenever Otto and I were together I felt like crap. He was wrong for me and I did nothing to change the course my life was about to take. If he happened to be seen with me in public, I felt every eye on me. That's a sickening feeling when you know it's coming from a bad place.

I said that I'd receive no more anonymous phone calls or letters, but I was wrong. I couldn't even control what was coming into my house, yet I still wouldn't let this man release his hold of me. Someone sent a note saying hell would freeze over before Otto would want me. I cried.

That note came the same day Otto received his blood test results. I don't know if I should say he passed or failed-but the baby is his. He failed three more tests after that. How was he making all these babies?

My Otto life returned with more power than it had before. I couldn't stand myself. My body couldn't stand it either. I went from a sexy size fourteen to a size twenty-two in a matter of four Otto months, and weighed two hundred and thirty-three pounds. I didn't care anymore.

Luckily, Esta was married before I ballooned out of control. She found out I was Otto's patsy because he was my date at her wedding. Esta knew I wasn't happy with him either. She told me to leave him; he could give me a disease or something worse.

"Esta, what could be worse than that?"

"Once I heard this woman got cancer because she was with the wrong man and they didn't mix well. These things happen sometimes so get out now before it happens to you."

A few seconds of silence passed, and then came hysterical laughter from both of us. If I died at that moment I would've been satisfied. Knowing Esta wanted happiness for me and loved me unconditionally was all I'd ever need. We hung up and I knew I had to do this. He had to go. Esta was willing to walk through fire for me. What was I willing to do for myself? Lonely or not, he has to go.

The words sounded so good in my voice. It's too bad I never put them into play. I wanted to take control of myself but I still did anything Otto wanted. The desire of needing him in my bed at night, even if it was only to sleep, had more authority than it should.

Otto made many requests of me during my relationship with him. I used to hate to think about them, let alone talk about for someone else's ears to hear. I'm over that part of my life now so I don't want to hear any judgmental remarks from any of you. Yes, I used to baby-sit for him. There, I said it. Why did I do that, and how could I have been so stupid you ask? Well, I'll tell you. My twisted reality with Otto made me think we'd raise his puppies, I'm sorry, children together. I figured if I babysat for him he would want to marry me. Dumb ass.

I was only going to tell you half the story but I might as well cleanse my soul. While I cared for his dog pound, he'd be out with the mothers or who ever he picked for the night. Dumb ass.

My brain was so far into depravation when it came to him. One time we went out for dinner and a movie and were having a very enjoyable evening. I'm sure Otto had multiple personalities because on the ride home he asked me if I loved him.

"Yes, Otto, I love you. Why'd you ask that?" I should have said hell no, or just kept my mouth shut.

"Baby, if you love me, I want you to walk naked in front of the car with the headlights beaming on your beautiful round ass. I'll never cheat again if you do."

"Otto, I can't do that! What if someone sees me?" I was bewildered.

"Don't worry about that. I'll go to the parking lot behind the auto shop. There's a junkyard back there and no one will be on that road tonight. Please do it, Lynnde. It would turn me on."

Yes, I did it. But wait, listen, don't throw this book down just yet! For the first time in our relationship he admitted he was cheating and said he'd never do it again. Before, when I'd ask him why he did certain things he'd simply say, "It's a man thing," and leave it at that. Maybe if I did this he'd change.

I took all my clothes off, including my shoes, in the middle of December, when it was thirty degrees outside. Disgraced to the point of wanting to drop dead got worse when two cars rode by and honked their horns. Otto had the high beams shining on all of me so the drivers and occupants saw everything God gave me. My humiliation of myself lasted for ten minutes. When I put my cold as a warehouse full of frozen chocolate ice cream ass back in the car, my tears started. If he says one word to me, I'll kill him is what I thought.

"Lynnde, I'm going to make you mine." *Start killing. Oh, you're such a liar.* "That was beautiful. I'll drop you off at home and be back later. I forgot about an appointment I have."

I sat in the back seat and thanked God he had a truck because my big ass needed all the room I could get. On the ride home he blasted his stereo with incomprehensible music, and said nothing more. Maybe I didn't understand it because I was trying so hard to hold back tears that came anyway. I couldn't concentrate on anything else.

When he pulled up in front of my apartment, he didn't give me a kiss or anything. He pulled off before I was barely out of the vehicle. Standing on the sidewalk I bawled out loud then wondered what had I just done. I was lower than the earth beneath me and on my way to hell.

After that evening I didn't see Otto for two weeks. He'd call sometimes and make dates that he never kept. I was so disgusted with myself. Otto slept all over town with anyone who smiled at him. He made a total of five puppies that I knew about and all kinds of breeds called my house looking for him. That's when I hated myself. After his last request, I hated him. I didn't have to ask him to leave my life, he just did.

It was a Saturday afternoon and I had the day off. My parents and I were going out for dinner at six that evening, and Otto showed up at 1:13. I was surprised to see him because he hadn't called and he never left work to visit me.

Otto didn't love me, like me, or even care if I existed for that matter. He asked me to show him again how much I truly loved him. A female walked in and he added if I did this, we'd go and pick out a ring first thing in the morning. Why did I allow him to take me down so far?

"Otto, who is she? What's going on?" These words came out in my getting ready to cry voice before the tears stream. You know, in that wiggly, wobbly, coming unglued voice.

"Lynnde, I love you. I've always loved you. I just want to be sure that you're the woman for me before I give up the single life. You understand, don't you? Just do this one last time, and I'll know you're the one for me, okay?"

I didn't want to marry Otto, nor did I love him. All I heard him say was he loved me. That's all I wanted. Someone to love me. I had people who loved me but I didn't have a man of my own who did. He said we'd be married after this one last request. I believed him. I needed a man at any cost. I paid with my self-respect and my self-esteem.

Otto wanted me to kiss and lick his nasty black ass while he had sex with this woman. An ass one day I thought would be all mine. I never saw the woman before, but she was very attractive and looked like she was too young to be involved in something like this. She eyed me without any facial expression and never said a word. Oh, I was so stupid.

They began getting undressed and I did nothing to stop them. Next, they started kissing and touching as if I weren't in the room. Was this really happening? Was I in a Three-D nightmare?

The realness of it hit me when I heard the words created by fucking. He was tearing her and me up at the same time. Otto began his sexual voyage with this woman and I watched from eyes that weren't mine. He never made love to me like that and instead of stopping his madness; I wanted to ask if I could be next. Was I going crazy? My mind had gone to the lost and found and hid in the don't nobody want this shit section. I had no sense of right or wrong. I'd have to move into a padded cell after this.

What kind of woman would let the man she loves have sex in her bed with another woman? And I'm not talking about the freaky people so don't down me for not being with it. A woman with nothing to give to herself, or to the world.

The sad sickening part is that I not only watched, I participated in it. I held on to his thrusting body and allowed my tongue to slide across his backside. I cried the entire time. Did anyone find a gun yet?

He finished, after being with her longer than he ever was with me, and they both got dressed. Otto told his partner to wait outside in the car; he'd be down in a few minutes. I stood up facing him without any feeling in my body; not believing this went on in my apartment and in my bed. The phrase, you are what you eat came to mind. It's true. I felt like shit because I ate shit. My feast didn't come directly from the source but it was shit just the same. Otto's next words confirmed his hate for me.

"Lynnde, I never want to see you again. You disgust me. You're not good enough to be Mrs. Otto Parker, or any man's wife for that matter. Don't ever call me or come looking for me again. Your fat ass will do anything for anybody. I never loved you. I was doing you a favor by fucking you. Here's some money; buy some respect."

He then walked out of the door, leaving it ajar, and never returned that night. I didn't say one word. I stood there with trembling lips, eyes full of tears, stinking breath, and dollar bills scattered at my feet. Three years. Three years of his sorry ass. Who did he think he was? Who did he think I was? Who did I think I was? Nobody. I didn't think I was special, and I deserved the pain I felt. I'd gotten rid of my baby and this is what I received in return. I fell to my knees and cried, "You dumb ass bitch," for whoever I was to hear.

Three hours passed before I was able to move again. Once feeling returned to my body, I took the sheets off the bed and threw them in the trash. History was repeating itself and I called for death to make an introduction. Death took too long, so I walked into the kitchen with a vengeance. I didn't need a man. What I needed, I had right in front of me. Food. Glorious food. It always loved me and made me feel complete. It was never disgusted with me, and I could have as much of it any, and every time I wanted it.

As I opened the refrigerator to begin my heavenly climb, the doorbell rang. I didn't care who it was; I wasn't answering it. They could ring that thing until it broke. I had some serious eating to do, and I wouldn't stop for anyone.

Then I had a crazy idea that it was Otto coming back to apologize to me. I walked to the door faster than I had moved in weeks. My last thoughts before I swung the door open were for Otto to please be standing on the other side.

Someone much better than Otto stood before me. My beautiful mother. I burst out crying and sunk into her arms. She must've summoned strength from somewhere deep inside because she held me and helped me walk to the couch. I was two hundred plus pounds and she was only one hundred and thirty. Why couldn't I be stronger? Why did she have to see me like this?

My mother loved me no matter what went on in my life. My mother, Cecelia Marie Lee, maiden name Bonam, the most beautiful fifty-year-old woman I'd ever seen. Why couldn't I be like her? She still had the shape of a twenty year old and always wore fitted dresses with matching sweaters. Her hair was still its natural color of black and she wore it in a neat pin curl style. Recently, she started wearing glasses and chose a style from the fifties that made her even more beautiful. I don't know what kind of luck my father had to marry her.

We sat on the couch and listened to my howling dog cries. My mother held me, rubbed my back, and told me to let it go and let it out. Everything would be fine now that she was there. I wanted to say I was sorry for acting this way and that I should be stronger, but more cries filled in for the words. She held on to me tightly and spoke words I needed to hear.

"Baby, I knew you were hurting. I should've done something a long time ago. Don't you worry none. Forget about that boy child. That wasn't a man you were with. He didn't treat you with the respect you deserved. You'll be all right. Mama's here now, it's going to be all right. You're strong, smart, and beautiful. The right one will come along, you'll see. Every one makes mistakes and you have nothing to be ashamed of. You just keep on living, you hear? Just keep on living."

All I could do was nod to let her know I understood.

"I love you, Lynnde. Before any man calls you baby, know that you'll always be my baby first. You can come to me with anything. I'll take care of you. I don't care how old you get, and it doesn't matter what the problem is. Just come to your mama."

My tears fell harder.

"That's right, baby. You let it out. Let it all out. Love's gonna come my baby's way soon enough. You just wait. Just wait for love."

I was a twenty-four year old successful shoe store manager who was acting worse than a two-year old. My mother was right. She told me these things in the past, but I didn't want to listen. My mother always gave me life talks to help me in my journey. Being a hardheaded person made me hear them as talk down speeches. I learned the hard way that I was wrong. My mother was talking to me. Giving me her wisdom and knowledge to help me avoid the pain I felt. When God returns the privilege of having children to me, I pray they listen and don't make the same mistakes I have.

I never think about how much I love my mother. Just telling her I love her isn't good enough. I'm ashamed to admit I let a bad relationship lead me astray from the good relationship I had with her. We used to talk on the phone everyday and go out to lunch or dinner at least three times a week. All of that changed when I fell in love. I remember my mother's exact words when I said I was going to move out.

"Twenty-one is just an age and doesn't qualify you as a worldly adult. Don't be in such a hurry, Lynnde."

She'd say whatever it took to keep me at home. My mother just didn't understand that it was time for me to venture out into foolville. I moved out for all the wrong reasons but from here on out, my reasoning process is going to change. The only thing I'm going to concentrate on is my family, and put in some serious work on me. No men this time, just me.

# Headed In the Right Direction

Six months have passed since my journey into the underground. My life can be described as average I guess. I still work, eat, and sleep, so I'm doing okay. I'm trying to make my life as normal as possible. It would be a big help if I knew what normal was.

The best part about my life now is the reconnection made with my mother. We are back on track, and I don't know which one of us was happier. The night of my ass taste test, you know, freak lesson 101, her showing up was the best thing that could've happened to me. I never told her the truth exactly. What mother wants to hear her daughter eats animal ass? Well, would you tell? Not that you would be so stupid as to do what I did. I really don't want to bring my level of intelligence into question so as they say, let's not go there. My mother figured I caught him in bed with another woman, and she seemed satisfied with my version of the truth.

That night I wasn't worth anything. My mother gave me a bath, brushed my teeth, and made my couch nice and comfy, seeing it would be my bed for the evening.

"We'll get rid of that bed in the morning and get a new one okay, baby? All you need is a fresh start and everything will be fine. Now baby, don't forget, you can always come back home. Think about it, you hear?"

"Yes, Ma. I hear. I'll think about it."

"Good. Now, baby, you didn't do anything wrong. Don't be ashamed of this. Morning will come and mama knows you'll feel better."

I cried again. I didn't want my mother to leave but was too ashamed to ask her to stay. She called my father and told him she was going to spend the night with me because we were overdue for a girl's night. I heard her say, "She's alright, everything's fine. And no, you don't have to come over."

I was happy that my father asked about me. I thought my moving out would spare them the aggravation of worrying about me and seeing my pain. Once again, I failed everyone's expectations. My mother had to come to my rescue. Did I even deserve to be rescued?

That night seemed to pass slower than time usually allowed one to suffer but morning finally came. I opened my eyes to see my mother sitting up in a chair facing me. She looked as if she'd been studying my face for hours.

"Hi, Ma. I'm sorry."

"Oh, baby, don't you say sorry to me. You have nothing to be sorry for. Just remember, you never have to feel pain alone, you hear me? You tell your mama and let me feel it for you okay? You talk to me anytime about anything, you hear?"

"Yes." The only word I was capable of saying.

"Good. Now don't be upset with me but I called your job and told them you wouldn't be in today. I said you had an upset stomach, okay?"

"Thank you, Ma. I planned on calling in myself."

"Now, baby, I want you to keep a good head about this. Don't go and do anything crazy. He ain't worth it, you hear? Do you feel like some breakfast? I can cook you something special or take you out. Whatever you want is fine with me."

"I'm not hungry. I promise I won't do anything crazy. Things were over between us a long time ago. I'm sure I'll be fine."

"Now, that's my baby talking. That's my Lynnde. You'll see baby. You'll be better than fine. Just wait and see."

While we were telling each other this situation would pass, someone knocked on the door. Yes, Otto's name went through my mind but it was my father. He had come by with our neighbor, Mr. Thompson, to remove the evidence. My mother meant what she said by getting a fresh start. She called him back during the night and told him what happened. As my father and Mr. Thompson came in, my mother held me and said, "Lynnde, he's your father and he loves you the same as I do. He's here to help and you have nothing to be ashamed of. He's not here to judge you, but to love you. I want you to let him do just that, you here?"

As my father walked towards me I nodded. Once he reached me, he didn't say a word. He stretched his arms out, pulled me towards him, and gave me a hug. I felt like I was seven years old again. Yes, I hugged him back and did what I do best, I cried. He didn't say anything. He just squeezed me tighter. My mother took Mr. Thompson into my bedroom while my father and I stood in the middle of my living room. He spoke stern loving words to me, which made me wish my parents would move in with me.

"Baby girl, whatever man you meet, you tell him if he don't treat you right, you don't give a damn. You already have a man who loves you and that's your daddy, you hear? You tell him that for me."

As I sat on the couch feeling so sorry I ever wished him dead, he walked away with pride in his step. I can't believe what I just heard. My mother hurried out of my room and sat next to me.

"See, I told you your daddy loved you." She then hopped up and went back into my room. I wrapped my arms around my chest hoping to feel my father's presence once again. I'll never wash these pajamas. I'll wear them until they fall from my body and shout no more.

I'll get over this. I know it for sure now. I have the love of my parents and have the love of myself to help me. My life will prosper without what's his name and I'll be better than good. Lynnde is going to be all right.

After my bed was removed, my mother and I cleaned my apartment from head to toe. I didn't think I'd feel good at all that day, but my mother had me laughing out loud, singing songs, and even dancing. I didn't move too fast but I did okay. I told her I was going to take control of my weight, and she gave me much needed encouragement.

"Every thing will come in time, you'll see. Just take your time, baby. Don't be in a hurry. Uh-uh. No need to rush along the beauty you already have."

Even though six months have passed, some days I don't understand my feelings. Work is going well and I've managed to make a few new friends. I know I don't love Otto, but he always seems to find a way into my thoughts. He shows up at the strangest times. Sometimes, I'm in the middle of a meeting and hear a word that's nowhere near his name, and his face obstructs my sight. When I'm at home, he shows up first thing in the morning. Sometimes I wake up and say his name aloud. When I go to bed at night, I say his name as I 'm drifting off to sleep. It's really weird when I wake up in the middle of the night, thinking the doorbell has rung. I get out of bed, run to the door, and open it to find no one on the other side.

I don't have any desires to be with him, and I wish he'd stay out of my thoughts completely. Even after seeing him with her and her and her, he's still beautiful to me. I wonder does he ever think about me, and if he does, are they special thoughts? Does he treat anyone the way he treated me and why did he treat me that way?

When I was one month into withdrawal, I kept wondering if he'd ever call me again or if we were going to get back together. I told myself things would be so different because I'd treat him much better. Then I thought what could I possibly do to treat him any better? I worshiped the ground he walked on and gave him my heart on a gold edible platter.

When I see Otto with the woman of his choice for the day, he never says hello. And if he looks my way, it feels like he is looking right through me, which makes me hurt. I wish he wouldn't even come to the mall. Doesn't he know how much I loved him and wanted to be with him forever? Sometimes I thought about paying him to be with me. Has anyone out there ever done that?

Thinking of all the bad times we had helped me move on. People were always looking at us and laughing at me. I thought of all the times I kissed his ass to keep him coming to me before I did it, literally.

My mother and Esta tell me to wait for love but I don't want to. Why should I have to wait when they both have someone in their lives? I want someone, too. He had to love me. He had to. You can't spend three years with someone and don't feel anything for them. That makes no sense. What about the other women? The hell with the other women! His love for me is all I'm concerned about.

I think that's why I'm having such a hard time getting over him. I want him to tell me that he did love me and that it wasn't me, it was him. My heart beats in overtime telling me it's way over; you're not the one for him. Then my head asks for one more chance, saying it's willing to wait for him. That's when my senses come back. I tell my head that I'm going to get my chance at love but not with him. I'll be patient and wait. Humph, I wish my life were like daylight savings time; I'd turn it ahead.

# Don't Be Fooled By the Wrapper

Work has been better than usual. I recently received a pay raise and was picked to manage a new store opening up in a shopping center. After seven years at one store, a change of scenery is better than any all you can eat buffet for me.

Esta is working at a fashion boutique and has a plan in motion to open up her own soon. She's always been business savvy, so I know if she wants it, it'll happen. My girl is coming home in three weeks to celebrate her parent's anniversary. Lord knows I can't wait for her to get here. When I told her I stopped seeing Otto, she cried. That girl loves me. She said I should learn to live with, and love me.

"You'll see, Lynnde. You'll love yourself just as much as I do." How did she get to be so smart, and how did I get her for my best friend?

I took her advice and have been spending time by myself. I hate it. Not because I don't like the company, but it seems I eat to entertain myself. If I'm watching television, reading the paper, washing clothes, or doing nothing, I'm eating. Food gives me comfort, which makes me feel needed, and that's what I like.

My weight's been on a seesaw since my Otto breakup. When a month passed, I went on a food rampage. When I weighed in at two hundred and forty-two pounds I decided to start a diet. Within two weeks, I was amazed I'd lost five pounds. I celebrated for a week and weighed in at two hundred and forty-eight pounds. Depression started to set in and I stopped the diet and weighing myself after that. I'd love myself more if there were more of me.

Miss Optimistic became my middle name after staying up late one night watching television. I ran across an old black and white movie but didn't get the name of it. In the movie, a woman explained to her friend that there's a big difference between being alone and being lonely. She said, "As long as you love yourself, you'll never be lonely because there will always be someone with you who loves you." Get it? I didn't get it at first either, but I did in time, and I'm sure you will, too.

Being alone is no big deal. You're usually alone when you use the bathroom, bathe, or get dressed, so a little alone time is good for the soul. Day after day I repeated what I heard in the wee hours of the morning and managed to get my weight down to two hundred and ten pounds. I'll be all right. Yep, I'll be all right.

Every now and then I go out with a girl who worked in the mall two stores down from me. Esta told me it's okay for me make new friends as long as she remained my best friend. That deal is sealed in a time capsule that will never be unearthed.

Tori Ladd is my cohort's name. She's the manager of a women's clothing store called, It's Your Size. It's a plus size store, but she's not fat at all. Do you ever notice when you go into a plus size store all the women workers are quite large? Some people think a plus size store is the only place heavy people shop so that's the only place they can work. And I thought I have issues.

I like Tori though. We met on a customer level when I'd shop in her store occasionally. Once I reentered the single life that I didn't know I was always in, we began going to lunch together. She's a very attractive chocolate chip cookie brown, without the chips-five-feet-nine inch, slim, one hundred thirty-five pound slinky thing. I always try to figure out what someone weighs even though I promised myself I wasn't going to do that anymore. Looks aren't everything.

Tori and I go out sometimes and we always have a good time. She likes to dance and can stay on the floor all night. When she drinks, she makes me think of a Hershey's chocolate bar. She's pretty brown on the outside and nuts on the inside. That girl drinks entirely too much. I wouldn't call her an alcoholic, but she can hang with an old drunk that was locked in a liquor store on his birthday. Do you see what I see? I've seen her drink until she throws up.

Ugh. Once she's brushed her teeth and gotten herself together, she continues her affair with the DRINK.

The first time we hung out was during my, "I'm so lonely" phase. Tori invited me over to her apartment, and I had the best time since my days with Esta. I'd forgotten what it was like to have a girlfriend. We had dinner, talked, and yelped off key to songs we didn't know the words to. Her next-door neighbor, Mrs. Lipton, came over and asked if she could join the party. She did a three-sixty turn when she saw it was no men and just us. She did take a drink of cognac with her when she left, though.

One conversation we had that night was about her brother. He was her twin, but he was the ugly one. See, there I go talking about the way someone looks. Well, I have to describe him to you, so it's not the same as just dogging someone, is it? No, I didn't think so. I'll never understand how two people can have the same mother and father, be twins, and one is good looking and the other isn't. In this case, the ugly one would be Desmond.

That name is wasted on him. He comes into the shoe store sometimes, always smiling and trying to make conversation. I've seen and smelled his feet, so maybe that's why I think he's so unattractive. Desmond has corns, bunions, and crust all rolled up into one on his paws. He needs to get those things amputated and start all over again.

Yes, I know that wasn't nice, but it's the truth. Straight up slave feet. I bet every time he hears the word master his feet start hurting. Okay, okay, I'll get off the man's feet.

Another thing is he's shorter than Tori, which makes him shorter than me. He's only five-feet-five inches tall. I don't want to be the next Sonny and Cher or for techno-colored purposes, the next Marilyn Mckoo and Billy Davis Junior. Sometimes he looks like a bird that was kicked out of the nest too soon. I have visions of eating the last worm, rolling over, and crushing him. I'm not going to jail for that.

He's not too skinny or anything. He's an average weight for a man of his height, but I'm a lot larger than he is, and he doesn't look like the picture framed in my mind. Excuse me for a minute, will you? My phone's ringing.

"Hello?"

"Hey, Lynnde, girl. What cha doing? Getting ready for our big night?"

"Hi, Tori. No, I'm just sitting here relaxing before I take a bath. What's up?"

"I hope you won't mind if I invite my brother along to hang out with us tonight. He's been having a real hard time at work, and he needs to get out and have some fun. Do you mind?"

A massive attitude massaged my shoulders before I responded.

"Did you ask him already?"

"Relax would you. Yes, I asked him. But look at it in a positive way. It's a big club and it's not like you'll have to spend your evening talking to him. But will you please be nice?

"Okay. I'll be nice and I'm sure we'll all have a good time. Now let's get off of this phone and start getting ready for our night of partying."

"Thanks, Lynnde. Desmond and I will pick you up at 9:30. I want to get there early so we can get valet parking and see what's going on, if you know what I mean."

"Yes, I know what you mean. I'll see you later. Bye."

"Bye, girl."

Damn, there goes my little high I was on. Desmond's feet just skipped through my mind and left a dust trail behind. *Be nice, Lynnde.* I'll be nice to him, but I'm not going to spend all evening with him. I know Tori's going to wander off somewhere and I'll get stuck with Doctor Dolittles, "I can talk to the animals," illegitimate child. *Stop it.* Desmond is probably a really nice guy and a good time will be had by all this evening. I have to stop judging people by the way they look. There are good people in my life and they don't do that to me. If they did they'd have to judge three people. They like Lynnde for Lynnde and I must learn to do the same of others. I'd better get a move on; it's 6:42 and I still haven't decided what to wear.

After frying my brain, I picked out a long dress with a matching coat and low-heeled shoes. I want to be sexy and comfortable at the same time. I'll have to take what I can get, so comfort it is. You're going to have to excuse me again, the phone's ringing. I can go days without getting any calls and now in the middle of my conversation with you this thing wants to act up.

"Hello?"

"Hello, sexy."

Oh, hell no. It's Otto. Six months had passed without one word from him and in two days it would be seven. What does he want and what made him think he could call me? I'm not going to lie, his voice still sounds good, but it's irritating at the same time. My tone went from pleasant to the starting point of digging in your behind time. "What do you want, Otto?"

"Hey, sexy, don't be so mean. I called to see how you've been doing. I miss you. I can't get you out of my mind."

"Otto, I'm not in the mood for any of your shit right now or even later for that matter. I'd appreciate it if you never called me again."

"Baby, I can understand your anger and I can accept that. I just can't accept us not being together anymore. What do you say to a get back together dinner? I miss you, Lynnde."

My anger came to me in hot hell flashes, and my voice reached a pitch I'd never heard before. I'd suppressed so much these past three years towards Otto, that now it was exploding out of me in the most ugly way imaginable.

"You doggish bastard fucker! What makes you think your nasty ass can just call me like it's all so good? I'm gonna set your fucking ass on fire right now so you can start your trip to hell! That way when you get there, the burning feeling won't come as a shock to you. I should hate you,

Otto, but I don't. I hate what I let you do to me over and over again. So accept the fact that hell no we can't go to dinner or do anything else together. Accept the fact that I don't want you, need you, or care to have sex with your limp dick ass ever again. Oh, and one more thing, accept the fact that I don't ever want you calling here again. Now you talk to Mr. Dial Tone. Here's what he has to say."

The phone cried because I slammed it down so hard. To calm down I walked around in circles. I felt very hot and my heart raced, but I felt good. I was over him. Yeah, I told him what he needed to know. If I didn't get the chance that dummy had just given me, I was still over him. I'll round off my six months to seven since I only have two days to go, and say it was a hard seven months but I did it. I moved on and didn't even know it. It wasn't so bad after all.

I don't love Otto, and going down a dead end road is just that, a dead end. Seeing myself in a new light and getting stronger makes me feel special and worthy. Gosh, loving myself feels good. Wow, look at the time. I have a date with life tonight, and I must be on time for this one.

Twenty gallons of new blood went carousing thru my body, or at least I felt like it did. Listening to a little party music and washing my entire rump to a new tune added to my happiness. Otto probably called because he saw me a few days ago at the mall. Yeah, I checked him out but not in a wanting kind of way. He looked like he gained a good thirty pounds and his face was fuller. His sexy piercing eyes were no longer there. They looked a little closer together so his face had some sort of ape effect going on. He looked decent though. He was with two women and three kids so one can only imagine what was happening with them. But you're right, who cares. Oh good, the Ladd's are here. When I get in Tori's car, I'm going to disconnect her horn. She's going to wake up the entire neighborhood with the way she's laying on that thing.

Why can't I fast forward my legs and get to the car sooner? I'd do anything to make Desmond stop staring at me. I guess he's decent looking enough with his feet and hungry bird features. So what does he see in me? There I go, backsliding and putting myself down. What doesn't he see in me? It doesn't matter anyway. I'm not going to think about a man or his feelings towards me tonight; I just want to have a good time. Oh, what a gentleman. He's getting out to open the car door. I guess the time to start being nice is now.

"Hi, Desmond. How are you? Are you ready to enjoy yourself tonight?" That sounded sincere didn't it?

"Why, Lynnde. I'm fine, and it's so nice of you to ask. I'm sure we'll have a good time. I hope you'll dance with me. You're looking so pretty."

Nerd, but who am I to talk? "Sure, I'll dance with you. Hey, Tori Ladd. What's up, girl?"

"Girl, I'm ready. You look nice. As you can see, I put on the tightest clothes I could find so ladies, watch your men."

Laughter filled the car followed by a brief moment of silence and then Desmond.

"Lynnde, I hope we can take a picture together because standing next to you will only make me look better."

"Desmond, it would be my pleasure to make you look better."

The car grew silent after my response. Within seconds, hysterical laughter took the wheel, and I don't know when it let go. When I was finally able to catch my breath, I earnestly apologized to Desmond. I told him I didn't mean for it to come out that way. That's what I get for talking about his feet; I just put mine in my mouth.

Desmond offered up a cheerful smile. "No harm done, Lynnde. Someone as sweet as you would never say anything mean."

He should've met me two hours ago. That comment would never have come from his mouth. I saw Tori looking at me from the corner of my eye, so I figured she wanted me to say something nice in return.

"Thank you, Desmond. You look mighty nice, also."

Tori smiled, so I'm sure I did a good deed. Desmond thanked me and the conversation turned to Tori's day at work. I caught a glimpse of Desmond in the rear view mirror in his attire, which consisted of a black suit with a white shirt and black bow tie. He'd be the neatest looking penguin in the bunch. See, I can give a compliment.

We were a few minutes away from the club and my enthusiasm grew. I'd only been out a few times since, him, but I never felt this good. For once, I wasn't thinking about meeting a man but instead, listening to some good music and actually dancing. Usually, I just sit at the bar and people watch but not tonight. This was going to be a celebration.

My twenty-sixth birthday was three months ago. I spent it at my parent's house and received a phone call from Esta. When I went home, I sat on my couch and cried until daylight greeted me. Sometimes the tears were happy ones, and sometimes they were tears of self-pity. I cried because I wished I had a man and cried because he was out of my life. Those were supposed to be happy tears. I cried because I was on my period and couldn't be touched in a special way. I cried thinking if I could be touched, there was no one who I could call to touch me. Maybe it was just my hormones or me being stupid, but not tonight. Tonight, I plan to celebrate my life turning down a two way street for the first time. I'm really not paying attention to Tori or Desmond. I'm in my own zone thinking about how I'm going to put more effort into learning to be grateful for the breaths I take. I'm grateful for the chance to better myself, even though I took that chance away from someone else.

"Okay, Lynnde. Snap out of your trance and let us in on where you've been. You haven't heard a word I've said have you?"

"I'm sorry. I was just thinking about something I have to do at work first thing Monday morning."

"Enough about work. We're here and this club better be nice. It's opening night and first impressions mean a lot sometimes, if you know what I mean."

"Yeah, Tori. I know what you mean. Girl, do you know, Tina? She usually works the register in the mornings during the week?"

"Yeah, I know her. The real skinny one who thinks she's superfine. One of these days I'm going to tell her she looks like a Twix stick that's lost it's wrapper - skinny, black and bumpy. What about her?"

"Her boyfriend, Donnie, is one of the clubs part owners. She told me this place has something for everyone. It has three levels and each one has a different theme."

Tori slowed down and placed a cute smart look on her face. "Is one floor for the sexually disadvantaged?"

"No, but if one was, I'm sure you wouldn't be checking it out."

"Put your fangs back in, Lynnde. I was asking for you, not me."

I saw Desmond looking at me in the rear view mirror with a crooked smile on his face. Not tonight tweety bird, get that thought right out of your mind.

"Tori, for your information, I wouldn't be interested either. She said the second floor was strictly R&B, and the third floor was for jazz lovers. She didn't know what the music would be on the first floor. There's also a restaurant on the third floor."

Desmond chimed in with, "Wow, this place really sounds classy. I plan to frequent this establishment often, and Lynnde, you're more than welcome to join me."

"Thanks, Desmond." I responded rather dryly, but I didn't mean to. I wasn't going to come back here with him on a date and would find the right polite words to tell him so. Why is he here?

Maybe he'll get lucky and meet someone tonight. Probably not. Big Bird doesn't have a sister, and if he did, she wouldn't come here. *Stop it, Lynnde. This is a celebration, remember?*

Tori pulled up in valet parking and went into diva style before she got out. As Desmond and I were getting out, he told me he was a poetry writer and hoped one day to write a poem for me. Where in the world did that come from? See, that's why I didn't want his homely tail to hang out with us. I want to be with the man of my choice tonight. Not the man that no one else wants, and since I'm a friend of his sister I have to do the right thing and get stuck with him.

"Desmond, that's so nice of you to want to write a poem for me. I can't wait to hear it." Liar, liar, my whole body is on fire. I don't want to hear a word he has to say. If that poem sounds anything like he looks, I'm purchasing a set of earplugs. *Get off the looks. Exactly what is it about Desmond you don't like?* He doesn't fit my vision of what a man is supposed to look like for the umpteenth time. Just because someone is digging on you doesn't mean you have to settle for him or her does it? I know I've had a few losing rounds, but I'm not ready to throw in the towel. I want what I want and maybe it'll be what I need. All right, all right. I'll get to know him, but I'm telling you I won't like him. Aside from his feet, his penguin flair, and the in-your-face fact that he's shorter than me, he may be a decent man. Nobody's perfect, especially me. I shouldn't ask for something I can't give myself or to anyone else. It's time for me to open my mind and go deeper than the surface. My problem is my perceptions about sex and I can't see myself having sex with Desmond. Sex shouldn't come first in a relationship anyway. I need to get to know the person first. I'm going to study that fact and make it part of my knowledge.

*Club World.* Hmm, I think the name is a little tired, but I'm the one paying fifteen dollars to get in, so I'll just keep my comments to myself. Desmond offered to pay my way but I declined. Accepting his offer would seal my fate for the evening. The place is packed and I see people I haven't seen in ages. Tori's mouth is in overdrive and her voice is a few octaves higher, so I know she's going to party hard tonight. Desmond is standing next to me bobbing his head as we try and make it to the second floor. At least he has the beat. The first floor is country and western and we couldn't get in if we wanted to. People are lined up in the hallway and out the door waiting to yeehaw to the country beat. Maybe one day I'll come back and check it out.

I can hear Janet Jackson singing Control loud and clear, as we get closer to the entrance. Control. That's the word that best describes me. Control. From now on, that's what I have. Total control of my life and the people I let share it with me.

As we walked in the door, I felt like running to the dance floor before my new anthem went off. I changed my mind when I noticed the platters of food and glasses full of free champagne lined up for the taking. Since it's my life's rejuvenation celebration, I must do my share by drinking as much of it as possible. Someone has asked Tori to dance and before she wiggled her slim frame off to the dance floor, she turned to me and flashed her best ho girl smile.

"Lynnde, girl, this place is jumping! I know I'm going to get more than a few numbers tonight! What about you?"

"Girl, I just want to enjoy the atmosphere, the champagne and Desmond, of course." I had to add that last part because his eyeballs were damn near down my throat. We gave each other a hug, and she told me to make this the best birthday celebration ever.

"Lynnde, would you like me to find us a table?"

Penguin time. "Yes. That would be nice."

"Okay. Wait here and I'll be back as soon as I can."

"Alright. I won't move." From that point on my night went downhill. I'm sure Desmond found a table but I'm not positive. I don't remember. I can't remember much of anything on my own except being at home on my knees in front of the toilet with Desmond rubbing my back telling me I'd be okay; everything would be fine. I don't think I've ever felt that ashamed or embarrassed in my entire life. Too much champagne. Too much vodka. Too much rum. Too much idiot for one person to bear.

Everyone I came in contact with bought me a drink. I drank too fast and too much, was drunk early in the evening, and told anyone within my voices range it was my birthday. Just because they offered me a drink didn't mean I had to accept it. I drank shots of tequila followed with beer chasers. I don't know what got into me. Oh wait, yes I do, too much liquor.

The music was good, the food was plenty, and the champagne flowed like an endless stream. At what point I took the drink that began my avalanche will only be remembered if it was caught on tape. Desmond told me when I drank some of my shots I licked his cheek. I thought that was a fantasy of his. He had to make that up, the midget liar. Three other people told me the same story so he wasn't lying. I must've looked like a hippo cleaning off a newborn kitten. It didn't even belong to me. Ugh. I made a total fool of myself.

The worse part I do remember is asking Desmond to help me to the bathroom. I was too much woman for him to control drunk and I tripped over a chair leg. There my big ass went along with a chair, no, make that two chairs and a table. I hit the floor hard, not because I remember the pain, but because my skin is bruised in three places. If this thick skin is bruised, I wonder how the floor is holding up.

While I was sprawled out on the floor someone yelled, "Get her drunk fat ass out of here!" It took three men to get me up and Desmond wasn't one of them. The next day, someone from the club called and said they had my shoe and my dress coat. I'm such an idiot.

Desmond and I danced quite a bit, and I danced with this guy named Steve. Or maybe I just ended up between him and his dance partner. I danced by myself and was really swinging my round rump so I'm sure a few dance couples were interrupted.

My behavior at the club was superior compared to what I did in Tori's car. I know you don't think there could be anything worse but there is. I'll tell the plain truth and say I peed on myself. Not just for my knowledge but for Desmond's, also. It started as soon as I was plopped down in the car by whoever helped me up off the floor and down two flights of stairs. It didn't stop until Desmond helped me out of the car twenty minutes later. Twenty minutes of a slow piss stream soaked Tori's front seat and floor mats. She drove a white four-door Nissan Sentra that she owned for five years, and was proud to never have had an accident in it. Tori was going to hate me when she found out.

I don't know where she was but I was glad she wasn't with us. The seats were cloth and I super soaked the passenger side. No amount of cleaning would do them justice. I'd have to get a second job to pay her new car note.

Desmond managed to maneuver my soggy rank self out of the car. When we were halfway up the walk, I told him how I destroyed Tori's car.

"Oh, don't worry about that, Lynnde. I'll clean it up and it'll be as good as new. Tori won't suspect a thing."

This came from a man who just received the worst first impression ever. Where did I get the nerve to say I didn't want to be bothered with him? I wished a sniper would pick me off. One bullet straight to my head and into my brain. At least there'd be something in there. I didn't know how to respond, so I did what I do best and started crying. I felt so stupid trying to stop tears that came harder. My tears were running neck and neck with my pee.

I was drunk and smelled like a case of cat piss without the litter box, and my dress was stuck to me. Stuck so far up my crack I would have to use a crowbar to get it out. I saw a picture of me lying on a psychiatrists couch. I need help.

As soon as we entered the front door, my stomach started to rumble. Thru my sobs I managed to say bathroom. I made it to the toilet in time, so at least I could be proud of something. The toilet held me up for forty-five minutes and thankfully my tears and vomit decided to stop. Desmond was by my side the entire time. I wanted to flush myself down the toilet with the rest of the shit but I'd probably plug it up. Shit just didn't want to leave me alone.

I held my head over the toilet; shame wouldn't let me look him in his face.

"Lynnde, a good hot bath will make you feel brand new. I'll start the water for you, okay?"

I nodded because I had no voice to answer him with; it went down the toilet with the rest of my insides. I prayed he didn't want to help me undress. There was no way he was about to see me naked. What do you mean he's already seen me naked? You're right in a sense, but I meant physically. Tears, pee or vomit cannot compete with my weight.

Desmond turned the water off and said he'd be in the living room waiting. Then he helped me off the floor and walked out of the bathroom, closing the door behind him.

The person I looked at in the mirror brought tears to my eyes again because I didn't recognize the face. Why did I do this to myself? I thought about the time when I was eight years old and snuck a drink from my fathers gin bottle. When the disgusting taste touched my lips, I dropped the bottle on the kitchen floor. Gin and glass went everywhere. A piece of glass hit the floor and came back up and cut me on the neck. I received a super deluxe mega size butt whooping from my father. Not for trying to drink but because the glass could've slit my throat and killed me. Why didn't that glass do a better job and spare me from the life that's destroying me now?

My father hollered and shook me while saying, "Alcohol is no good for you so don't ever drink it." He still drank after that happened, so enough of that lead by example stuff. First gin then bleach. Was I ever going to get it right?

I kept a pair of scissors in my bathroom cabinet and no, I wasn't going to cut my wrists or my throat. The scissors were the only way I'd be able to get my dress off. Why bother taking it to the cleaners, it was ruined. I stepped into a bathtub that was the perfect temperature and had the right amount of bubbles. Desmond wouldn't want anything to do with me after tonight. He was only being nice because I was his sister's friend. Tori did say he was the perfect gentleman. She told me many of the women he dated used him because they could get anything out of him. He worked at a collection agency, had no kids, and drove a Volvo. A black male catch in his thirties usually meant one of two things, you either hit the jackpot, or he was hitting the wrong pot. Desmond was probably very careful when it came to the opposite sex. He looked to be the type that wanted to be married before he had kids and that's the best way to be. Well, if he wanted to get to know me after this night was over, I'd let him. He didn't have to do anything he did to help me, and for that I'm grateful. No, I'm not settling. I'm giving someone different a chance.

As I lay back in the tub and closed my eyes, I saw Desmond's face. I'd say his skin color was that of a peanut butter cookie that wasn't too brown or too light, but just right. I know I used cookies to describe Tori and Desmond, but you know food is my favorite thing and they are twins. He had a thin mustache that fit his face and lips, and he wore square tinted glasses over his hazel colored eyes. Desmond doesn't look like my man but what was it I had to learn?

I washed my body at least four times and stepped out the tub feeling fresher. My head was killing me and I was still a little sluggish. A large bottle of aspirin was in the medicine cabinet, also, and as I swallowed a few of them, I thanked God my robe was hanging on the back of the bathroom door. I didn't want him to see a trace of me naked physically. It made no sense to prolong my embarrassment, so I opened the door and walked to the living room, half hoping Desmond would be gone. He wasn't. He was sitting on the couch reading an outdated magazine. Desmond stood up and smiled when he saw me.

"Hey there, good looking. How are you feeling?"

I smiled halfheartedly and said I felt okay.

"I'm sorry you got sick. You'll feel much better after you've had some sleep."

He was sorry I got sick? With a stupid sheepish grin I replied, "Thank you, Desmond. Thank you for everything. I'm sorry I ruined your evening."

"Ruined my evening? A lovely lady like you? Never. Just being with you made my night. You were celebrating and I should've done a better job taking care of you. I hope you'll give me the chance to make it up to you."

"Huh?" Now who's the dork?

"Forget about tonight and get some rest. Everybody has bad days. If it wouldn't be too much of a bother, I'd like to call you tomorrow, just to make sure you're all right? I'll call in the afternoon so I won't wake you, okay?

My head pounded, my stomach bounced, and I know the look on my face was similar to a dusty donkey's ass. What planet was Desmond from?

"Yes, Desmond. It's okay. Calling me won't be a problem at all. Anytime will be fine."

"Wonderful. I'll go now. You need your rest. If you need anything, call me. I wrote my number down on that piece of paper on the table. I have your number because Tori gave it to me. Is that alright?"

"That's fine, Desmond."

"Okay, Lynnde. I'll talk to you later. Make sure this door is locked; I don't want anything to happen to you. Sleep well. Bye."

"Bye." We smiled at each other as I closed the door behind him. I locked it, turned off the lights, and went into my bedroom to lie down slowly. When my head hit the pillow the bed spun halfway and stopped.

"Please," I said aloud. "There is nothing else in me to come out. I'll never drink again." I guess my bed was satisfied with my answer because it spun no more.

There should be a limit to the amount of stupid one person's allowed at a time. I say when you pass it, death is the fine you have to pay. Let me do the world a favor and die tonight. My head is killing me; maybe I'll get lucky and die from a headache. I sound like a slightly retarded monkey. *Go to sleep, Lynnde.* I swear I'm never leaving this house again. Well, only to work, to my parents, and maybe grocery shopping, but that's it. Dummy. Dummy. Dummy.

I must have some kind of gene in my body that activates itself when I need to be brought down a rung or two. Tonight it was on full power. I thought I was so much better than Desmond by feeling he didn't deserve the right to be in my company. For once I saw a strong woman in me and I loved it. Thinking I could walk on water didn't give me the right to drown Desmond in the process. I'm better than no one, and have no more right than anyone else to be on this earth. *Go to sleep, Lynnde.* Desmond should be disgusted with me but he isn't. His treatment of me tonight went way beyond his duties to his sister's friend. He's going to clean Tori's car to spare me her five octave screeching voice. He made sure I arrived home safe and didn't leave until he knew I was all right. I owe Desmond a lot more than what I gave him tonight. *Go to sleep, Lynnde.*

Shit, no one in the club is going to remember what a good time they had or who was there. All they're going to remember is the fat girl. The big fat girl who made a fool of herself. The big fat-assed girl who ate too much. The big, sloppy, fat-assed girl who drank a case of champagne and anything else that came in contact with her mouth. The big, sloppy, fat-assed clumsy, girl who knocked over, and probably broke a table and two chairs. I'll be the talk of the town for weeks to come.

Desmond was right there by my side. Did I say anything to hurt his feelings? I'd never know it by the way he acted. God must put some people on this earth to show other's how not to live their lives. I'm definitely a teacher. *Lynnde, go to sleep.*

There's nothing I can do to change what happened this evening so when people ask me what happened, I'll tell them the truth. I'll say Desmond was trying to get a piece and he put something in my drink. It was his fault and not mine. Oh, God, help me. After all that man has done for me, how could I have a thought like that? Take me now please, I'm waiting. *Lynnde?*

Control. What happened to my control? Dummy. Tomorrow I'll start fresh. I'll take control tomorrow. Tomorrow, I hope you never come.

# Do I Really Love Him?

Life is so good. My world has been on a serious upswing and I have so much to tell you. A new year has come and things have been wonderful. I've received another promotion at work, and now I'm the district manager of seven stores. I love the responsibility, and the pay raise has enabled me to upgrade my Escort to a Taurus. I'm styling now.

My father was so happy for me that he rented a large banquet hall and threw a party. I couldn't believe he footed the bill for it all. The dinner was buffet style and included shrimp, lobster, beef, pork and chicken. Let's see, there was rice, potatoes, macaroni and cheese, vegetables, collard greens, oh, and ham, too. Who else was there? Let me finish telling you about the food first, that's still a special subject to me. We had all kinds of breads including cornbread, muffins, and five different kinds of salads. The dessert table was a mile long, and there was plenty of champagne for everyone. I only had a half glass though.

Why are you in such a rush to know who was there? Oh, all right. Esta and Larry flew in and surprised me, my coworkers, many of my relatives, Tori, and I can't forget about my man. Who is my man? How dare you ask who! My man is Desmond and don't you forget it.

I'll shout it to the world if I have to. Desmond Ladd is mine! Life is something else. Would you ever imagine that we'd be dating after the way I talked about him, not to mention the first impression I gave him. I forgot to tell you earlier he cleaned out his sister's car and she never smelled a thing. Don't ask me how he did it but he did. She thought he was doing her a favor, but we know the truth and don't you ever tell her.

Our relationship is going rather well. We don't crowd one another, but our time spent together is perfect. I'm learning I can be in a relationship with a man and not give up my life. My parents love him and Esta says, "So what he's shorter than you? He loves you, Lynnde. As long as you're each other's main concern, you don't need to worry about what everyone else thinks." Now that's a best friend.

While Esta and Larry were home, the five of us went out to dinner. Desmond and Tori love the Wilson's, that's Esta and Larry's last name, and the Wilson's love them in return. My family is growing and I couldn't be happier. Esta and I made plans for me to visit them in California and she even wanted Desmond to come along. I love him, but I want them all to myself on my first trip. I'll bring him next time.

Desmond makes me feel so secure in our relationship. I felt comfortable leaving him and wasn't worried about him straying. My mother said the pain would go away and it did. For the longest time I never thought I'd feel pleased about my life. It helped when I learned I have to live my life for me.

My mother and I still do our lunches, and Desmond joins us on occasion. He loves the relationship I have with my mother. He knows my father and I had our difficulties, but says just love him. His mother is deceased and his father lives in another state, so his advice to cherish my parents is sincere.

I know no one is perfect, but Desmond is close to it. He always opens car doors for me and sends flowers just because. He cooks breakfast, lunch, and dinner, and always makes sure I have everything I need. His hobby is poetry, so he pens me the most beautiful poems. Desmond recited his first poem to me two weeks after we decided to date one another. We decided to date one another three days after we decided to become friends. Our first three dates were sweet but the fourth one was magical. That's when I heard my poem for the first time.

He talked me into going back to Club World and having dinner on the jazz floor. I didn't want to go at first, but my incident was over a year old and my body size changed once again, so I didn't think any one would recognize me. The only person who would've identified me was my coworker's boyfriend, but he lost his share of the club. He was caught stealing belongings from coat pockets when they were in the coat checkroom. I always thought he was a little strange. He talked with a lisp, stuttered, and told the dumbest jokes. Sometimes he'd come into the store and I'd bet money he talked to the shoes. With the way his mouth was moving, I thought the shoes answered him back. He made me think I could ask a new pair of pumps not to hurt my feet and they'd understand me. Like I said, he was strange, high altitude cuckoo's nest strange.

Desmond arrived at my apartment with one red rose in his hand, wearing a tuxedo, and not looking like a penguin at all. A limousine was our transportation for the evening. Earlier in the day I received a dozen red roses at my job. I was walking on air and wasn't about to come down for anything. His message on the card said he couldn't wait for our precious evening to begin and hoped it would last forever. I called Esta right then and there and my mother, too. Esta screamed, "He's the one for you," and my mother said, "I knew he was the one for you." What were they trying to tell me?

Desmond and I rode in the limousine for half an hour before going to the restaurant. While riding, we drank white grape juice from champagne glasses, and nibbled on a fruit, cheese, and cracker tray. I wore a black halter-top dress with a thigh-high split, and two-inch open-toe heels. I wanted higher heels, but can you believe the store didn't have them in my size? I would correct that Monday morning. You thought I was going to say I didn't get higher heels because Desmond is shorter than me, didn't you? Well, the way he treats me outweighs all of my dumb hang-ups. And speaking of weight, mine is now one hundred and eighty-six pounds, and I love the way I look. Desmond says whatever size I'm happy with is the size he's happy with. He loves me regardless.

We arrived at the club and rode the glass elevator up to the jazz level. While gazing at a three story illuminated water fountain, we enjoyed an appetizer of mushrooms stuffed with crab and a lobster spinach dip. Desmond said he could prepare it and put this restaurant out of business. He was an excellent cook, and you know I couldn't wait to taste it.

I didn't listen to jazz much, so Desmond told me the song playing was by an artist by the name of George Howard. The song was titled *I Want You For Myself.* Desmond hummed along with it, saying every time he heard it he thought of me. He asked me to dance, and I was glad he did. For once, I wanted people to look at me and see how very happy I was. Maybe they were looking at the height and weight difference, but I didn't care about any one's opinion but mine.

I hadn't told Desmond yet, but I was in love with him. On the dance floor, he pulled me close, and we swayed as if we were one with the rhythm, making me want to stay close to him forever. He didn't seem to be that short to me anymore. I don't know if he had on platforms or if I was seeing him as the exceptional man he was.

I thought I'd explode from excitement when Desmond said he wanted to recite my poem. Someone on this earth thought I was special enough to give a poem to? *Uh-huh...*

The words I heard from his moist thin lips were the sweetest words spoken to me to date.

"Lynnette, Lynnde, the girl of my dreams, I knew it was you, always you. You are the woman for me. Fine beautiful woman. I need to love you. Let me love you. You fine, beautiful woman. Fine, beautiful woman. Sexy, chocolate woman. I love chocolate. I want to taste your chocolate flavor in my mouth until it becomes one with my tongue. Fine, beautiful woman. Fine woman you are."

We continued to sway from side to side, and I felt a tear rolling down my cheek. I don't know what's good or bad poetry, but that one is published in my heart. Desmond stepped back, looked me in my eyes, and asked if I liked the poem. All I could do was stare at him as he wiped the tear from my face.

"Don't cry, Lynnde. If you don't like it, I'll keep trying until I get it right. I want to make you happy."

"Desmond, you do make me happy. Those were the most beautiful words I've ever heard. Thank you. I loved my poem."

Is this really happening to me? Someone must be paying him to treat me this way. My eyes gave a quick glance around the room. I thought Roger Pitkins was there. Remember him?

Desmond and I walked back to the table, hand in hand. We dined on filet mignon, and I had the best conversation with a man I've ever had in my life. He wanted to know about me. What I loved, what I disliked, what were my future plans, and how could he share my dreams with me. We danced, talked, and I never wanted the night to end. In the past, I've often wished for death to come. I'm taking a rain check on it now. Pass me by, skip my turn and go sit on death row. Just don't show up.

On the ride home, Desmond asked again if I really liked my poem. I told him I'd never get tired of hearing it. He gave me a card he designed and the poem was written on the inside.

"Lynnde, this is only the beginning. We have so much to learn about one another and so much to give. We will only get better."

I feel so stupid when I don't have anything to say.

"Don't say a word. Just let me hold you until we get to your place."

I lie back in his arms and closed my eyes. A large round revolving bed with rose petals on it surrounded me. Desmond was walking towards me with a pair of blue silk pajama bottoms on. He reached me, ran his hands up my legs and over my... I can't finish telling you what happened because the limousine stopped and the door was opening. We arrived at my apartment too quickly, but before I could tell Desmond I wanted to keep riding, he was halfway out and reaching back in for my hand. We walked to the door, and I asked him to come in.

"I want to come in, Lynnde, but I'm going to decline. My thoughts are not very clear right now. I don't want to make any mistakes when it comes to you. I want to be with you for a long time and take things slow and be careful. Please understand? I want to do what's right by you."

Huh? "I understand. I don't want to make any mistakes either. (I just want to have a wild sweaty boot-knocking session with you, that's all) We can go slow."

He leaned forward and we shared a gentle kiss.

"Goodnight, Miss Lee. Lock the door behind you. I'll call you first thing in the morning. I have to go into work tomorrow for overtime, but its only a half a day. Would you like to go to lunch?"

"Yes." I sounded like a robot in a trance.

"Okay. Good night, Sweetie. And lock the door."

Desmond stood on the porch as I closed the door. It felt like I was closing it in his face, but I managed to lock it while leaning against it, trying to feel his presence. He respected me. I never had that from a man before. I'm not going to lie, though. My mind went straight to the bedroom and into the land of nakedness. I wanted him bad that night and have wanted him every night we were together. He was right in waiting. We became closer and he's my everything. What more could a woman ask for? Well, I wouldn't mind if he gave me a piece. Desmond says two people should be totally committed to each other before having sex. If he doesn't hurry up and drop his draws I'm going to just be committed.

All the time we spend together is beautiful, so I don't push the sex issue, but a little physical contact would be nice. Desmond says he loves me and that I'm the only woman for him. We've been together a year-and-a-half, and I don't know how he does it, but playing solitaire with myself (and I do mean with myself) all night long, is starting to get a little monotonous. I want someone else to play with me for a while. I'll never stray from Desmond. His making me wait has made me want him even more.

My birthday was coming up once again, and his present to me was a round trip ticket to California. He said he had to make sure I came back. For him, I'd fox trot back. I'd be there a week and Des said he had something special planned for me when I returned. I thought about marriage, wondering was he going to ask me, and said a prayer every day that it would finally be my turn at happiness.

I love Desmond and have even changed my ways of thinking about sex when it comes to him. I'd never been in charge when it came to physical relations, but I plan to make him relate to me in ways I never thought of before. Sometimes he'll give me full body massages, or talk to me on the phone so seductively it makes me feel like physical contact has taken place. I added another chapter to the karma sutra simply from thinking of positions with him. I saw us on the kitchen table at two a.m., the bathroom floor at 5:45 in the evening, and standing up in the closet wearing a coat that was still on a hanger at the stroke of midnight.

If I mention the thoughts I have of food and him, you'd think I was pure dirty. Desmond makes my mind dial 1-800-What-a-Freak and I love it. Waiting is making my hormones go into overdrive and good things come to those who wait.

Desmond drove me to the airport the day of my departure with my mother in tow. My father offered to take the day off to ride with us, but I had a flashback of the last time my family took a trip to the airport. I didn't want to witness a part two.

Larry and Esta were waiting at the airport with a big sign that said Happy Birthday Lynnde! We Love You! I cried for the entire state of California to see and didn't stop until I was at their house.

Esta had opened up her own boutique and was doing very well for herself. She designed clothing for celebrities and had some outfits for me that she had to take in a few sizes. It was only one size, but it added to the high I was on. We talked about Desmond, and Esta gave me nothing but praise.

"See, Lynnde girl. I told you to wait. Your man has come and found you."

"You were right, Esta. He said when I get back he has something planned for me. I hope it's some sex."

"Oh, Lynnde. That man knows what he's doing. He wants you to be his wife and there's nothing wrong with waiting until you're married to have sex."

Why is it when someone else is getting it on, they tell you it's okay to wait?

"Esta, dear. Did you wait until you were married before you had sex?"

"Ahh, no. But mine was a special circumstance. Larry was leaving for the Marines, so technically, I wasn't doing it for myself, but for my country."

I love, Esta. She can still make me laugh until my eyes are nothing but tears.

My week with Esta went much faster than I wanted it to. We both cried like wailing fools at the airport, and even Larry was a little misty eyed.

My plane ride home was filled with thoughts of Esta's wedding. I imagined mine would be the same beautiful, classy event that hers was. When we were in our teens, she often spoke of how her wedding would be. I always saw the same vision she did until she talked about jumping over a broom. Every time she mentioned the broom, my vision of her in a bride's gown, and Larry in a tux, turned to one of her in a dusty beige frock, Larry in cut off pants and a ripped shirt, and neither of them wearing shoes. She'd always say, "Oh, Lynnde. Don't be so closed minded, it's going to be beautiful."

Somehow, I never saw what she did until the day they were married. Once again, she was right. It was beautiful.

Esta was gorgeous. The broom belonged in a world record book - it was a sweepers dream. Her gown was a form fitting, lacy silk and satin creation with a million rhinestones on it. She said her train was only ten feet long, but I said it had to be thirty.

Even though it was her wedding day, it was the best day of my life. A wonderful part of me had found happiness. I cried tears of joy but was sad at the same time. Her wedding day marked the beginning of our separation.

The wedding was beautiful and the reception was described as the ball of the century. But I knew this day, like all the rest, would soon end. I hugged and held on to Esta as if she were one of my extremities about to fall off. I never wanted to let her go. If I did, I felt a part of me I enjoyed everyday would only be used on special occasions. Esta was the special occasion in my life, and she'd be thousands of miles away. I felt selfish. Even though she just joined her life with another's, I still wanted her all to myself. I was happy she had Larry, but she had me first. I didn't want her to forget it.

Our parents stood side-by-side holding hands as Larry and Esta drove away after their reception. I looked at them and my body felt serene. For the first time I realized you can get love from everyone in your life, not just your man. And the reality of it came right on time.

Oh, please don't let me make a fool of myself and put words into Desmond's mind or mouth that aren't there. If he doesn't want to marry me now, then I'll wait. I'll wait for him as long as I have to, because when he's ready, my wait will be over.

# Not For the Rest of My Life

Tonight's the night. When Desmond picked me up at the airport, he asked if we could have a special date in four days. He said he had something very important to talk to me about and the four days have come and almost gone. Tonight has got to be the night I receive my first and last marriage proposal. It's been eighteen months, three weeks, two days, six hours and twelve minutes and counting since we met.

We've gone the entire time not engaging in sexual intercourse, so he has to know I'm as committed to him as he is to me. I did try things at times to get him to break, but they never worked. When he'd come over for dinner, I'd wear the nastiest, sexiest, you might as well be naked outfit. He'd tell me I looked eatable but wouldn't disrespect me. I'd beg for some disrespect, but he never gave in. That made me love him more, and see all love between a man and a woman doesn't have to be physical.

For my twenty-seventh birthday, he bought me a diamond link tennis bracelet, and we enjoyed dinner and a movie. I thought that would be the night. It wasn't. He took me home, made sure I was safe and sound, and went home and called me. That night, we had phone sex that was better than any physical sex I had to date. We are committed; we are one. I'm sure he's going to ask me to marry him. I can't lose him. His height, his looks, and his feet are perfect for me. Big change, huh? Pure love will do that to you, and I want it to do it to me for the rest of my life.

Desmond should be here any minute. I've prepared a meal of scalloped potatoes and braised pork chops. I never thought the combination was anything spectacular, but Desmond enjoys them the most. He says they remind him of his mother's cooking, and eating them always makes him feel thankful. I hope he gets here soon; I'm about to burst.

How stupid will I look if he doesn't ask me? What if he wants my opinion on a new suit he bought or something about his job? He has been working quite a bit lately. He's always on top of his work affairs so it can't be that. If he doesn't ask me to be his wife tonight, I'll never eat again. Too drastic. I'll come up with something.

The doorbell buzzed and I panicked for a moment before running to open it. *Don't break your neck getting to the door, Lynnde.* I won't. I opened the door and saw excellence. Desmond and I looked at each other for a few moments and he spoke first.

"Hey, beautiful. I've been waiting all day to see your face. How about a little suga'?"

We kissed, and then stepped back from each other to catch our breath as he came in. He turned his nose upward with sweet curiosity and said, "Lynnde, sweetie, something else besides you smells good in here. Is it what I think it is?" "Yes, Des. It's your favorite. Now come in here and eat before it gets cold." He walked to the couch and summoned me to do the same.

"I'd love to but dinner's going to have to wait. I have to talk to you, and I want to do it now. Come over here and sit down, please." "What is it? Is something wrong?"

"No, Lynnde. For once in my life, everything is right. Now please, sit down."

"Okay." I walked towards him with a little shake in my body. I don't think he noticed it, but I was on the verge of tears, and my stomach purchased a new jump rope. As I sat down, Desmond started getting down on the floor on one knee. He took my hands when he reached the floor and my tears began.

"Lynnde, this past year and a half with you has been perfect. I've waited for you for so long. Now that I have you, I'm never letting go. I love you more than I thought was possible and will love you forever. I want my children to call you mommy. I want a baby girl that looks just like you. I want to wake up to you when we're ninety-five years old; my love for you will still be brand new. You're all I need. You're the woman I have to have. Please make me your husband. I love you, Lynnette Donna Lee, and I'm asking you to become my wife."

He then reached into his pocket and pulled out the biggest diamond ring I'd ever seen. It was the three-carat princess cut diamond I saw in the jewelry store. It caught my eye when we went to get a few links taken out of the tennis bracelet he bought for my birthday. My vision went from his face and then to my hand, and back repeatedly.

"Lynnde, please say yes."

"Yes, Desmond. Yes. Yes. Yes." I slid down on the floor with him and started to laugh and scream through my tears. He laughed right along with me as he placed the first kiss of our engagement on my lips. This was real and it was going to happen. Wait until I tell my parents. I have to call Esta, and Tori is going to flip, and my mind went on and on with my life's new preparations.

Desmond and I lay on the floor and talked about the kind of wedding we wanted to have. We discussed where we wanted to live to begin our lives together. He wanted to wait another year before we married because he was coming up for a promotion at work and wanted to be able to give me the life, and the wedding I deserved. Not to mention a cruise to a beautiful island for our honeymoon. Desmond wanted to pay for everything.

"Baby, we're a team and we're going to do this together. I make good money and there's no way you're going to do this alone. I won't let you kill yourself giving me nice things. You're the only nice thing I want."

"Lynnde, it's a man's job to provide for his family and that's exactly what I plan to do. My wife is not going to want for anything. I won't be a man if I can't give her what she needs and wants. You don't have to worry about a thing. Just tell me what you want. I'll make sure you have it, okay?"

"Desmond, baby, this is our wedding. Not just mine. I wouldn't feel right having you foot the bill, and neither would my parents. We're a family that's going to do this together. That's the only way it should be."

"You're my queen, and a queen shouldn't have to work for anything. Let me do this, okay? Let me provide for my queen."

I started to cry again. Desmond was too good to be true.

"Don't cry, Sweetie. I was born to take care of you. You're all I want to live my life for. Your happiness is my main concern."

"Thank you, Desmond. You're so good to me. But right now, my main concern is that you eat something. I have to make sure my husband's stomach is always full."

Hopping up and turning to help me he said, "Okay, I'll eat, but our evening is not over yet."

"What else is there? I don't think I can handle anymore."

"Yes you can. You can handle me for the rest of your life."

"Now that's the kind of talk I like to hear." I had a crooked, 'I'm gonna get me some tonight look on my face'. *You just don't get it?*

We held hands and walked into the kitchen to enjoy our meal. I'm right handed, but I ate with my left hand so I could see how my ring moved and shined. I was down to one hundred and seventy pounds so my fingers didn't look as fat as they used to.

Desmond is too good to me. I can't believe he really loves me, and that we'll be together as man and wife. The best part is that I'm the only woman he wants, just me. He says I am beautiful, and fine, so fine. Thank you, God, for sending Desmond to teach and show me what patience is. Patience is beautiful and something I'll keep in my life always.

After dinner, Desmond said he'd do the dishes. I couldn't talk him out of it, so I sat down and admired my ring. My mind fantasized about our wedding day. I saw fresh flowers everywhere, a live band, scrumptious platters of every delectable food you could imagine, and a wedding cake that would feed thousands of people. I know I'm exaggerating. I have a right to. This is my wedding.

What is Desmond doing in that kitchen? I know he's a clean neat freak, but this night is special. Just as I was about to call him, the doorbell rang.

"I'll get it, Des." I opened the door to see a flower deliveryman standing there.

"Are you, Lynnette Lee?" he asked.

"Yes, I am," I answered with a perplexed look on my face.

"Bring them up, boys."

I stepped to the side and he entered with two vases of red roses in his arms. Three other men who were all carrying the same thing followed him.

"Oh, my goodness. You must have the wrong address." Just then, Desmond walked up behind me and wrapped his arms around my waist.

"Lynnde, they have the right address. I told you, you're my queen. From now until forever, you'll be treated as one. I'll stop at nothing in showing you how much I love and appreciate you. When we watch TV, you always comment on the pretty women in music videos and how they get treated so wonderful. Tonight, I'm going to show you that your life is going to be better than a three-minute music video. I'm going to show you that my love is real. I want these roses to be a constant reminder of that."

I held Desmond tightly and felt different than I did a few hours earlier. My body and mind were going wild with anxiety, but yet I felt so calm, like Desmond and I had just fused together to become one. This must be what it feels like to have a soul mate. *Hmmm...*

The deliverymen paid us no attention and closed the door behind them after they made three trips apiece. I kept holding on to Desmond, and uncertainty entered my mind. It left once it realized my life was going to happen with or without it.

"Lynnde, look and see how beautiful you are to me. I know these flowers are only a symbol, but know that what we have between us will never go away."

I turned to admire the flowers and was slightly shocked at how many there were. He said each vase contained two-dozen roses, and that there were twenty-four vases. At that moment I couldn't add and didn't care how many there were. I only cared that he did all this for me. He wouldn't leave me alone after this. Desmond would become mine physically tonight. I don't care if he wants to wait or about his respect or whatever else he has in mind. I can't be without him any longer. He's changed my life and my living room halfway into paradise and can't leave until it's complete.

As my mild shock wore off, I looked him in his eyes. A different man looked back at me. For the first time, I saw him as my husband and he saw me as his wife. He knew he wouldn't deny me tonight.

"Are you sure this is what you want, Lynnde?"

"Let's not talk anymore. I love you." Desmond began undressing me, working his way around my body from top to bottom, and back up once I was unclothed.

"Lynnde, you're beautiful."

He continued to kiss me and helped me to lie down on the floor. This was worth the wait. I lay on the floor caressing my body as Desmond undressed himself for my eyes to see. This was going to be incredible. He was going to be marvelous for the rest of my life.

I admired Desmond's naked body, which was quite pleasing, until my eyes saw "it." What was "it," you ask? Nothing. Absolutely nothing. I'm not a day care provider.

Why did all of a sudden I feel like I was in nursery school? Now I know why he made me wait so long. He knew I wasn't going to get anything. I'd continue to wait if I'd known this.

Desmond's penis was the size of a Chap Stick tube. No, no it wasn't. It was more like the size of a Vicks inhaler that had nothing else left to inhale. Picture a sweet gherkin pickle? Or how about a fat free Vienna sausage? Does that help you to understand what my eyes didn't see? I can't believe I waited a year and a half for nothing. Good things come to those who wait my ass.

But, Lynnde, you love him. He's your soul mate. He's perfect for you. You want to spend the rest of your life with him. Look at all the roses. Think of the poems. Think of how nice he was to you when you got sick at the club, remember? You're his queen and he wants to take care of you. He loves you. He can't take care of anything with that midget dick of his. *Okay, okay calm down. Sex isn't everything. You can work this out.*

Oh no, he's coming towards me and rubbing that little creature up and down my leg. Ugh. He's having surgery. There has to be something out there that'll help. A transplant, implant or a pump. Wait, not a pump. A pump will just make it look swollen, like a fat lip or something. I don't want to do this at all. Right now, all I feel is disgust. He shouldn't take too long.

Damn, he's kissing me and saying sweet nothings, and I'm really emphasizing the word nothing. I guess he's really in the mood. My mind is so far away from this moment.

Now he's trying to enter inside me. Ugh. All I feel is aggravation. Desmond is really enjoying himself. He's really giving that little thing a workout. He keeps saying, "Oh, Lynnde, you feel so good." How would he know?

I guess I should look like I'm enjoying him, but all I want to do is tell him to get his earthworm out of me. I manage to say, "Desmond, you feel so good," and "don't stop." *Keep thinking how much you love him and how much he loves you.* Those thoughts aren't working. I want him to hurry up. Now he's making a screeching noise. It sounds like car tires on a wet road that have just run over a hissing cat. If this is what his orgasms are going to sound like, I hope I go deaf tonight.

*Stop it, Lynnde. Desmond loves you and will give you his world.* Good, he's done. I hope he doesn't talk. I hoped too late. He says he loves me and can't wait for me to become his wife. I barely get out the words I love you in return and hear snoring. Oh, hell no. No pleasure for me and he's asleep? *You love him. You love him. You love him.* That's not working right now. *Okay then, look at the ring and your roses.* That's not working either.

No wonder that fool spent so much on the ring and wants to pay for the wedding. And who does he think is going to water all these flowers, and clean them up when they die? *Lynnde, sex isn't everything and you know you love Desmond, right?* Yeah, right. But all of a sudden I feel used. He made sure I was in love with him before he let me see his Brown and Serve. Wait until we were committed to each other, my ass. He should be committed and promoted to the newborn baby club president. Ugh.

A tiny wet spot is on my inner thigh and I want to throw up. I sat up to take a closer look at what he thinks is a penis, but it retreated back inside itself. What I saw made me think if a fly had a penis this is what it would look like. Tsk, even his balls are little. They look like burnt, dried, button mushrooms. *Lynnde!*

Desmond's boxer underwear are lying on the floor. First thing in the morning, I'm taking them to the store and get his money back. I'll buy him a pack of toddler underroos to replace them. Disgust won't let me talk anymore. I hope I have some hard liquor in the cabinet because the only way I'm sleeping next to him is drunk. Hurry up tomorrow because tonight has got to go.

# When Is The Grass Ever Greener?

My life with Desmond went on as usual. We told everyone about our engagement and received the responses we expected. My father thought Desmond was the man for me and spent time with him whenever he could. My mother wanted to get started on our wedding plans right away, and every week I received different wedding gown designs from Esta. Tori gave me a list of their family members and friends, which grew every time I talked to her. Everyone was excited about my wedding but me. I know I need some kind of professional help now. I had a man who loved me, and I was letting one little thing get in the way. Yes, that was the wrong choice of words, but you know what I mean.

Once we had sex the first time, that little thing kept popping up and wanting to come for a visit. Every time we had sex, or whatever you called what he was doing to me, I felt sick. One minor flaw shouldn't mess up everything else. The only person I told was Esta. She told me talk to Desmond about it.

"Lynnde, you love each other. You'll find alternatives to the problem."

"Esta, how do you tell a man he's not pleasing you in bed because he has nothing to please you with?"

"Relax, girl. Just think this through and find the right words. Everything will be fine."

Everyone says things are going to be fine when they're not the one having any misfortunes. This would never be fine. Nothing could fix this. I feel like going into hibernation.

Desmond worked so much overtime saving money to give me the wedding of my dreams. Sometimes he gave me his entire paycheck.

"The world is yours for the taking, Mrs. Ladd." I hated when he said that.

I should've said something to him, but I didn't. I mentioned my feelings of doubt to my mother, but I never told her my reasons.

"Oh, baby. It's okay to be a little nervous or scared. That happens to everybody. Don't you worry about a thing. Desmond is going to take care of you and give you the life and love you deserve." I always told her she was right but I knew otherwise.

The wedding I couldn't wait to have was coming too fast for me. We decided on the date of August 28th, 1989. The day came and went, but my wedding never did. I didn't realize until many months later that I made the biggest mistake of my life. I had someone who wanted to share his life with me, and instead of talking to him and coming to an understanding, I turned to someone else.

In preparation for my wedding that I didn't want to happen, I'd begun to work out at the gym full time. I wanted to be the sexiest bride that ever walked down the aisle. That's where I met Terrance Ramsey. I forgot about how good Desmond treated and respected me once Terrance talked to me. My looks don't matter point of view ceased to exist as soon as he opened his mouth.

Terrance looked like the man I was supposed to marry. He was six feet even, and had the complexion of a brown Crayola crayon. His body was tight, all of his skin was smooth, and his feet were well taken care of. He wore his hair in a low-cut style and had a shade for a beard. His eyes were dark brown and he was fine.

My weight was one hundred and thirty-six pounds, and he complimented me every time we saw each other. I never thought about getting married when I talked to him. We began talking at the gym, and eventually over lunch and dinner. We talked over breakfast after I started spending nights with him.

Being with Terrance made me think I was settling with Desmond. I thought Desmond wasn't good enough. Everything was wrong with him. He was too short, he chewed like a starving bird, his feet weren't smooth enough, and the list went on and on.

Even though looks aren't everything, Terrance was fine with and without his clothes on. I couldn't marry Desmond. He knew something was bothering me, and his way of helping out was to always treat me better. I wanted him out of my life when he did that. Somewhere inside I knew I was wrong, but I didn't care. I didn't want what I needed but what I wanted, and it wasn't Desmond. He would be hurt by not marrying me, but people change their minds everyday.

After weighing the pros and cons of our relationship, it always came back to breaking things off with Desmond. Terrance drove a nicer car than him; he was more attractive and had his own barbershop. Terrance and I looked like more of a couple than Desmond and I did.

You may think my reasons are childish and immature, but this is the rest of my life we're talking about. If it wouldn't have been Terrance, it would've been someone else. Desmond's sorry attempt at lovemaking would've driven me to it. I don't want a sexual aid all the time. If you can't teach old dogs new tricks, what exactly are you supposed to do with a dead one? Bury it. Let it rest.

I made the decision to tell Desmond that our relationship was over and regretted my decision often in the following years. At the time, all I could think of was the sex he wasn't giving me and never would. I was still very superficial, but didn't notice it and didn't care to.

One morning I called Desmond and asked him to come over when his workday was done. I'd been doing so many things with Terrance that I wanted him for my man. Desmond would have to go. I didn't love him anymore, and there was no sense in me leading him on.

Desmond arrived at my apartment at 6:34p.m. with flowers in hand. They wouldn't work this time. My attitude turned nasty when I saw him and I became dismayed. I didn't say hello or give him a kiss. I let him know my feelings and held the door open for him as he took baby steps to leave.

"There's no need for you to get comfortable. I wanted you to come over so I could tell you to your face. I want you to see I mean what I say. I don't love you anymore. I don't want to marry you. We're too different and have grown apart. I should've told you sooner, but that doesn't matter, you know now. Here's the ring back. I hope you find true happiness because you won't have it with me. There's nothing you can say to change my mind, so leave, now. I have things to do."

He stood staring at me with a pained look I'll never forget. Tears rolled down his face, and I heard a faint whimpering sound. I wanted to kill myself. What had I just done? Why did I do it? I saw Desmond's love for me and threw it away like a piece of scrap paper. When he started to cry out loud, my disgust returned. I told him to get out and don't plan on coming back. Someone else would be here taking his place. I wanted to tell him to hurry up and leave but decided to keep my mouth shut, he'd be gone soon enough.

I held the ring out for him to take as he walked towards the door with his head held down. I figured I'd be getting a new one soon enough; what did I need this thing for?

Desmond reached me and held his head up to face me. The words he said echoed at times when I least expected them to. At times they woke me from a deep sleep. I heard them when I was with Terrance, and they grew louder when all the disasters going on in my world came to a head.

"Lynnde, you may never love me like I need to be loved, but you will always want love like you need to be wanted."

"Whatever," and I slammed the door as he took his last steps out of my apartment. I thought to myself, "What in the world did that fool just say?" It made no sense to me at the time and didn't until I never achieved what I had with Desmond. I understood them one day when they caught me off guard. I wanted someone to love me the way he did, and desired the connection we had, and the happiness we shared. I didn't realize what happened until my heart was stuck under my shoe with parasites clinging to it deciding what part was theirs.

I thought I was it. I'd lost weight, made a few heads turn, and became a foolish woman.

The events that happened in my life were things that I didn't always feel I deserved, but my actions made them deserving of me. I wished for Desmond and cried so many tears because he was my love, my only love. My wait was over, but I was in too much of a hurry to see it. I made a choice to be someone else's fool.

If I was in such a rush to end things with Desmond, why didn't I tell anyone things were over between us? I couldn't. I continued to see Terrance, but waited for Desmond to come back. He never did. It was as if he disappeared from my earth. He never called, and I didn't see him again until one year later. He said hello and told me I still looked good. He was looking at me, but his vision had to be cloudy. My weight started to balloon again and I had two black eyes that no amount of make-up or big shades could cover up. I was ashamed he saw me, and my response to him was a blank stare in return. My plane was about to crash, and I would not eject myself from it. I wanted to crash and burn.

After I ended things with Desmond, someone else took control of my life. I waited three weeks before I told anyone. I told my parents first, and my father's relationship with me went back to square one. He took one look at me and shook his head in disbelief.

"I knew you were going to fuck this up. You can't control your weight, and I should've known you wouldn't be able to control getting married. Sometimes I wonder if you have a brain inside your fat ass head at all. That boy probably got a good look at you and changed his mind. I'm going to call that birth control center; you're going to be their next poster child, you dummy."

He walked away and didn't speak to me for two months. His voice was filled with so much repulsion; I decided not to say a word. I knew he never wanted me to be born. My mother said he was just upset, and he really liked Desmond. I'm sure it was more about the money that was nonrefundable. He paid for the reception hall, the catering, and new clothing for my mother and him. My mother told me she understood and kissed me on the cheek.

"Ma, don't you have anything else to say?"

"No, baby. Not this time. I'll support you no matter what. I'm not feeling so good right now. I'm going to lie down. I'll call you later, okay?"

"Okay, Ma." She walked upstairs, and I heard her bedroom door close. They both thought I was wrong but it was early yet. I'd show them I hadn't made a mistake.

I stood alone in the middle of my parent's living room feeling lonely. If I was going to be alone, I might as well go home and celebrate cutting an anchor loose without any misgivings. Although I alienated everyone with one action, things would work out in the long run.

I called Esta thinking she'd understand. Of course she said it was pre-wedding jitters and not to worry, they'd pass. Then I told her about Terrance and that twenty-eight was too young to put your sex life out to pasture. Terrance made me feel like a woman, and I couldn't get enough of him. When I was with him, I felt like she did when she was with Larry.

"But, Lynnde..."

Growing angry I cut her off. I was sick of everyone else running my life. "Look, Esta. I really don't want to hear it right now. You're talking to the new and improved Lynnde, and the only opinion that

counts is mine."

For the first time in our friendship we hung up without saying goodbye to each other or that we loved one another. She hung up on me. I wanted to call her back, but thought I'd better give her time to cool off. She loved me and wanted what was right for me, but she'd understand in time, also.

I felt I was on a roll and called Tori next. She said Desmond told her weeks ago. I asked her why she hadn't called me so I could explain.

"Fuck you, bitch! And fuck your explanation! I've loved my brother since birth, and the only thing that counts is the way he feels."

My face flushed shit that came out of my mouth. "But, uh, uhm, well, Tori, wait. You don't understand."

"No, bitch! You're the one that doesn't understand. He loved you and still does. You think because you're looking a little better you can get any man you want now? Well, shit-head, that's not how life is. You don't walk over people and think you can treat them anyway you feel like! I know about you and Terrance. Your ass don't know him yet, but I can't wait until you do. Don't call any members of my family, and you better pray I don't see you in the street.

I'll stomp your ass for my brother, and then I'm going to stomp it for me, and everybody else!"

I spoke for a few seconds before I realized the dial tone was my conversational partner. Why did I bother to call the enemy? Of course she's going to side with him. How did she find out about Terrance and me? Does Desmond know?

I'm not going to worry about her or anyone else right now. No one is thinking with a clear head, and it's my life anyway. Everybody else does what they want and now it's my turn.

My eyes are filling up with tears and I don't know why. I'm not crying for Desmond, I can't be. I see his face, but that's normal when you end a relationship with someone. I didn't make a mistake. I'll prove it to myself and to all of them, they'll see. Things will work out for everyone. I have Terrance, and in time, Desmond will have someone else.

I sat on the couch, crying out loud until my head hurt. Maybe it's the time of the month for my hormones to act up. The tears are not for Desmond or for the way Tori talked to me. They're not here because Esta hung up on me or because my father wished I were never born. Are they here because I feel sad for my mother?

I know it's a combination of everything but I'm not admitting it. I can't let them know they've gotten to me. They'll see in time. They'll see my decision was right, and life will return back to normal. I have to believe everything works itself out in time. Oh, God, please don't let the time pass too slowly. I need my family, and these tears have got to stop.

# Here She Comes

# May I Die Tonight?

Today, I lost my job. I know where it is; it just doesn't belong to me anymore. After fourteen years as a member of the Just Shoes establishment, I was fired.

I haven't spoken to you, dear reader, in five years. Many times I've wanted to, but was unable to. My jaw was either broken or my face was too swollen to move. I'm living at home with my parents and have been here for the last three years. I usually ride the bus when I want to go someplace because my car was repossessed two months ago. My life has not been good at all. I'm thirty-three years old and am feeling lower than I have ever felt.

My weight is back in the two-fifty plus range and I tried to commit suicide yesterday. I really didn't want to do it and didn't try very hard at all. I took a butter knife and slid it back and forth across my wrists until nothing happened. When I realized I wasn't going to get the desired effect, I used the butter knife to prepare a rather large sandwich. I'm so sorry and disgusting.

I thought long and hard about telling you what's happened to me. I'm comparable to untamed animal waste, and didn't think you'd care to know anything else about me. I don't have anything else to do now since losing my job, so I have more than enough time to talk.

The last time I spoke with you, I'd ended things with Desmond for a reason that makes no sense to me now. I had a new man in my life and thought he would make it all better. What made me think he loved me, I'll never know, but whatever my reasons were, they weren't correct. I told Terrance things were over between Desmond and I, and we could be together freely. He was a gentleman for the three months I saw him before breaking off my engagement. He treated me to candlelight dinners; moonlight walks in the park, and always told me how beautiful I was. And let's not forget about the sex. He made sure he didn't arrive at his point of pleasure until I was totally satisfied.

After I told him I could be his woman, he reacted as if he didn't care for me anymore. Of course, I could let no one know the reality of my situation. I had to portray to the world that I was happy with my decision and things were just fine.

The first time Terrance hit me my life instantly became composed of nothing but tumbleweed and dry cactus. Desolation was the only thing that surrounded me. I felt so bad afterwards that I missed three days of work due to the shock and disbelief that he'd hit me.

I'd gone over to his house unannounced, and he showed me, as soon as he opened his door, to never do that again. I felt so stupid. It was eleven o'clock at night, and I had on a trench overcoat with a bra and thong on underneath. The black stiletto heels I wore were so high that when he slapped me, I easily became off balance and fell. I hit the ground hard holding my face, wanting to know what just happened.

"Terrance, what's the matter with you! What did you do that for?"

Terrance stood over me and spit much too close to my face before speaking.

"Don't ever show up here again without calling first! You don't know what I may be doing!"

I wanted to jump up but my face stopped me. It didn't want to get hit again. "Why should it matter what you're doing? I'm your woman and I want to know what's going on in your life!"

"My life is on a need to know basis when it comes to you and you need to know what I tell you, understand?"

The coat had risen up my sprawled open legs. All of my business was out in the street and no one had asked me a thing. "Why did you hit me?"

"You needed it."

His right foot poked me in my side as he stepped back over me and slammed the door closed, with me on the outside, and still on the ground. He could've offered to help me up or at least apologized. I didn't knock again or demand more of an explanation; I went home and waited for him to cool off. We'd been seeing each other for five months and he was right. I should've checked with him first to see if it was okay to come over. He may have had other plans.

That first slap started the downfall of my working career. He hit me so hard my face puffed and had his handprint on it. There was no way I'd go to work looking like that. I'd never called in before, and since I was the district manager, I could appoint someone else to do my duties. I should've appointed someone else to take my place with Terrance. He was certified crazy. Well, I guess I should keep my mouth closed because I was crazy, too. I was ashamed to admit I made a mistake and instead, I put on a disfigured happy face to help hide the truth. I was fired today. I have nowhere to go tomorrow.

When my manager told me, I cried and begged him not to let me go. I said I'd straighten myself up and get back to the way I used to be. My request fell on a head that had no ears.

"I'm sorry, Lynnette. It's a little too late for that. You're constantly late and you've missed too many days. You're supposed to be a leader. It's too bad we can't trust you anymore since this last incident. You'll be hearing from our lawyers about the case against you. I'm sorry it's had to come to this. Concentrate on finding a way to pay back the twenty thousand dollars you say you didn't take. I'd hate to see you do jail time."

Dry heaves with tears came out with my shocked comment, "Jail time?" My immediate supervisor, Mr. Dewey, turned his back towards me and twiddled his thumbs.

"This is all the time we have for this meeting. Jack will escort you out of the store. We have all of your keys and business papers, so there's really no need for you to return here, not even to purchase shoes. I'm giving you notice that you're not welcome in any Just Shoes store until this case is resolved. Jack, get her out of here."

"But Mr. Dewey, please. Let me explain."

"I'm sorry, Lynnette. The only explanation that matters is ours. Goodbye."

I sat in the chair that I was interviewed in so many years ago and cried. This was the chair so many others sat in as I interviewed them. A throwaway dust rag had more worth than me when Jack, the security guard, helped me up out of the chair. Jack and I worked together since day one and this was just as hard on him as it was I. His broad shoulder held my dismal body as he escorted me out of the door, while speaking consoling words of encouragement.

"Don't worry, Lynnde. The truth will come out. I know you didn't steal the money and they'll know it, too. I'm going to miss you."

"Thanks, I'm going to miss you, too." We hugged each other, and I made the last exit from the first and only job I ever had. I'm glad this didn't happen at the mall store; everyone would've seen me get what I deserved. All personnel issues were handled at the home office store. No one I knew saw me walking to my car bawling or driving home quietly sobbing either.

Through my tears, I decided not to come straight home. I went to a buffet, a hamburger joint, a Chinese restaurant, and hit a convenience store to make sure the supply under my bed didn't run out.

It was going to be a long night.

The time I arrived home was the same time I would've come home if I'd been working, so no one suspected a thing. My mother left a plate of food for me in the microwave, which I ate before going up to take a bath and eat junk all night long. I told them I had an afternoon class to attend so I'd be sleeping in.

"Oh, baby, that's so good to hear. Is it a class that's going to give you another promotion?" My mother was so chipper it made my heart cry.

I responded with a vacant stare and burst out crying as they both looked at me with wondering eyes.

"I'm sorry. I'm a little tired that's all. I'll see you in the morning."

My father's look changed to one of, "I know you done fucked up again, but I ain't saying nothing tonight because I know your fat ass will talk soon enough."

I had to get back out of his house, but without any money saved, no job, and no ideas, I had no clue as how to do that. I was evicted from my apartment because my rent was three months late and Terrance had kicked my ass twenty-too many times in it. My landlord was sick and tired of making repairs. He had to replace the front door twice, all the walls either had to be re-plastered or repainted, and the carpeting in the bedroom had to be cleaned three times in one month. He made sure I wasn't going to do this again to his place or anyone else's.

My name must've been placed on some kind of list that alerts other landlords because no one else would rent to me. Terrance had moved in with me, so when I was evicted, I asked him to get a place in his name. He agreed, but said I'd have to pay the rent. I agreed, because under no circumstances was I moving back home.

When we moved to "our" new place, he kicked me out so many times it was ridiculous. Hotels were my home many nights, and in the morning when I came back to get dressed, he still wouldn't let me in. I would have to call in to work with some lame excuse as to why I'd be late or not coming in at all.

Terrance is the one who stole the money out of the stores safe. It was my fault for giving him the password and my safe keys, but I never imagined he'd steal. I don't know where he is now and haven't known for six months. When we were evicted from "our" apartment for fighting and disturbing the peace, he decided to move in with his brother. I cushioned the grenade that I should have let end my life, and moved back home.

We continued to "date," and he continued to treat me like we were in a heavyweight title fight. I did nothing to stop it and felt I deserved every blow I took. He beat me for my baby, for Desmond, for wishing my father were dead, for Otto, for Lamar, and he beat me for all the starving children in the world. He figured if I didn't eat so much maybe someone else would have a chance.

Terrance didn't have his barbershop or car anymore and had been driving mine. He told me he got rid of it because he wanted to save money for our upcoming wedding. The truth was the car was in another woman's name. When he missed two payments, she came and took it back.

His barbershop burned to the ground, and I thought he set the fire himself so I asked him. Terrance went berserk, punched me in the stomach and added two kicks as I fell on the ground while spewing, "You stupid bitch! So what if I did do it? What the hell are you going to do, tell the insurance agent with your fat ass?"

When the insurance company ruled it arson, with no help from me, he woke me up out of my sleep early in the morning with slaps, punches, and a new grip on my neck that any wrestler would be proud to own. He received the news the day before and stayed out all night drinking but still came home at five a.m. to show me it was all my fault, and teach me a lesson. As soon as he finished treating me to his early morning rage, he told me he loved me and said he was going to give me the best loving a woman could wish for.

One day I had to work in the store's office and Terrance surprised me with lunch. Using food was his way of getting everything he wanted. He knew I'd never decline a meal, free or otherwise. He came to get the store's safe codes. His plan worked flawlessly. I knew no one who wasn't an employee was allowed in the office, and instead of making him wait until I came out front to my own office, I like the fool I was, buzzed him into the back.

"Hey, baby. I bought you some lunch. They got my baby working hard, huh?"

"Yeah, just a little bit. What's up?"

Terrance's expression was very soft, and he actually made me think he cared.

"Just making sure you get something to eat that's all. What's all these numbers for any way?"

"Oh, just store business. Nothing that would interest you."

"Anything you do interests me, you know that. What, you think you can't trust me?"

"No, Terrance, no. It's not that at all. These are the numbers to the stores safe and only certain employees can have them."

Aggressively he replied, "Girl, you don't trust me, do you? I've been with you for three years, and yes we've had ups and downs, but I told you things were going to get better; I'm going to change. I've just been down on my luck lately with the barbershop. Now, tell your man a little store business."

Trying to hide my fright, I calmly replied, "What do you want to know?"

"I'm going to show you I mean what I say, and that you can trust me. Give me the safe numbers, and I guarantee nothing will happen. What do you take me for, a bank robber or something?"

"This isn't my business, Tee. It's the stores business, and I..."

In an I-am-your-boss-and-your-fat-ass-has-to-do-what-I-say voice, Terrance replied, "Don't you work here?"

"Yes."

"Then it is your business. Now give me them numbers."

I felt a punch coming on and this wouldn't be the first time he hit me on my job. Once, I was in the back taking inventory and he thought I was fooling around with one of the workers. He whacked me in front of two other people. I didn't say anything. What do you say in a situation like that? "Oh, no I'm fine. We play like this all the time," or "No, that didn't hurt?"

I stood and watched him walk away while my coworkers watched me watch him walk away. When he was no longer in sight, I excused myself to the bathroom and cried. I didn't love him or the fighting, so why did I stay? The naysayers would prove me wrong that's why. Somehow, I would make this work. All I needed was a lot of time.

When we'd go to my parent's house for dinner, or attend a social function, Terrance treated me the same way he did when I first met him. My parents thought things were fine between us, and I would wait until he became that man again.

Terrance stood staring at me with his, I'm-getting-ready-to-drag-you-across-the-floor look, and I suddenly became afraid. If I didn't give him what he wanted, he'd think I didn't trust him and would want to fight. If I did give him the numbers, and he stole money, I could be fired. I didn't feel like fighting, and knew he wouldn't steal from the store; that would be the same as stealing from me, and he'd never do that. He loves me and would never do anything to hurt me. Well, you know what I mean.

"Here, Terrance." *Will somebody set this dummy free?* "These are the numbers for the safe, but you can't get into it without this password and these keys. What do you plan on doing with them?"

"Nothing, baby. I just wanted to see if you trust me or not, that's all. I wouldn't do anything to jeopardize our money. If you really trust me, you'd let me carry them for a day. Then tomorrow, we can set a date and plan our wedding."

You know that's all it took for me. I wanted to be married and have someone love me.

"I guess it won't be a problem with you keeping them overnight. I'll get the keys from you tomorrow, okay?"

"Now, that's my girl." He walked out without saying goodbye or showing me any sign of affection. *And why should he? He didn't come to the store for your dumb ass anyway.*

Terrance didn't steal anything that day. He made copies of the keys and numbers and waited until two years later when we weren't living together anymore. He'd been sweet talking one of the girls who worked in the office and it took two years for her to let him in at closing time. We still "dated," but I thought he was living with his brother to save money for our wedding. How wrong I was; I was not part of his plan. He was seeing another woman and plotting and planning to rob the store, disappearing without a trace.

I never told my parents that I'd been evicted twice. I told them Terrance didn't want to live in sin anymore, and he didn't want me to live on my own. My ruse worked until he left town without telling me where he was going or that he robbed the store. I wondered how he was able to get away with so much money, so I called Jack, and he gave me all the information I needed.

Rita, the office manager, usually makes bank drops every evening before she goes home. For two weeks she didn't because Terrance the sweet talker somehow persuaded her not too. He wanted to see how much money would be in the safe and instructed her to only deposit one fourth of the stores receipts. She figured she'd deposit the full amount later and everything would balance itself out.

At the end of the second week, Terrance picked her up from work with his brother Teddy. Terrance kept her distracted while Teddy emptied out the safe. Rita was off the weekend and didn't notice what happened until Monday night. She didn't tell anyone else of her plan to let the money sit there, so when April, the girl who works the part- time morning shift came in, she thought everything was fine. When Rita came in and saw the empty safe, she asked April did she deposit the money. Of course she replied, "No." Rita called the police and all the head honchos came in.

After a month long investigation, the trail led back to me. I was fired for giving Terrance my keys, password, and safe numbers. Rita is on a two-month suspension and told me she wished my stupid ass were dead. She also told me she was having sex with Terrance, and he said she was better than I was. She didn't forget to add the part about me being nothing but a fat elephant doink and he was sick of fucking me. Rita was reprimanded before I was, so when I walked to my car, she met me in the parking lot. I thought she'd say she was sorry that I'd lost my job, but I was mistaken about her reaction.

"Lynnette, if I'd gotten fired I would've beat your ugly pig face until it was pretty! We both know that would be an all year thing and would never happen. Your retarded ass better pray we don't see each other again."

I was fired today. I keep saying these words over and over in my mind, and they still don't seem to belong there. I'm thirty-three years old and I live at home with my parents. Repeating this isn't helping me make myself believe it. If I don't pay back the twenty thousand dollars that was taken from the store, I'm going to jail. Where am I going to get that much money? Where in the world is Terrance? How could he do this to me? If this is what his version of love feels like, I hate it.

At one point in our relationship, I know he had to love me. It must've been before he started beating me. When I'd asked Terrance why he hit me, he always said, "A woman needs to be put in her place sometimes. If you don't like it, you can get out." If I left, I'd be considered a failure and I didn't want to fail.

I let go of the pride I didn't have anymore and told Esta what was going on. She told me exactly what I should do; just leave that man alone. We hadn't spoken to each other for three months after I told her I broke things off with Desmond. The first time we talked I called to tell her I missed her and that I was sorry for speaking the way I did. My personal stompings weren't received on a regular basis so I didn't mention the downside of my life.

"As long as you're happy, I'm happy. You know what's best for you, and I'm going to support you no matter what."

"Thank you, Esta. Do you still love me?"

"Girl, always. Now give me some more good news."

I proceeded to tell her about my love life and how I didn't have one thought of Desmond. I was lying. Desmond was with me constantly, and I knew deep inside that I'd made a mistake. Sure, Terrance was much more attractive physically, but he didn't love me. He never would. With Desmond, I felt like I could walk on air. The air with Terrance was suffocating. I should've told

Desmond I'd made a mistake and begged him to take me back, but, of course, I was too proud for that. I wasn't too proud to get my ass kicked, though.

I lost my job today. I'm sitting in my room eating chocolate bars with an orange soda chaser. Why should I care what I look like? No one wants me, and I'm not sure if I want myself. I'm already fat, and a few more pounds won't be noticed.

My visits to the gym stopped after the fourth beat down I received. Terrance decided to kick me in the ribs along with his other moves of torture, and when he finished, I couldn't stand up straight to walk. I allowed Terrance to treat me horribly while I waited on a day that would never be on a calendar. Leap year included.

Once I missed the first week of my exercise routine, my lifestyle of fitness was over. I was a size six when I met Terrance, and within eleven months I was a size sixteen. I hated myself because I did nothing to control my downward spiral. The only thing I did, as I destructed, was eat.

What difference does it make how big I am? Fat may come in all shapes and sizes, but it's still classified as fat. Who cares if you're a size twenty, or eighteen, or any of the other plus sizes as we so politely call them, you're still fat. It doesn't matter if you're a size twin-bed sheet. So what you're not as big as a king size? You're still fat. I stopped caring long ago, and the feeling is going full throttle now.

I made many stops to eat before arriving home, and once I got here, I ran to the kitchen and ate again. Now my fat ass is sitting in my room eating even more. Maybe I'll choke on something and die before morning comes. If I do, I hope I choke on the last thing in my stash box because I'd hate for any of these goodies to go to waste. What in the world did I just say? I sound like a combination of a pig, an elephant, and a hungry hippopotamus that'll kill for any meal. I need help.

What am I going to tell my parents? How am I going to tell them? Maybe I'll say their thirty-three year old waste of a child lost her job, was evicted from her apartment, and lost her car. In other words, I'm a fuck-up. That sounds believable.

The days following the repossession of my car I told them that Terrance's car was in the shop having major repairs done. The lie increased when I added that he was driving mine and he'd take me wherever I had to go. Instead of me paying my own car note, I gave him the money, and he was supposed to pay it for me.

Wrong again. He was paying a car note, but it wasn't mine. He used my money to pay Rita's car note and work his way into the store's safe. Terrance intercepted all of the notices I received by mail, informing me of my upcoming repossession. Words cannot describe the sick feeling I had when Mr. Repo Man came to my job and drove away with my Ford Taurus. I asked him for an explanation, and he said the finance company had given me ample time to make up my late payments. He told me of a notarized letter they received from me six months ago saying all monies owed to them would be paid in full. The letter included a schedule indicating how the payments would be made. They received the last payment three months ago and tried to contact me, but couldn't.

"I've been at the same address for months. There must be some kind of mistake."

Mr. Repo Man didn't stop his particular movements of seizing my car as he spoke. He walked around it as if he'd just bought it, and paid no attention to my whiny pleas.

"Look, lady. I'm sorry for your misfortune, but don't take your frustrations out on me. I'm just here for the car."

I stood staring at him with my mouth wide open. The fumes that escaped smelled so bad that bugs bypassed the opportunity to enter it. Although I knew nothing about what he was saying, I knew it was true. I asked to see the notarized letter, and Mr. Repo Man told me that was not his area of expertise. He repeated the fact that he was only there to pick up the vehicle, and I'd have to call the finance company for any more information. Then he drove off in my car with me standing in the parking lot of Just Shoes, watching someone who did not belong in my car drive it away. Shock prevented me from crying at that point. Terrance, I hate you.

I haven't seen or heard from Terrance in six months, and know I never will. This is all his doing. When he left town, I began making my own car payments, but my money wouldn't even cover the late fees. How am I going to prove I didn't sign a notarized letter? Who's going to believe I was so stupid to let him handle my finances? I'm living at home with my parents because I can't get my own place; I threw away the man who loved me, the man I thought I loved threw me away, and my car was repossessed. I was fired from my job today.

Everyone will believe I have serious issues. Everyone I come in contact with will take one look at me and know I have nothing for a brain. I deserve this for always being in a hurry to have what I want. Is this the way I want my life to be? It would seem so by the choices I've made. There was no green grass on the other side. I looked at dirt-covered cement and tried to make it look like a healthy lawn. I should've opened my eyes and saw the real picture. Well, I'm feeling it now. I've hit the ground hard and it's very painful. There's no need to dust myself off because I'll be down here a while.

What am I going to do all day tomorrow? I know, I'll look for another job. It won't be too hard to find one in New York City. Wait a minute; no one is going to hire me. When I tell them I was fired from my last job and what the reasons were, I'll get thrown out the door.

Hear come the tears. It seems like tear production is the only thing I know how to do. I'll tell my parents the truth. They'll understand that it's not their fault I grew up to be a fool. It happens all the time. They'll understand that I'll never be married and will always live at home making minimum wage, if that, because I let someone else lose my job. I'm sure they'll understand that I'll have to drive their cars because I let someone else ruin my credit and I am unable to get my own. They may not know exactly how I managed to ruin my life, but they'll understand.

I'm positive they already know Terrance doesn't exist. I make up fake dates that we're supposed to go on and go and sit in the garage until the wee hours of the morning. Thank God they were always in the bed when I came back in because I reeked of gasoline.

"Why won't Terrance come in and talk for awhile, Lynnde? Is something wrong?" That's a question that came from my mother.

"No, everything is fine. We're just running a little late that's all." That was the excuse I used when I first lost my car. Before that happened, I always said I was going to pick him up and ended up in a fast food parking lot until it closed. Then I'd move on to another one.

Terrance didn't even tell me he was leaving or say goodbye. That would've given me insight on him robbing the store, so I guess he couldn't. I found out he was gone after waiting three mornings and three nights for him to pick me up from work. When he didn't show up on the third night, I took a taxi over to his brother's apartment.

My car was parked on the street with a pile of tickets stuffed under the wiper blade. Still, I thought he must've overslept or something. I couldn't call him because they didn't have a phone and couldn't reach him at work because he didn't have a job. As I walked up to the door, a man on the front stoop told me the boys that used to live there moved out a few days ago.

"Huh? You must be mistaken, Sir. That's my car and my boyfriend's been driving it. Maybe his brother moved."

"No, I'm pretty sure both of them left. They had themselves a fancy long black car, and two women were inside it with them. Looked like a cross between a Cadillac and a limousine. My eyesight ain't the best, so I really can't tell you what kind of car it was." The man was eating peanuts and lifted his hand in an offering. He felt he had to do something to help ease my pain.

"That was probably Terrance's brother and a friend. We're going to get married, so I know it wasn't him."

"You knock on the door and see, but Terrance gave me this watch and some clothes for my son. Teddy gave me this nice gold chain. It's too flashy for me, so I'm going to give it to my son."

My knees buckled when he showed me his jewelry. Those were things that I'd given to Terrance on his birthdays. My eyes filled with tears, but they didn't fall. I knocked on the door and it opened. I saw bare rooms that once looked lived in as I continued to walk through a scavenged site. The only thing that was left was a crumpled picture of me on the floor. My tears had streaked my face as I made it to the front door, and the old man asked was I was okay.

"Yes. Everything is fine." What happened was the only thought that sat next to the rotten pea in my mind.

I decided to take my photo and give back to Terrance once I saw him. I still have the photo. Before going back outside I cleaned my face up, not wanting the old man to know he was right. His voice cracked as he asked, "Did you find who you were looking for, Miss?"

Lies took me hostage at that point. "Yes. I completely forgot he said he was going to help his brother move. I was to come by and pick up my car. I guess it's those pre-wedding jitters. Thanks for your help, bye."

"Bye, Miss."

The old man knew I was lying and looked down at the ground as I walked away. Before getting into my car I turned to face him - he was still looking at the ground. I guess he didn't care to look at the fool of the year.

That happened on a Wednesday night, and I had no idea of the news I would receive the next day. Thursday morning would be the day my downward spiral gained its full momentum. The store's investigation into the missing money would start, and I still had no idea the trail would end with me losing my job. I think they, meaning the head honcho's at Just Shoes, knew all roads pointed to me long before they told me. Maybe they were giving me an opportunity to fix the mess I didn't know I made before they fired me. Damn. Whatever the case, its still a fact that I was fired today. I have nowhere to go tomorrow.

I never realized how much of my life depended on my job. I feel worthless now. Getting fired makes me feel unneeded by the world, like no one wants me, like I'm not good enough and have no more importance. What have I done with my life? Where did it go, and why did it suddenly decide to leave me? Am I really that bad?

It's 4:12 in the morning. I've asked myself the same questions over and over and have no answers. The only thing I accomplished was eating everything in my junk food box. I never told you it's actually seven junk food boxes, one big box can't fit under my bed. My weight is close to three hundred pounds. If I had the chance, I'd leave me, too. I have to tell my parents tomorrow. Holding the truth in will make matters worse, and I can't hold any more misery. There's no room for it with everything I've eaten today.

My father and I were getting along until I dumped Desmond. I might as well let him get his hate for me all out in the open. I said I never wanted to hurt my mother, but I'm going to do it anyway. I can't do anything right. Maybe when I lay back and close my eyes a massive coronary will come. I have no brain, so taking my heart away won't bother me at all. God, take me now.

11:56 a.m. is the time I woke up. Is this what unemployed people do? The desire to get up and get dressed isn't here and I have nowhere to go. I might as well stay in bed a little longer.

I want to talk to Esta for comfort, but I'm too embarrassed to call. She's four months pregnant with twins and I don't want her to worry needlessly about me. This is a wonderful time for her, and I'm really glad she's happy. Saying that isn't very convincing because everyday I wish I were the one who was married and about to have children. My life is so far from that it's pitiful. Esta has three fashion boutiques and I don't even have a job. She has a husband and is pregnant with two of the most beautiful babies that will ever enter the world. I have no man to speak of, and look three years pregnant with the most disgusting fat that will never leave.

There are so many medications to take for headaches, colds, backaches, or whatever ails you. Why isn't there something to take to make your life all better? Why can't I be a chalkboard for two minutes and erase everything bad that's happened in my life so far? I'd cease to exist then. That wouldn't be so terrible either. Who am I kidding? I'm not capable of committing suicide, and I don't want to die because then I wouldn't be able to eat again.

I lost my job yesterday. The words still have the same meaning even though it's a different day. I have no car. People say materialistic things may not mean everything, but they account for a lot. My worth was valued by the position I held and the type of car I drove. What is my worth now? Please, don't answer that. If you're saying,

"Don't worry Lynnde, things will work out," thank you. I can't see a rainbow or a pot of gold anywhere. Maybe I need glasses.

What I do see is my mother looking hurt, and my father talking to me exactly the way I deserve. She'll be home at 2:30 from the hospital, and my father usually gets in around 3:15. I'll tell them then. It makes no sense to prolong the inevitable, and as they say, the sooner the better.

As I trudged out of bed to the shower I decided to do a little housework. On the walk downstairs to begin cleaning the living room, the kitchen told me it had something to ask me. I started a conversation with the refrigerator and didn't stop talking until 2:25, when I heard my mother's keys turning in the lock. She walked into the kitchen to see me polishing off the final noodles from last night's spaghetti dinner. It wouldn't have been a big deal, but I was eating from the glass container, never bothering to heat any of it up. I ate the spaghetti after I ate all of the lunchmeat, pickles, mayonnaise, butter and cheese, and drank every beverage in the refrigerator.

When my mother's and my eyes met, I burst out crying. She dropped the bags she held and ran towards me, hugging me tightly while fighting back tears I heard trying to come through her voice.

"Oh, my baby girl, what's wrong? What's going on with my Lynnde to make my baby cry?"

I felt shame, pity and fear all at once. I blubbered pretty well at that point, so the words I attempted to say made no sense to her or me.

"Calm down, baby, and tell me what's wrong. Whatever it is, we can fix it and make it all better. Tell me what's wrong."

"Oh, Mama. I'm sorry. I don't know what's wrong with me. I lost my job because I was accused of stealing, my car was repossessed and I was evicted from two apartments. I'm sorry."

There, I said it. All my dirty deeds were out in the open. I felt my mother's hold on me get tighter as she rubbed my back like only she knew how.

"Now, Lynnde. You stop all this crying, you hear? We're going to work this out, the three of us together. Did this Terrance boy do this to you? Where is he?"

"Terrance did have a lot to do with this, but I don't know where he is. He stole the money from the store, but I'm the one who gave him the information. I don't know what to do."

"That's what your daddy and I are here for, to help you. Don't you worry about a thing. You can always get another apartment, another job and a car, but you only get one life here on this earth. This is the time for you to start living yours for you."

My mother sighed heavily and squeezed me tighter.

"I thought something wasn't right between the two of you. You never want to open up to me, and I didn't want to meddle in my baby's business. Let this be the last time you don't come to me, you hear? Did he hit you?"

My cries were her answer.

"Oh, my baby. Why didn't you come to me, Lynnde? You know I'll be here for you no matter what. I told you that before, remember?"

My head hurt and slob ran down my mothers arm. A two-year old having a temper tantrum was a prettier sight. "I didn't want you to worry, or be upset. I wanted to handle things on my own."

"Baby, everybody needs help sometimes. Now you, your father and I are going to sit down and work this out. Your father and I figured you weren't seeing Terrance, but why didn't you tell us about your car? Your daddy told me not to ask about it, that you would let us know in due time."

Shocked I asked, "Daddy knows I lost my car?"

"He didn't say those exact words, but I knew what he meant."

"Ma, I'm so sorry. I'm sorry for moving back home because I had no other choice. I'm sorry for losing my job and my car. I'm sorry for growing up to be a failure. What am I going to do?"

All my life I wanted to be a grownup and here I was, at the age of thirty-three, still acting like an innocent child. I did everything wrong. When I had to fix things and make them right I went to my mother in the form of a ten-car pile up for answers.

"Lynnde, baby, this is not the time to start feeling sorry and put yourself down. Sometimes when people come into our lives, we forget that they are actually in our life and we start living for them. When you think you're in love, it's easy to let go of yourself and forget your values and worth for the sake of trying to get what you want. Many people make the same mistake. Don't you cry over that. Uh-uhhh, don't you cry. You're a strong, beautiful, smart woman and I want you to never forget that, no matter what a man tells you."

My mother rocked me and spoke with a humming rhythm in her voice. She pressed my head into her bosom and wiped my tears away with her words.

"One day your true love will reign supreme. When it does my baby will know. Don't be in a hurry, baby. True love will never let you forget who you are. Your little light will always shine, you hear? This too will pass, baby. Yes it will. One day at a time. One day at a time."

I couldn't speak. I love my mother. She was always right when it came to me. I was always in a hurry. That's why I make mistakes. I promised myself a few years back I'd never be a fool again. Trying to have the man I wanted, instead of the one I needed, made me a liar.

Life is bad enough with strangers' lying to you. When you start doing it to yourself, something is definitely wrong. I closed my eyes while my mother held me, wishing hard that when I opened them I'd be six years old again.

"You go on upstairs and get yourself together. I'll tell your father first, and then we'll all sit down and talk this out, okay?"

I wanted her to take away all of my heartache so I agreed without a fight. "Okay, Ma. Thanks. I love you."

"I love you even more, baby. Now go on."

I stood and walked away listening to my mother call on Him to guide us. I cried a bit more but I kept on walking. I should be able to tell my father myself and feel very ashamed about that. I'll be honest and tell you I'm afraid. When it comes to telling my father anything, I turn into the little girl who sat on his lap and was called pet names for comfort. I guess I'm not as grown as I think I am.

I walked into the bathroom to stare at my face in the mirror. I asked it, "Mirror, mirror on the wall, am I the most fucked-up person of them all?" The mirror didn't give me a fairytale answer but showed me that my face is triple it's normal size. I have two chins and my eyes are early morning vampire red. I'm truly ugly.

At one time, you'd still see my pretty brown, almond-shaped eyes when I smiled. Now, with all the fat on my face, a smile makes them disappear into small, cracked slits.

Four times in my relationship with Terrance he made them disappear. Three of the four times they disappeared together. He must've went to school and earned a degree in the art of how to give someone a tailored black eye. My eyes were the same ugly blue, black, red, purple color, and they were always swollen just right. That's the way they looked to me, but I couldn't see very clearly.

My overly chubby hand is very shaky as I raise it up to touch my brittle hair. It used to be so soft. I haven't bothered to take the time to care for it since Terrance pulled it out in patches and cut some of it out while I was sleeping. I usually wear a wig. A wig was the only thing, besides shaving my head bald, that helped out the style he left me with, which was a mangy dog do with Alopecia.

Terrance never loved me. He cut up my clothes, threw away things that belonged to me, and watched me look like an idiot trying to find them. If I cooked a meal he didn't want to eat, he threw it on the walls and floor. Sometimes he'd ask me to prepare certain things and still throw them all over, or smash them in my face and say, "A dog wouldn't eat this shit, but you will. You eat anything."

One time, he was going to pick me up from work and never showed up. In my taxicab ride home, I saw him with another woman. I rushed out of the cab, ran over to my car, asked what was going on, and who she was.

Terrance took a drag on his cigar and leaned to one side. I'd seen that pre-slap position before, so I took a few steps back to insure he'd miss me. He surprised me by saying, "This is my sister," and nothing more. Right.

When I went around the car to open the door, I planned to throw her out, he pulled off, and the half open car door hit me in my leg and knocked me to the ground.

There I lay in the middle of the street with car horns honking for me to get out of the way. The main horn was the taxi driver. He yelled at me in his native tongue and motioned for me to get back into the cab. No one bothered to help me up. *And why should they?* I didn't want to get up. My time on the ground felt normal, and I prayed I'd turn into a manhole. No such luck.

I limped back to the cab hearing curse words coming from every direction. On my ride home, I thought about Terrance, not about saving myself. He never mentioned her before or after he came home at two in the morning. I confronted him before he made it to his destination of the bathroom. He turned to me enraged, and blasted my soul.

"Bitch, shut the fuck up and get your fat ass back in the bed! I ain't gotta explain shit to you! You should be glad I even come home since no one else wants your stankin' ass!" Then he slammed the bathroom door in my face.

What did I do? I did exactly what he said. I walked into the bedroom with my head down and got back into the bed. What was wrong with me? I had no self-respect and only thought about how my leaving would make my ending things with Desmond show everyone I made a mistake. They all knew I made a mistake, and I knew it, too. I just didn't want to say it out loud yet.

I was already evicted from my first apartment, and even though this one was in his name, my reasons for staying and paying the rent were nowhere in sight. A miracle was not going to happen in my life. Maybe I should try to get a place on Thirty Fourth Street.

Before forcing myself to sleep, I sat in bed thinking of Desmond and how right he was to speak his last words to me. I wanted a love like we had and knew it wouldn't come from Terrance. How could I have been such a fool? Talking about it over and over again didn't help me out either. I need to change my life's course, but I don't want to be alone, no matter what the consequences are.

Please try to understand. Many of you are most likely wondering how can I ask you to understand when I don't know what's going on myself? I'm just talking out loud, not loud enough for Terrance to hear, I don't want to upset him, but loud enough for an answer to respond. Terrance is never going to love me, this I know. So what's the problem, you ask? Why don't I leave? Maybe somewhere in my mind I'm hoping he'll kill me, and the world will feel sorry for me.

When I heard him coming towards the bedroom, I lay down and pretended to be sleeping, but should've been packing my bags and getting out of this life. Instead, I lay in the bed and continued to play my role as the defeated contender in a freak combination boxing and wrestling match.

I was on my side with my eyes closed, and my body was turned towards the wall with my back facing Terrance's side of the bed. He walked to my side and stood silently. I wanted none of him or his problems tonight, but what difference did that make? He never cared about what I wanted or what mattered to me.

Upon hearing his voracious breathing, I cracked my eyes open slightly to see him looking down at me. He was totally naked. I thought not moving would make him leave me alone. I was wrong. Thinking he wanted to use me like a bathroom, a urinal to be more accurate, would've been correct.

He walked closer to my face and began to pee on me while threatening me not to move. He added that if he saw me breathe, tonight would be the night I died. So much for wanting him to kill me. I didn't move. I cried, but who could tell pee from the tears in the dark. A wet face is a wet face. He laughed during his urination process and told me a fat ho will do anything for a man.

While receiving my golden shower, I thought of the time I urinated in Tori's car. I'd much rather receive Tori's wrath than this, but thank you for sparing me, Desmond. Sometimes coming full circle isn't a good thing. I hate you, Terrance. I hate you.

Tears fall down my face as I continue to look in the mirror. Instead of getting ready for a life planning session with my parents, I'm making it look worse. I can't get the thoughts of that night out of my mind.

When Terrance finished soaking my face and hair, he told me what he thought of me.

"Look at you. Look at your sorry stank ass lying in piss. Even animals don't sleep in their own shit. If you ever confront me I'll break your neck. I'll fix your mouth so I'll never hear it again, bitch. Now get your nasty ass up and clean this bed."

He walked out of the room and went and slept on the couch. I did what he told me to do, crying through my every motion, cleaning the bed before I cleaned myself. I thought Terrance might want to sleep in it with me. *You need help.*

I didn't sleep on his side either after I washed myself. My side was soaking wet, so I slept on the floor, afraid he'd come in the room and see me. This was my life's normal routine, cleaning up after someone else's garbage. I knew my lifestyle was wrong, but somewhere down the line, I decided to wait for a change to find me instead of finding it first.

While cleaning Terrance's piss, the memory of licking Otto's ass brought more tears to my eyes. Damn, I must be nasty. In the morning, he came and woke me up in his usual make up manner. He entered me without my consent and humped until he felt he'd done me a favor. I hate you, Terrance. Terrance, I hate you.

I'm staring at my face in the mirror and wondering if my life is capable of improvement. My insides boil when I think of the money he stole, and how I'm never going to prove I didn't willingly assist him.

My reflection brings back times with Terrance I made myself forget. I thought of the time he held my head in the kitchen sink when it was full of dirty dishwater and screamed, "Swim, whale! Swim!" Once, he cut my thigh with a butcher knife. He said he wanted to roast my meat and find out what whale tasted like. My weight was out of control, and he reminded me of it every day. Terrance hated me. Every time he beat on me, I ate. He told me he was going to beat my mouth swollen shut, so I couldn't eat any more. I'll admit that Terrance was a pro in the butt whooping category, but he'd never stop me from eating.

I knew I was wrong for staying with him, but I also knew something was wrong with him. Instead of taking care of myself, I did a little investigating to find out about Terrance. When he'd come into the fitness club where we met, he sometimes came in with his friend, Markus. Terrance never spoke of any ex-girlfriends or family, and after a year and a half of his fury, I wanted answers.

Markus was a willing participant and gave up information about Terrance that disgusted me. Terrance's mother sent him to New York from South Carolina to live with his father after being in and out of detention homes. He stole money from his father at age seventeen and has been on his own ever since his father kicked him out. Markus told me horror stories of Terrance beating girls in the street, in dance clubs, at grocery stores, anytime of the night, or in broad daylight for the whole world to see when a woman wanted to break things off with him. *Run,*

*Lynnde. Run.* No one knows where he got the money for the barbershop from, and he's been shot at twice. *Faster, Lynnde, Faster.* He'd been beat a couple of times by a few dudes for messing with their women, sisters, or whatever dirt he decided to play in.

I stood listening to Markus and didn't say a word. Tori's voice said, "Hello," but I still said nothing. Markus told me he liked Terrance, but thought he needed professional help. I needed help. I knew his background, was living proof it existed, and did nothing to get out of the situation. Was I scared? I don't think so. I thought he loved me, and thought he was going to change. He did change, but it wasn't for the better. Terrance was a derailed freight train that hadn't crashed yet. He was off track but still moving too fast, destroying himself and everything that came into his path.

I can't stop looking at my face in the mirror. Am I somewhere inside there? If I knew who I was supposed to be, maybe I could find me. Maybe someone special will return one day. I was fired from my job yesterday. I have no job to go to today or tomorrow.

Wondering if my father made it home, I opened the bathroom door to hear muffled voices. I couldn't understand what they were saying so I returned to the black maze I was in. I didn't want to think of the past years I had with Terrance, but thoughts of him wouldn't leave me alone. Maybe this is some kind of therapy for me, believing my very unpleasant memories of him really happened. Not suppressing them may help me move on. Accepting the fact that I allowed him to treat me the way he did, and it was no one else's fault, could be my first step to regaining Lynnde, or at least getting reacquainted with her.

I remember watching a talk show when I was dating Otto about women in physically abusive relationships. Otto never hit me, so in no way did I think of our relationship as abusive. I thought those women were stupid for staying with the men, thinking someday they'd change or that they'd never be hit again. I swore that would never be me and boasted that I was too smart for that. "A man will never, ever put his hands on me, and if he does, that will be the end of us." I wish I did what I said.

I heard the expression to hell and back and often wondered what someone was going through if they felt they'd been in hell. Now I understand it completely. The question I ask is, "Will I be able to make it back?" Feel free to give me an answer at anytime because I'm clueless at this point.

My mother's statement that everyone needs help is true. If I'd opened my mouth sooner and forgotten about the pride I no longer had, I wouldn't be in this situation. I told myself before I was going to concentrate on me, but I never did. Now I've given myself no other choice. Well, from now on, I won't allow anyone else in my life that'll cause me harm; I've made my mind up on that point. As we all can clearly read, I'm doing fine in that area all by myself.

Do you mind if I ask you a question? Thanks. Do you ever wonder if you were here in another life? Lately I have. I could never figure out what, or who I was, or in what period of time I was here before. Today, as I stare at myself in the mirror, my past life tells me exactly what I was. I was a dog. It doesn't matter what breed or if I was male or female, just that I was a dog. I was a stray dog that no one wanted and barely escaped getting caught by the dogcatcher and being put to sleep.

That has to be the reason for the pattern of my life. I put myself in bad situations, and just when I think death is my only alternative, something from someplace inside of me saves me. It's the same as a stray dog that's in the pound waiting on death and is adopted at the last minute. When he gets to his new home, he's not liked and it's back on the street he goes. I wonder, though, if I choose to kill myself, will I come back as another stray dog? Is that the thought stopping me from committing suicide? If I can break the cycle of destruction I'm in, it would most likely be easier for me if I were in human form. Besides, I'm making sure I get dogged just as much as I would if I were that stray dog, running from it's certain death. No one treats a stray dog with kindness. It's always told to get out or to go back where it belongs. No one wants you. We understand that it doesn't know where it belongs. I can relate, because I don't know where I belong either. I've been dogged so much I should be eating Alpo as a snack or better yet, an entire meal.

*All right, Lynnde. Stop this nonsense talk. You know what's happened in your life. Now it's time for you to do something about it. Stop bringing up the past and start making plans for a better future.* I will. I promise, I will.

Right after, I get the thought out of my mind of Terrance saying my mother was a dumb bitch for having me, or the time he cut up my clothes and hung them up in their proper places without me suspecting a thing until I put them on. He slashed all four of my car tires while I was working and made me think someone else did it, gave the TV I bought to another woman because he said all I watched were commercials about food. He used my toothbrush to clean his sneakers, put it back in its holder, and watched me use it to brush my teeth. Terrance would spit in the cartons of juice and smile as I poured a drink from them. Then there was the time he showed me the front row tickets he bought to a concert and made me chauffer him and his "sister" that he never mentioned there.

Terrance made up a game called Choke A Hog. He said he had to wrap his hands around my neck, squeeze my throat, and count how many minutes it took for me to stop breathing. As soon as I stopped breathing, he'd let go. I didn't tell him I didn't want to play as I watched him walk towards me. When he put his hands around my neck, I cried. He called me a punk bitch, punched me in the eye, and the list goes on and on.

I know you think I'm a stupid person. You have to think so after what I have and haven't told you. Don't think you'll hurt my feelings if you admit it. I think I'm stupid, too. I was fired from my job yesterday. God, help me please.

"Lynnde. Lynnde, baby, come down here. Your father and I would like to talk to you."

It's time for me to behave like an adult. "Okay, Ma. I'll be right there." An adult should be able to maneuver stairs that they've walked up and down many times before. I don't want to travel them this time because I feel like a dead man walking. I can prevent them from feeling any more agony over me; there's still time. There has to be something in this medicine cabinet that can help me out. I'll drink the bottle of mouthwash or eat some facial cleanser. I'm so dumb.

"Lynnde? Baby are you coming?"

"Yes, Ma." Before opening the door, I turned once more to look at myself in the mirror and saw sweat beading up on my face. Come on, Lynnde. Don't fall apart now. A brief rush of strength came to me, but left once my foot touched the top stair. My mother stood at the bottom with a comforting smile on her face. The calm before I dive into the burning pit of hells lava I guess. I reached the bottom, and she put her hand in mine and guided me into the dining room.

"Don't you worry about a thing, baby. We're going to work this out, you hear?"

I didn't answer her because my voice had just walked out of the bathroom and was on the top step. We reached the dining room and my father stood up, walked towards me, and gave me a hug.

"Are you are alright, girl?"

"Huh?"

"I said, are you alright?"

I didn't mean to say "huh" out loud, but the disbelief of my father's question took me for a loop.

"Yes, Daddy. I'm okay."

"Lynnde, why didn't you tell us what was going on? You know we love you and will help you with whatever you need. I don't give a shit about that boy. Tell me what happened with your job and your car."

Who was this man? He looked like my father, Lynndon Donald Lee, and his voice sounded exactly the same as his, but the man holding and speaking to me was not him. Please let this be real and not some kind of sci-fi episode. What did my mother say to him is what I want to know?

We all sat down and I began to tell my father how I trusted Terrance to pay my car note, and the unappealing story of how he got important information to steal from the store. I told them the higher-ups at Just Shoes felt I was an accomplice so I was let go. The only voice that was heard was my rickety one but I creaked on. Once I finished my tale of doom, I held my head up and looked my parents in their faces. I expected to see a look of love on my mother's, but not on my father's. I couldn't believe his look of sympathy and was half shocked to see a trace of tears. What did my mother say to him?

A few moments passed before anyone spoke. My father wiped his eyes before the tears rolled down his face and told me his plan of action.

"Baby, this is what we're going to do. Right now, don't you worry about getting a job. We're going to straighten this situation out with the shoe store, and you're going to need all of your energy for that. No one will ever accuse a Lee of stealing and get away with it. I know you're a smart girl. You used bad judgment, and you ain't the first person to make that mistake. We're going to get a private detective to track this sorry thieving ass boy down and make him pay for what he's done to you. He can't be that smart and know how to disappear without a trace. I'm not stopping until his ass is in jail." I sat still and opened my mouth to speak. I needed to ask this man his name.

"Let me finish. I want you to write a letter to the finance company and explain what happened. I promise you they'll work out some kind of payment arrangement. I've never known any place of business to ever turn down money. Don't worry about how you're going to pay them either, I'll take care of that. We're going to work together as a family and straighten this out."

My father spoke with a controlled, soft voice. I sat mesmerized in his words. My eyes focused on his mouth as I tried to look down his throat to see if someone else was in there.

"I know it's your life, but whatever good or bad goes on with you, happens with us. That's how a family operates. I may not have been the father you needed in the past, but all that's going to change, starting now. I need to make a few phone calls to get the ball rolling. Think about what you want to say in the letter, so we can work on that later, okay? Don't make yourself sick worrying about this either. Everything is going to be alright."

My father stood up and walked towards the kitchen to use the phone. When he past me, he put his hand on my shoulder and gave it a squeeze. I looked at my mother with something that hadn't been on my face in a long time, a smile.

"See, baby. I told you things would be all right. I told you we'd put our heads together and figure this out. We love you, and no one's going to hurt our baby girl. Now I want you to take two aspirin and go lay down for a while. The words for the letter will come. I'll start dinner and will wake you when it's ready."

My mother gave me a hug and went into the kitchen. Tears filled my eyes. I did it again. I managed to shut out the two people that would never hurt me and would always help me. Did they make me pay for my mistakes? No. They accepted my problems as their own and took charge of my situation. My father's words to me earlier on in life of no matter how old I get, I'll always be his baby girl, are true. I may look like a grown woman on the outside, but my insides feel like a needing little girl. Regardless of what you think of me right now, I'm not ashamed to say I love feeling like this. No, not the feeling of falling apart, but the feeling of love, protection, and loyalty I just received.

For the first time, I realize I can work my problems out no matter how bad they are. All I need to do is be truthful to myself, and let the truth show itself to everyone in my life. I was honest in telling my parents about the mistakes I made and they saw it. They were willing to help me with no holds barred. What's really a shock is the fact that my father doesn't want me to work right now, and instead, concentrate on getting myself together.

Where is his fatherly instinct coming from? Could he have had it all along? I can't believe he didn't bring my past up. One of my problems is I'm always so negative. From now on I'm going to think positive thoughts. He does want what's best for me, and maybe he didn't want to help me until I asked for it. I wish I'd asked sooner.

My entire body should be made of rubber. Maybe then the bad that bounces into my life will bounce right back out of it. See, there I go again. Putting myself down. That could be a reason why I always end up with negative results. What you project to the world are the thoughts you have of yourself. I never think anything positive about myself until someone negative tells me it's okay. I'm going to teach my brain that I don't need a man to survive. My body already knows it by showing the world I never miss a meal.

Okay, no more put-downs. My father's the only man that's ever shown me I can trust him and it's about time I start doing just that. *Admit it. At thirty-three years of age, admit that you love your father. Even if more bad times lie ahead you'll still love him. He's shown his love and no matter what, you need to show him yours in return.* Oh let me get upstairs. I hear my mother and it sounds like she's coming this way.

As I walk past the kitchen I see my mother looking in the refrigerator and my father sitting at the kitchen table deep into a phone conversation. I wish I could freeze this moment in time. This is for me. They're doing this to help me. Lynnde. The girl who won't talk to a mistake until it turns itself into a disaster. The girl who's always in a hurry to run home crying but doesn't realize it until she gets there.

If I were in college and failed all of my subjects, what would I do? I don't think I'd drop out just yet. I'd stay in school and sign up for different ones, ones that were more suitable for me. Subjects that made me prosper in life. That's the plan of action I'm going to take starting now. I'm going to get through this and sign myself up for some new courses. Courses that allow me to travel down six lane highways instead of one-way dead end roads. With the help of my family, that I'm admitting I need, I'm going to embrace my life with a more beautiful open mind. Think positive girl. I'm going to love Lynnde first, with all of her imperfections included, and give the world the greatest gift I can, me.

# Getting It Together

Three months have passed since the dining room talk with my parents and my affirmation for a new lease on life. Listen up and open wide dear reader, because, boy, do I have some talk for you. I'm so anxious to talk, and I have to tell somebody. I'll begin by bringing you up to date on my personal statistics first.

I'm still living at home and things couldn't be better. Yes, you heard what I said. Things couldn't be better. I'm attending a local college and taking two courses; one in business, and one in fashion purchase in an attempt to put myself on the right course. I promised Esta I'd work for her since she told me I was the only person she'd trust to run her New York store. Finding out that Lynnette isn't so bad after all is wonderful.

I've lost a few pounds; thirty-two to be exact, and have decided to take it slow. I have to try and do the right thing when it comes to my weight. The large up and down swings are not good for my health, mind, or my body. Talk about confusion and stretch marks. I've got them so bad. My stretch marks argue with me over which ones belong to them. I'm not kidding. They have spawned generations that have their very own colony. My thighs look like mini-malls and the election for mayor is coming up any day now on my stomach.

I don't know the proper definition for the other signs of plumpness on my body. Some call it cellulite. Please. The dents, ridges, and valleys in my skin have a life and mind of their own. I'm going to take charge and handle them, but I have to sneak up on them slowly, so they don't have time to organize a plan of attack.

You may think I'm giving my fat power, but I'd bet money it has a seat in the United Nations. If you've never been overweight, you may not understand exactly how I feel. Trying to get a visual of what I'm saying may help. Let me give you my top five reasons why I'm sure my fat does as it pleases.

1) My fat has a mind of it's own because when I turn to the left, some of my body stays to the right.

2) My fat never stays inside my pants or shirts when I sit down; it somehow manages to wave at whoever passes by.

3) When I walk past a mirror, my fat takes it's slow sweet time and doesn't look at itself until my eyes are too far ahead to see it.

4) If I make the mistake of trying to put on a shirt and sweat at the same time, my fat decides to make the shirt roll itself up into a ball and stop below my breasts, never making the long journey to my waist a very pleasant one.

5) I know my fat is thinking for itself when I take a long hot bath. It always gives me a hard time and tries to prevent me from washing myself below my waist. It usually

wins because I work up such a sweat I have to take a shower instead.

Now do you see why I say what I say and I know what I know? My fat may be independent, but it's going to have to listen to me when I tell it to go. I'll make sure it doesn't have a place to stay so it'll have no choice.

The word obesity is used to describe my body's condition and I'd like to tell the person who gave that word life, thank you. I want to thank them for making me be considered a freak by this society's rules, and thank them for the confidence that word took away from me. I understand I have a problem with my weight, and I let the troubles in my life be comforted by food. But in no way do I, or should I, be considered by anyone else as gross. That's one of the words used to describe the word obese. Degrading myself in the past was the thing to do, but no more. I've let myself know that I belong, and society is going to know it also. If a fat person disgusts you, try taking a blinds man approach, you won't have a problem then.

Okay, enough about my body. I'll move on and continue to bring you up to date on the situation that brought my life to this point. My father said he was going to hire a private detective to find Terrance, but he didn't have to. Two days after our dining room talk, the eleven o'clock news told us exactly where he was. There'd been a car accident on a highway in South Carolina and Terrance was involved. He was driving a stolen Cadillac and fell asleep at the wheel. The car ran off the road, hit a tree, and his brother, and another female passenger, were ejected, and killed. They were returning home from a nightclub and Terrance was driving drunk, so drunk that when the police asked him who he was and what happened, they weren't able to understand what he was saying. No one in the car had any identification on them, so a grisly accident picture with Terrance in it was flashed on the screen. A phone number was shown for anyone to call with information about who he was or the accident.

When I gave the shoe store Terrance's name during their questioning of me, they went to the police and an APB was put out on him. I didn't know about this and was fired anyway. He was arrested for drunk driving and vehicular manslaughter and went to jail. Two police officers and a lawyer went to question him about the store's robbery, and he admitted the whole thing. That came as a shock to me. He probably felt guilty about causing his brother's death and wanted to clear his mind of some of his wrong doings.

Terrance committed suicide after being in jail for two weeks by hanging himself with a bed sheet. An investigation was held into how he managed to do it because there was no place for him to hang from. Prison officials found out he tied one end of the sheet around his neck, and the other around the bars on his jail cell doors and rocked back and forth in a chair until he lost consciousness. He was found with shallow breathing and died shortly after.

One of my former bosses called and told me about Terrance's death and his funeral. They thought I might like to go, even though we didn't have a good relationship and offered to pay for my flight. I went to South Carolina for the wake and sat in the back of the church, but I could've sat anywhere because only his parents and a handful of other people were there. My going was for a sense of closure, I guess. My father went with me. He offered to be my bodyguard, and his company was exactly what I needed.

I stood over Terrance's coffin and stared at him for a long time. He looked like the beautiful man I'd first met, not the man that caused me so much pain and heartache. I didn't bother to introduce myself to his parents. They wouldn't have known who I was anyway.

Terrance looked like his mother, and for a split second, I was glad to have known him. I thought I heard Terrance ask me for forgiveness through his mother's eyes, so I looked at her and forgave him. My mother said forgiving helps you to heal, and I want to get over this as quickly and correctly as possible. I've had good feelings about myself since starting over and haven't thought much about Terrance. I've filed that chapter of my life with him away with the title, The Story Of A Fool, Part Three. I don't plan to ever read it again.

My old boss offered me my old position, but I decided not to take it. I didn't take the manager job back because I felt it was time for me to make a change. Working there again might make me think of Terrance. I'm looking forward to running a fashion boutique and shoes are a part of fashion. Looks like I'm going to have the best of both worlds.

The finance company worked out a payment plan with me after I explained all of the events that transpired. My Ford Taurus was already sold, but I will be able to finance another car once I'm gainfully employed. I plan to work part-time on the weekends and concentrate fully on my classes.

I called both of my ex-landlords, told them about Terrance, and apologized for the destruction I caused while living in their buildings. The first landlord accepted my apology, but the second one wants to take me to court. He won't be able to because my name wasn't on the lease. He let me know with a few choice words that he was glad Terrance was dead, and he hoped no one ever rented to me again. There was nothing for me to say, so I thanked him for his opinion and hung up. Life goes on.

As for my personal life, my mother wants to introduce me to one of her hospital volunteer friend's son. I told her no way, that I want to be alone with Lynnde for a while and get myself together. She didn't hear a word I said.

"I understand completely, baby, but this one here is a nice church going fella, and he's not bad on the eyes at all. Think about it, okay? I'm not talking marriage, just a friendly dinner. You need to get out and do something else besides school, you hear?"

"Yes, Ma. I hear you. I'll let you know later, okay?"

"What time later?"

"Maaaa."

"Okay, baby."

I love my mother. We've become closer than ever since I'm living at home. She bought a king-sized bed for me and sleeps with me sometimes. We stay up late on the weekend watching movies, and talk about the course she wants my life to take.

"Don't worry about the past, baby. It just helps us prepare for our future." She says that every time we talk to each other.

Not watching the steps I took as I rushed into the world to become a grownup made me fall more than once, flat on my face. Everyone says be careful of how you treat people on your way up the ladder; you may meet those same people on the way back down. I hate finding out some things to be true.

On one of my worst days, I saw Desmond and Tori. Terrance didn't pick me up from work and I had to walk home. He dropped me off that morning, and before I could get my needs for the day out of the car, he pulled off. My purse was one of my needs; it contained my money, which is why I had to walk home. I didn't want anyone to know that Terrance failed to pick me up once again, so I waited until everyone else left before I started walking;

wondering if I should even go back to the place where I began my blur of a day.

Terrance started a fight with me that morning over my use of water. He said I should pay the water bill, along with the rent, because I was bigger than him and used more of it. It was early and I was cranky from not having much sleep the night before. He had his friends over for an all night party on a Tuesday. None of them had jobs, so no one had anywhere to be but where they were. I didn't feel like hearing what he had to say, so I replied with a smart quick tongue, hoping to silence him.

"That's the stupidest thing you've said to date. I guess you expect me to pay the cable, gas, light, and phone bill as well since your pathetic ass isn't man enough to do it. Shut up, Terrance. It's too early for your mouth."

My response caught him off guard because his reply to me was that of silence. I started walking towards the bathroom to get dressed when I heard him running up behind me. My face was met with his head when I turned towards him. The fool head butted me. His exact target was my eye. I fell backwards on the floor and grabbed my face in pain. Gray stars and filthy vultures circled my face and moaned a song of gloom; it hurt so bad.

While I was on the floor crying and screaming how sick I thought Terrance was, he started kicking me in my back, sides, and face, while yelling in crazy man lingo.

"Don't you ever talk back to me, you fat, sloppy bitch! Your stupid ass is going to pay every bill that comes into this house whether I have a job or not! Now get your sorry ass up and fix me some breakfast!"

He stopped kicking me and walked away muttering words under his breath that only a psychotic nut would understand. I managed to get up and went into the bathroom to look at my face. My left eye watched my right eye swell up, and my right eye noticed my left eye was red and puffy. My black eyes were on their way. I took my nightgown off and looked at my stomach in the mirror. It was bruised and I imagined my back was, as well. There was no need to look because I'd felt this way before. I wanted to call into work, but I was already absent two days that week and couldn't afford to miss anymore.

My right eyeball was no longer visible, and I'd have to wear a pair of light colored shades all day as I'd done before. I was at the point of not even bothering to put on makeup to try and cover it up, knowing what I was hiding, as did everyone else. I'm not sure who was who, but I came out of the bathroom to see Dr. Jekyll or Mr. Hyde standing in my living room in the form of Terrance's body.

"Hey, baby. I have some interviews to go on today, so I'll drop you off at work. I put your purse and jacket in the car, and I want to stop and grab you some breakfast, so hurry your sweet self up."

He walked out the door and I stood in the middle of the room waiting for an answer. Someone needed to tell me Terrance was sick and I wasn't the person that had his cure. Sure, I had the answer; I just didn't feel like talking to myself.

The distortion set in as soon as I got into the car to begin going through my workday wearing fake prescription shades and willing the clock to speed up. Time needed to pass quickly and when it stopped, I wanted to be eighty-five years old and have Alzheimer's disease. I never wanted to remember this day as being real.

While walking home, thoughts of dumping Terrance were the only things on my mind. I gave him too much power, and the only way to take it back was for me to get rid of him. This is what I was thinking when I turned to the left to look inside of a restaurant window. The moment felt weird because Desmond and Tori were looking right back at me. I stopped walking and stood still for a moment, then reached my hand up to manage a pathetic hand gesture.

Desmond returned with a wave and Tori gave me the ultimate black girl eye roll. He was being polite. I'm sure he didn't want to ever see me again in life. I deserved Tori's reaction. Desmond got up out of his seat as I turned to continue my forty-five minute trek home. We reached the entrance to the restaurant at the same time. He looked at me and smiled while I gave him a stupid grin and stood like an idiot the rest of the time. Anxiously he spoke. "Hi, Lynnde. How are you? I haven't seen you in so long. How have you been?"

"I'm okay. How are you?" Dryness choked my body but still I stopped the cooling tears I had saved for him from coming.

"I've been good. Are you still at the shoe store?"

Wanting to say I wish we were together and will you marry me was on the tip of my tongue. The only thing that came out though was, "Yes."

"That's good to hear. I told you one day you'd own one. When you do, I'll be your number one customer. I'm still at the finance company, and I'm thinking about branching out. If you ever need any help, let me know."

"Thank you."

"I won't hold you up any longer, but you're still the finest woman I've ever seen. Take care, Lynnde."

He walked back into the restaurant, and I turned my head towards the ground. Why was Desmond so kind to me? If someone treated me the way I treated him, I'd never talk to them again. Wait, who am I kidding? Terrance treats me the same way, and I still talk to him and more.

I watched him reclaim his seat and saw Tori's mouth start to move five miles a minute. As she was talking, Desmond turned to look at me. Not being able to stand myself at that point, I began walking again. The impulse to run to him and beg him to take me away from my life consumed me, but he deserved better, so I kept walking and began to cry. He saw my beat up face and said I was fine anyway. Could it be at all possible that he still cared for me? I said a quick prayer for the answer to be yes, but knew I couldn't go back. Things would never be the same between us. I made sure of that with my hasty and wrong decision to lead him out of my life. I'd always wonder if he truly trusted me, and Tori would make sure that he didn't.

After I'd been dating Terrance for two years, I ran into Tori in the mall shoe store. I'd gone there to check on some paper work and she was trying on boots. I said hi to her, and her facial expression let me know I should shut my mouth. My reaction was fake. I acted like the look didn't bother me, and went over to a display trying to look interested in it. She walked towards me, and I put a smile on my face in anticipation of having a pleasant chat. My smile ran away after she said what was on her mind.

"Well, well, well. If it ain't Miss Love Them and Leave Them. Have you gotten your ass kicked lately?"

I didn't say one word. My feelings of love for Tori were somewhere inside of me, and I relied on them at that moment. I know I hurt her, but I thought she'd gotten her rage for me out during our phone conversation two years earlier.

"No need to answer me. I heard all about you getting evicted from your apartment and the ass whoopins you've endured from day one. I thought I'd be glad that this is happening to you. At the beginning I was. You need to use your brain, Lynnde, and leave him alone."

Her face softened, and I felt safe enough to ask her a question. "How do you know about what's been going on with me?"

Tori's mouth twisted as she shook her head for my shame.

"Lynnde, have you gone entirely stupid? I fucked Terrance a few times before you. He's still trying to get some and still calls me. He tells me your business and talks about you like you're his trashy possession. I told you, Lynnde. I told you. I knew you'd see how he was soon enough. What, do you like getting beat on? Is that why you dropped Desmond? Is that why you're still with Terrance?"

I didn't answer her because I didn't know why I was with Terrance and not with Desmond. Tori faced me with a half look of concern and a half look of, I want to slap the shit out of you. She saw tears welling up in my eyes and spoke to me in a gentle voice.

"Look, Lynnde. Everyone makes mistakes. Get yourself some strength from somewhere and get rid of him. You managed to dump Desmond so you can dump his ass, too. I have no hard feelings for you, but don't think of getting in my brother's or my life again. He's finally found someone special who loves *all* of him. He doesn't need to be bothered with you. You need to concentrate on yourself and get Lynnde together. Now, can I get a discount on these over priced boots?"

I smiled then. I knew Tori was right in all her words. I couldn't go back to the past we all shared together, but I could fix the present. I gave her my discount, which amounted to her getting them free, and felt good about having once been her friend. I never saw her again until the night I saw them at the restaurant, and I haven't seen her since.

Many years later I found out that Desmond was the reason I was able to reach a friendly agreement with the finance company. I didn't exactly do business with him, but he was a friend of someone who worked at the company I went through. He put in a good word for me. I never knew he was a secret angel working on my side. Not being able to turn back the hands of time is bothersome, but I'll always have my memories and be grateful for the few people that contributed to the good ones.

I'm looking forward to my new career in the fashion industry and new life experiences. My mother asked me to attend church with her one Sunday, and I told her no thank you, the church thing isn't for me. I've always believed in God and asked Him for His help, but I never once was a guest in His house.

"Lynnde, baby if you asked one of your friends to come over to your house and they asked you to come to theirs in return, would you go?"

"Yes, Ma, of course I would. That's what friends do."

"Well, the Lord is your friend, and He has been in your house all the time. I think it's time for you to visit His." My mother knows everything, and she is always right. Dear reader, I know you love her. It's hard not to.

"What time should I be ready on Sunday, Ma?"

"9:30 a.m. will be fine, baby. Just fine."

The first time I went to church, I thought I'd feel out of place, thinking people would stare at me because they knew I hadn't been there in years. I kept waiting for someone to tell me it's about time I turned to someone who could help me. That wasn't the case on my first visit or any of them after that. I started to look at all the areas of my life in a positive way and dropped the feeling of being scared of change and trying something new. I was afraid of negative results, but how will you know if you never try? I wish I'd learned this sooner.

Timing is everything, and it feels so good to me to learn it right now. The appreciation I feel is genuine. One thing I can honestly say I know for sure is that from here on out, I'm opening my mind along with my ears and eyes. I'll always look at the situations and people that affect my life. I know I'm not cured from making the wrong choices and may even stumble and fall again.

If you're thinking I'm looking forward to making more wrong choices, you're mistaken. Help me out here and think positively with me, will you? My future will be positive because if I do stumble and fall, I can get back up and continue my journey with my head held high. I must remember to carry this knowledge with me always. Cloudy days will not be in my life forever; the sunshine will eventually find me. And when it does, I'll know how to let it shine on all of me, never bothering to use sun block either.

# I Am So Beautiful

I have four months of business classes left and finished my fashion purchase class three weeks ago. My father hung up the certificate I received on the living room wall, next to my high school diploma. He was teary eyed at the ceremony when my name was called, and I never would have believed it if I hadn't seen it.

Three weeks ago my parents and I celebrated my thirty-fourth birthday quietly on July twenty-fifth, and I wouldn't have had it any other way. Most of my time is occupied with them or working a part-time job at a small fashion boutique on the weekends, while waiting for Esta to come home and open her boutique here. She gave birth to twin boys four months ago, and like the third wheel I'm accustomed to being,

I went to California two weeks after they were born as a surprise with her parents. The babies are beautiful and resemble Esta and Larry. If I were younger, I'd probably wish for Esta's life. On this visit all my thoughts were for her. Not once did I think about wanting to be married or being someone I could never be. For the first time since my birth, I was happy with who I was and the direction my life was going. Esta mentioned she noticed something different about me, and she wasn't talking about my weight.

She never did talk about my weight, but you know what I mean.

"Lynnde, you look beautiful. Have you been keeping a secret from me, girl?"

"Why, Esta, as long as you've known me, I know this isn't the first time you think I'm beautiful?"

"No, that's not what I'm saying at all. You just look different. Could it be you finally think you're beautiful, also?"

"Yeah, girl. You guessed that one right. For once I'm loving me and feeling it. Some of my confidence must be showing."

"It's showing and it sure looks good on you. Confidence is something you wear very well."

We did the finger snap circle routine and burst out laughing. Although I don't wish for Esta's life anymore, I do wish we lived closer together. She's planning to come home in nine months to check out some buildings for her boutique, and my job is to scout out some locations and have a nice long list waiting for her. I love her for wanting to include me in her business life and for trusting me to do the right thing.

Esta's parents and I stayed in California for two weeks. Upon leaving, her mother was the only person who cried. The sadness I used to feel when we parted wasn't there, even though I wanted to stay longer. I felt nothing but happiness for her, Larry, and the babies, Lester and

Chester. But I wanted to get back to my life. I've never felt like that before.

When we were about to board the plane, we hugged each other tightly while she said her favorite words for my ears only.

"Lynnde, thank you for coming. I love you, and I'm glad to finally see you love yourself. Remember to be patient and wait. Wait for love because it's going to find you. Wait girl, because it's coming and you'd better be ready. You're so deserving. Someone as beautiful as you will not be passed by. Just wait, girl. Wait."

We hugged each other for a few more seconds before I saw my reflection in her tears. I knew her tears were happy ones, and I wouldn't feel sadness if she cried for me just this one time.

As we boarded the plane, I felt comfort hold me. I was thankful for Esta and her family, thankful that they wanted me to be a part of it no matter what I was experiencing. It had taken me too long to understand that the real love I wanted someone to feel for me was already there and had been there since the beginning of my existence. I always had the love of my parents and the love of the Phillip's family, who've been a part of me long before I knew what life was all about.

During our flight home I heard Esta's words many times. I was going to wait this time. Yeah, I told myself I was going to wait before. The difference this time was, I wouldn't just say those words, I promised myself I'd mean them.

# Girl No, Not Again

A new car was my graduation gift from my parents. I didn't ask if the car was for my graduating from the class or my gradual return to life. Once the mild shock wore off, it was a gift I was more than happy to receive. My father didn't buy me a car when I graduated High School, and I thought he should die for that. I cursed myself for that thought.

It was a nineteen ninety-five two door blue Nissan Sentra. As my parents and I were walking outside to the garage to get my gift, the idea of a car never came to mind. I'd been losing weight at a slow, steady pace, so I thought about a bike and would've been happy with that. Of course when I saw the car I did what I do best - I cried. On our ride around the block, I received a lecture from my father on the maintenance and upkeep of foreign cars. I smiled the entire time and never wanted him to stop talking. I told you I've changed.

It sounds like I've gotten my head on straight and have my life's plan worked out. I've found work I love to do, not that the shoe store wasn't fulfilling, it just took a tragedy to show me it was time to move on. Yes, I still live in the home, and sleep in the room I grew up in, but I'm looking forward to moving out one day. I'll move on knowing this time my reckless life won't be the reason I have to return.

For the most part, my life is peaceful and going along at a smooth pace like I've always wanted. I've changed for the best in many ways, but like all things, a complete change takes time.

Close your mouth. I'm not going to tell you another how-Lynnde-became-a-dumbass tale. This time I won't let that happen to me. I've promised myself I'm going to be patient in life and wait for the man I'll have true love with to show his face. I'll wait until gray hair and arthritis become a part of me if I have to.

But in the meantime, it wouldn't hurt for me to have a little sexual gratification, would it? Oh please, give me a break. I know many of you dear readers out there are getting it from places you have no business being in. And shall I add the part about getting it from people you have no business being with? At least I'm being honest and telling you I'm one hundred percent human. I've been very busy getting back on track, but that doesn't mean I haven't thought about sex. It's been a long time for me, with Terrance being the last man I was with over two years ago. We were still a couple, well at least I thought we were, but he never made love to me towards the end. The term of "knocking the boots" applied to me in a different way. I know his leaving me was a blessing in disguise, but the plain fact is, I need a man to cure this ailment. Yes, I said 'need' and 'ailment.' If you're getting it on a regular basis, you may find the terms I use amusing, but ha-ha hell. This qualifies as a need.

Some of you out there know and feel exactly the same way I do, so look to me as the voice of millions. Yes, I know how to add and I said millions. I'm going to do right by Lynnde, but does my journey to the path of righteousness mean I can't make a rest stop in the road?

What's wrong with turning down a different path and getting reenergized for my continuing travels? I don't know why all of you are making me feel so guilty about admitting my feelings. I've told you every other intricate detail of my dusty road travels above and underground. What do you mean don't I know sex before marriage is a sin? Yes, I know. Don't bother giving me that just because you did in the past, doesn't mean you should do it in the future crap, either. Honestly people, I know how to handle this.

When the average smoker quits, the taste of cold turkey always brings back the memory of how good a cigarette used to be. When an alcoholic walks those twelve steps, I guarantee you one of those steps is inside a bar. That's the way I feel now. I've taken a break from men, but it doesn't mean when I see one I don't think about being with one in a sexual way. I'm going the right way, honestly I am. It won't hurt me to backtrack just once. No, I'm not trying to convince myself I won't be a fool again. I know I won't.

Who am I trying to convince then? I'm not trying to convince anyone. This is the part of the story that comes next that's all. Well, you can sigh and huff and puff. I'll even take those, "Oh, I know she didn't," looks, but yes I did. I wanted to tell you sooner but I had to tell you all the good things first. That way, when I got here you wouldn't think that bad of me.

I've come a long way in a short period of time, and yes, I do have a long way to go. (The but comes next) But I've tried to take care of my other problems, so why not get this one out the way, too? Stop the teeth sucking and listen up. Here it comes.

A few months ago my mother tried to get me to go out with her friend's son. I told her I'd think about it, and she reminded me of him three days later. Mrs. Lee would not let this rest until I did exactly what she wanted me to.

"All right, Ma. Give me his number and I'll set something up."

"Oh, baby, that's good. He's a nice fella, and I'm sure you'll get along fine."

I could tell by her double-o-seven undercover agent smile she knew my response wasn't the total truth. I'd take his phone number, but I didn't plan on calling. I'm glad my mother knows me as well as she does. She gave him our number and he called me. The non-existence of sex in my life usually popped up when I saw a happy couple together or heard a nice love song. I wanted to do something about my need, but I didn't know very many men and never really thought about my mother's friend as an unknowing victim until I saw him. If she had told me what he looked like, I would've dialed his number first. She said he was a nice looking fella, but should've used the word fine. No,

I'm not going to get caught up again in the cycle of what a man looks like; I'm just describing him to you. I learned the hard way that a fine man doesn't necessarily mean a quality man. Now, for all you fine, quality brothers out there, don't take offense to my last statement. Everyone has different variations of fine, and I'm letting the world know I've finally bought a new measuring cup.

A belief I have for myself is that I'll never again judge a human being by their outside appearance. I believe that like I believe in eating a good meal, so you know that one's solid.

Our first conversation was on a Saturday afternoon. Taylor Stewart. His voice sounded like a sexy midnight quiet storm radio disc jockey. He did most of the talking, and I didn't mind one bit. For a quick second, I hoped his face matched his voice but a sparerib flashed before my eyes. I remembered my belief and never thought about his looks again. No matter what, I'd always believe in eating.

Taylor was thirty-five years old and never married but had been engaged twice with four children as reminders of his engagements. He worked as a nurse's aide in a retirement home and was going to school to become a registered nurse. It didn't bother him that his friends picked on him for wanting to do woman's work.

"Shoot, Lynnde. They can talk about me all they want. I've wanted to work in healthcare ever since seeing the show Julia when I was a child. I figure if I become a nurse, I can meet a woman as beautiful as Diahann Carroll."

"Ha, ha, ha, ha. That's funny, Taylor." When I didn't hear anything but him breathing, I stopped laughing, realizing he was serious. We talked for thirty minutes and decided to go to dinner the coming Wednesday. Wednesday was his night off and he offered to prepare dinner for me at his apartment. Believe it or not, I declined. As much as I like to eat, and as horny as I was, I thought before I acted. I didn't want to put myself in an uncomfortable situation and suggested a Mexican restaurant in a highly populated area. See, I've learned something from my past.

This would be the first date I'd go out on without all the hoopla that surrounded me when I left home. I didn't have Esta to fix my hair and face, or pick out an outfit for me. My mother would be at bible study and my father said he was going to play racquetball with one of his olden days drinking buddies. After he told my mother what his plans were, he turned to me and gave me a quick wink. When my mother left the room, I asked him what the wink was for.

"What wink, baby girl?"

"Daddy, you know what I'm talking about. What are you up to?"

"Nothing, baby. I had something in my eye and don't you tell your mother you saw me get it out, you hear?"

His last remark was followed by laughter on his part. As he walked out of the room his laughter grew louder and became the reason for his crooked, bent over posture. I figured he was going out for a few drinks with the boys and knew my mother wouldn't like it one bit. She told me once that you should never tell a man all of your business, and there's nothing wrong with a little secrecy if the deed was legal and no one would be hurt. I guess it goes both ways.

I don't know if I felt strange because I wanted my departure to my first date in years to be like the good ole days or because it wasn't. My earlier attempts at dating never turned out having positive results, so the word good applies to my actual departure. Quietly complaining about all the fuss over me wouldn't happen this time either because I know it was out of love.

If I had a genie in a bottle that would grant me three wishes, all three would be for one of those moments to return. Appreciate, dear reader. Appreciate all the good you have in your life. Some moments pass you by, and when they're gone, they're gone. Never returning your way either. Don't take the time to wonder why a blind man smells flowers he can't see. Take the time to smell a few yourself. Appreciation of every moment in life is another one of my beliefs that sits next to my trust in food. It's real.

A nice casual black pantsuit, not too fancy or revealing, but friendly, would be perfect attire for my first meeting with Taylor. Six p.m. approached much too quickly and I had to meet Taylor at seven, so I hurried myself along and walked out of my parent's home at 5:50 feeling a little lonely. I missed my old farewell parties, but I was glad to have the memories.

It would take me about twenty-five minutes to arrive at the restaurant, and I never thought about being fashionably late. Eating dinner was more on my mind than meeting Taylor, and the sooner I arrived, the sooner I could eat. Am I obsessing over food? No, I haven't eaten all day, that's all. We know I love to eat, but my admiration of food has changed. I know it is a necessity for survival, and I've accepted the information that I won't die if my stomach isn't full to the top.

I took an evaluation of my eating habits one night when a small amount of depression paid me a visit. My life was content, but I thought about what could have been. Where would I be in life if none of the mess I allowed to happen ever existed? My size eighteen was fine, and I was well on my way to the goal of being a size eight one day. Thinking of harsher days and the many times I didn't feel needed or loved, I let the memory of bad times and the food that was always there to comfort me take over. It was 10:20 on a Thursday night and my parents were asleep. The thoughts of my past clouded my prospering present, so I went to go find solace. I never felt satisfaction that night, but I looked for it at four fast food restaurants, an ice cream stand, and in our refrigerator. Of all the times I've filled my stomach to the rim, this was the first time I ever felt sick doing it. I'm sure I felt sick in the past, but was too worried about the reason I was eating to notice it.

When I arrived home after my rampage, I finished off everything that wasn't tied down in the refrigerator. I gorged myself, and felt disgusted when I noticed I was spreading jelly on a can of uncooked biscuits. I'd already eaten five of them and started to feel food I invited into my stomach trying to go to another home. I kept eating the biscuits, and told the food it had a one way ticket inside of me, it was there to stay. It didn't hear me or just plain didn't care, because it started leaving anyway.

Sitting in a chair at our kitchen table at 3:42 in the morning throwing up on myself is something I never imagined I'd do. I never ate and vomited before and wasn't about to start now; I'd never do that to myself. I wouldn't accept that I was doing it now, but I was. Maybe it was because the room was different in that I wasn't hanging over a bathroom toilet with my finger down my throat.

I ate until there was no more room left inside of me for anything. The food could do nothing to tell me, so it showed me the only way it knew how. The sickening part is as I was throwing up, I was still trying to eat the last of the uncooked biscuits. There were only two left, and they shouldn't have to go to waste. I hated myself with a vengeance and only stopped trying to eat the biscuits when I was putting one in my mouth, and some of my previous food met it before it met my teeth. Regurgitated food brought me back to my senses. I didn't stop vomiting until my insides were sitting in my lap, rolling down my legs, and putting a nasty shine on my mother's highly polished floor. I sat for a moment in disbelief not knowing if I should move and wondering why I didn't choke. Why did I do the stupid things I do?

The stupid thing I was referring to wasn't my ability to make myself sick for no reason but allowing my vomit to touch my mother's floor. Why couldn't I make it stay on me? Disbelief flooded me as I looked around my body, and at the gruel like stench I created on the floor. I started crying when I saw the biscuits on the table that I wasn't able to eat. Was I crying because I didn't eat them or because I was still trying to, knowing I wouldn't be able to save them from the garbage can? I was disgusted and ashamed of myself but wanted more food. I decided to clean myself up before eating again. What was wrong with me?

Taking off all of my clothes while sitting at the kitchen table was the first step I took to clean myself. Thank God no one was an eyewitness to that. I let my clothes drop to the floor but I still had my sneakers on. My pants were down around my ankles, and when I tried to stand up to take a step out of my un-artistic creation, I stumbled and fell in my slop. When I hit the floor some of it splashed up and hit me in my face. I was naked and lying in vomit. Instead of trying to get up immediately, I lie in it and cried. I deserved to feel like this. Nothing on this earth wanted me to be a part of it. My baby hated me for wishing her away and went to be with someone else. Every man I met hated me and did everything in their power to let me know. The one man who did care I threw away like any fool would do.

And now by the looks of things, food detests me. The one thing I turned to in my time of need, the one thing that never told me no, or denied me its pleasure. The one thing I could have any second, minute, and hour of the day, wanted a part of me no more. Didn't this food know I'd give my life for it, sell my soul to the devil for it, and steal a teenager's first paycheck from his paper route job just to have a taste of it? Please don't leave me this way! I'll promise you I'll do better. I promise you I'll eat you in the right amounts and treat you with respect. I promise.

The toilet flushing upstairs made me realize I was lying on the kitchen floor naked, in my vomit, and talking to it as if it were human. I started to pray silently and hard that whomever it was using the bathroom wouldn't come downstairs. Hearing my parent's bedroom door close was my sign of relief that no one would see the traveling circus act of the ass in slop in their kitchen. I managed to get up on my knees, moving slowly, and was careful not to slip again. The kitchen drawer that was used for dish towels was within reach, and I took all of them out, and began working from the outside of my hell ring; pushing the contents towards the center, and created a pile that was contained by the dish rags. It was nasty. I was naked in the middle of vomit. It was nasty.

I crawled towards the broom and grabbed it along with a few garbage bags, then carefully made my way back towards my vile formation. After two hours of sweeping, wiping, and mopping, the floor was restored to its original form with a little less shine, but would pass for clean.

Although this wasn't the correct washing procedure, I washed the dishrags and my clothes at the same time. I then quadruple bagged my insides, hid them behind the washing machine, and would wait until daylight to throw the bag away. My life was so connected to garbage bags. I'd taken off my sneakers and thrown them in the washer so I was completely naked now. I was a size eighteen, but I was a round, jiggly eighteen. In other words, I was fat. I was a naked, fat, sized eighteen child in my parent's basement who somehow managed to ruin her life again. It was only a short period of time, but I still messed it up.

My mother always kept up with the laundry so there wasn't one article of dirty clothing around to cover myself with. It was going on six a.m., and I had to get up the stairs and into the bathroom before my parents began their day. I never did much exercising but the grand idea to run up the stairs and tiptoe at the same time was my solution. I was naked. I had thrown up. I was nasty.

God helped me because my last thought occurred as I was closing the bathroom door. A scalding shower was all I could think to do next, somehow wanting to burn myself to death. I'm still talking, so I wasn't successful.

After my shower, I sat at my vanity and inspected the girl I saw in the mirror. Where did she come from and where was she going? When she gets wherever she's supposed to be, will she know what to do? I couldn't answer the questions, but I didn't start to cry. Instead, I made a long hard evaluation of myself. I'd been doing okay up until I went berserk and wondered what made me treat my body so bad? Did I do it because no one else made sure I had my daily dose of rejection?

Pondering these thoughts made my conscience explode. *Enough of this self-depravation, Lynnde! Stop relying on your past to indicate what your future holds! Get yourself together, girl. Don't be afraid to move on and see the good the world has to offer you.* Wasn't my mind made up to do that? *Obviously not.* Humph, leaning on the crutch of not having a man made me feel the need to go in search of extra comfort.

That's when my attitude about food changed. I try to eat three meals a day and in moderation, and always eat until my stomach says stop, not my brain. Yes, I still eat an occasional sweet snack, and as good as they taste, I don't go overboard. So now when I say I'm hungry, I really am hungry. That's the reason why I want to get to the restaurant and eat this man. I mean, eat dinner with this man.

I pulled up to Mexican Amigos and luckily found a parking space right in front. As I walked closer to the entrance, a man came from behind me and called my name. It was Taylor. He was close to my height but was more likely five-feet-eight or five-feet-nine, and had a slight muscular build. He had on navy blue dress pants and a navy blue shirt with the top button open. I noticed a silver chain around his neck and I saw myself kissing it. I'm horny remember?

His face was clean-shaven; his skin tone was the color of honey mixed with light brown sugar and he looked sweet enough to lick. Taylor would definitely be the man I got my next taste of sex from. Leave me alone, will you? His hair was a not so greasy low-cut jehri curl, and his facial features would allow him to model men's skin care products. When he smiled at me, I noticed a nice gap between his front teeth. It was the perfect size for any piece of my body's skin to slide through. I don't want to hear it.

"Lynnette, hello. I'm Taylor. It's nice to finally have a face to match the voice."

"Hi, Taylor. It's nice to finally meat (oops) you as well. Have you been here long?"

"No, I got here a few minutes ago. You look very nice."

"Thank you. You look nice, too." We hugged, and he opened the door for us to go inside.

"This restaurant is nice, Lynnette. Do you eat here often?"

"I used to. The food is good, and if you like Mexican you'll love this place."

"I haven't had much Mexican food, but I'm sure you wouldn't lead me in the wrong direction."

He thought his comment was funny and began laughing. I giggled also, but not at his comment. My amusement was due to the sound of his laugh, which was loud and had a funny rhythm to it. He snorted a few times before he finished and that made me chuckle even more.

We sat by the window and both ordered chicken fajitas, margaritas, and munched on chips and salsa while waiting on our meal.

"So, Lynnette, tell me about yourself."

I hadn't been asked that question in years and didn't know how to respond. "What do you want to know?"

He leaned forward and placed his arms on the table. His movements made him look interested. His face adopted a serious sexy look, and before he spoke he raised his arms to resemble a church steeple. "Everything you want to tell me. I want to get to know you."

Huh? *Relax, Lynnde.* I told him about the classes I was taking and of my plans to work with Esta when she opened her boutique.

"That's very interesting. What do you do for entertainment?"

"Well, I really don't do much besides school, but I guess I like to watch TV and occasionally read a book."

"I'm going to have to get you out more if you don't mind. Would you like to go to a movie or dancing one evening?"

My insides skipped as heat ran through my body. "Yes. That would be nice. I haven't done either of those activities in quite a while. Thank you for asking."

"You're welcome. It's nice to do things with the fellas, but being in the company of a beautiful woman makes it much better. I hope you don't mind me saying this, but I think you're very attractive."

A compliment? What do I say? *Geez...* "No, I don't mind you saying it."

"I knew you were going to be special, but Lynnde, you're something else."

Taylor laughed again and I wondered if he was something else. What was so funny about what he said? He managed to stay in his chair as he rocked from side to side, cracking up all by himself. I looked at him strange but kept a smile on my face.

The rest of the evening progressed smoothly. While his voice fit his personality, his laugh took him over the top. He told me stories about the nursing home, and we both laughed after every one of them. They were very funny. For the first time in a long time, I was actually enjoying myself with someone of the opposite sex. He never said anything out of bounds and our conversation moved along at a nice pace, which resulted in our evening ending much too soon. Since we both had early mornings, we made a date for the upcoming Friday, going to dinner and a movie. We walked to my car and he had a faint swagger in his step. He was comfortable and I'd make sure he stayed that way. Tsk, whatever, dear reader.

Taylor slowed a bit and took my hand into his.

"Do you mind if I pick you up this time? I'll understand if you want to take separate cars. I just want to be seen having a beautiful woman enter and exit my car."

"After you've said that, how can I resist riding with you?"

"Oh good. Is it Friday yet?" Taylor burst out laughing and I joined in. While writing my address down I wished my car wasn't parked so close. He took my keys, caressed my cheek, and opened the door.

"I don't know if this is the appropriate behavior, but would asking for a kiss be wrong?"

I'm glad he didn't know how I felt at that point. He could've kissed me on any part of my body, and I wouldn't have cared. Keep your comments to yourself, please.

"No, Taylor. A kiss shared with you would be fine."

He pulled me close, and I embarrassed myself by damn near choking him with my tongue. I had it so far down his throat that my tongue introduced itself to his tonsils. I'm so stupid. He didn't push me away, so I guess he didn't mind. We kept kissing until we felt the need to stop.

"Wow, Lynnde. That was nice. I haven't kissed a woman in a long time. Your kiss made my time lapse worthwhile."

I didn't respond with a comment but gave him more wattage than I'm sure he'd ever been accustomed to. A brief moment of silence engulfed us before he took my hand and helped me inside of my car.

"Lynnde, I'll follow you to make sure you get home safe if you like. I don't mind." "Thank you, Taylor, but that's not necessary. I'll be fine."

"Okay. I'll see you on Friday at 7:30. I'll count the minutes until then."

I wanted him to ask me to go home with him. It was my hornymones talking, so I took control and started my car. I waved as I pulled off and blew my horn. When I glanced in the rear view mirror to sneak a peek of Taylor from behind he was still standing in the same spot. Stupidity controlled the steering wheel because I almost ran up on the curb and knew he saw my poor attempt at driving. As I turned the corner, I blew the horn again. He waved and started walking towards his blue Chevy Cavalier. I couldn't wait to be seen in it.

Taylor was very nice and made our first meeting more than pleasant. Maybe I should rethink my decision of just using him for my love slave. *When will you ever learn?* He was very courteous and considerate and seemed to like all size eighteen of me. Whatever skinny person said no one likes a fat girl made a mistake with that statement.

Am I going to stay fat for him? No. I'm not going to lose weight for him either. My weight issue is something only I can deal with, and anyone who desires me is going to want me for the person I am or will become due to my own decisions. Now, if I could make my mind stick to the things I say that make sense, I'll do okay. I've gone this long without sex so waiting until I get to know Taylor better wouldn't make much of a difference. Maybe he's just looking for a female friend to hang out with and doesn't want to be in a relationship? It would be in my best interest to find out before I make a fool of myself by trying to give him something he has no desire to receive.

I'm learning, dear reader. I'll get there one day soon. I may not get there the same time you do, but hold on, Lynnde girl is coming.

# This Is Lynnde's World

I graduated from the business course and was ranked number three in the class. You don't need to know that there was only ten of us in the class, only that I was number three. I have a full time job as a fashion consultant at The Fashion Track, and I'm readying myself for Esta's trip home. I can't wait to get started on her boutique. She found a location two weeks ago and should be here sometime this month to finalize the paperwork.

I'm making pretty good money now and feel it's time for me, once again, to leave the nest. Not because I'm thirty-four years old and by an unprinted law, am too old to live at home, but because I'm ready to become the independent woman I know I am. Living on my own will give me an extra boost of confidence. I've become a smarter person by caring what happens to me, and I have control of my life. And this time when I say move out and live on my own, that's exactly what I mean. I don't need or want a man in and out of my home, going through my things, treating them like they belong to no one. I won't give my apartment keys to any man but my husband or my father. For now my father will be the only man with a set of keys.

This move is being treated the same as if it were my first. I'm a new person, so I want everything to feel like a new experience. My parents offered to buy me new furniture and whatever else I needed, but I declined their offer. I told them all I wanted from them was their support. They agreed but bought me an overly expensive piece of black art for my foyer.

My personal life is going okay. For once, I'm focusing on what I need to do to better myself, instead of how much better a man can make me feel. I've been seeing Taylor, and yes, we had sex. I'm sorry if you think I moved too fast in the underwear department, but chile', I needed a new pair and Taylor was a perfect fit. We went on six dates before we had intimate contact, so give me credit for not attacking him too soon. For you holier than thou readers out there, yeah, yeah, whatever. But thank you for your concern.

Our first five dates consisted of activities that placed us in the outside world, but the sixth one was dinner and rental movies at his place. Unbeknownst to Taylor, he removed my panties when he said he was in the process of looking for a home so his children could have a place to live with him. That scored points with me, but with the way my hormones were raging, he could've said anything. If he said he needed a place for his dog, I wouldn't have cared.

Taylor treated me kind and always seemed to be attentive to my thoughts and the way I felt. He said he found me attractive mentally and physically and wouldn't mind getting to know me better. I enjoyed hearing the words, but this time I didn't flip out and let my thoughts automatically take me into I have to have him mode, giving him everything I thought he needed. Thanking him and adding he'd be welcomed as a friend was my response. I honestly wanted to get to know him, as well. The ice was broken after that, and we began talking to each other on a daily basis.

The night I went over to his place, I didn't plan on making an intimate connection with him, yet it was on my mind. I say this because during our dates, the farthest we took any connection was kissing or handholding. He never mentioned anything sexual that pertained to me or anyone else.

Taylor was a gentleman, but I wanted him to show me how he made his children. I thought he may have been turned off by my weight until he said sexy women come in all sizes, and having a little extra never hurt anyone.

During our conversations, I gave Taylor a brief history about my past. Many details were left out, but I bought him up to speed on my life changing events.

"Everyone has endured some grief in life. I'm glad you came through yours and were able to meet me."

"Thank you, Taylor. That was very kind of you to say." While driving to his place, I added ten points to the Taylor chart and made up my mind that if he didn't bring anything sexual up, I wouldn't either. I didn't want to show him the undersexed woman I thought I was, and that I could make a dirty movie. Before pressing his bell I closed my eyes and half wished that we had sex and then wished that we didn't. Taylor opened the door with a light white haze surrounding him and wearing a long green apron that was covered in flour.

The frown I didn't suppress was no indication of how I really felt. "Hi, Taylor. Am I too early?"

"No, you're right on time. I've never have much luck when I work with flour. Excuse my mess."

Relaxing I said, "Oh, you look fine. Do you need any help?"

"No need, beautiful lady. I'm just about finished. Come on in and get comfortable."

I walked towards his kitchen, but he nodded in the direction of the living room. His home was very comforting. The sofa and loveseat were midnight blue overstuffed pieces and had many different pillows propped up neatly. The carpet felt plush under my feet. It was awkward walking over it in my shoes. His walls had minimal pictures but the wallpaper design was bold blue and had bits of silver specks throughout. It didn't look as if it should be covered up.

"You have a nice place, Taylor."

"Thanks, Lynnde. I can't take all the credit, though. I have two sisters, and one of them is an interior designer. I told her what I wanted, and she made it look like the total opposite."

Taylor burst out laughing and had to sit down to compose himself. I hope he never tries stand up comedy. He might get shot on stage.

After wiping the sweat from his brow he said, "Lynnde, I have some wine if you like. If you want something with more kick to it, I have rum and gin. I wouldn't mix them together, that'd cause an explosion in your stomach."

Why did he find that funny? When his laughter started to die down, I told him a glass of wine would be fine. My stomach grumbled asking what was for dinner, but I kept my mouth closed, figuring it was something fried and took a ten-pound bag of flour to prepare.

I could see Taylor in his kitchen. He moved with ease as he watched boiling pots and took on the role of a bartender. It took him three long steps to reach me and he took them like a satisfied pimp.

"Here, this is White Zinfandel. I hope you like it. I wasn't sure what to cook, but I decided on fried chicken, mashed potatoes and green beans. Nothing fancy, but that's really the only meal I've perfected."

I took the glass slowly. Our movements looked like an eight track tape soundtrack. "Whatever you made would've been fine, but fried chicken is way up there on my list."

He'd taken off his apron and had on a nice pair of pressed blue jeans and a white polo shirt.

"You look nice with and without the flour." My legs were crossed and I said this as I traced the rim of the glass with my finger. Smiling he added, "Thanks. So do you. You always look good to me, though. I'd love to continue talking about your beauty, but it's best to eat my fried chicken while it's hot. Let's get started." *Bingo!*

I followed Taylor into his kitchen, and aside from the flour, it was well kept. He pulled my chair back and I flinched. That was due to a flashback from Terrance. I thought he'd pull it all the way back and I'd end up on the floor. He did it on many occasions, and after the first time, I should've learned my lesson. A quiet sigh of relief came when I ended up in the chair at the table, not rolling on the floor listening to someone who supposedly loved me call me names.

"Lynnde, if you don't like it, you don't have to be polite and eat it. I'll understand. We can order something in instead."

"It smells delicious, and I'm sure it tastes the same. Don't worry about a thing."

"I hope you feel the same way after you taste it."

Both of my thumbs went up with a smile. We laughed as he placed a heaping serving of food before me. He then sat down and said grace before eating. I took a small bite of chicken and was surprised at how tasty it was.

"Taylor, this is delicious." Excited I asked, "How'd you learn to cook like this?"

He sat back in his chair relieved. Our eyes met. There was a tinge inside of me that he sensed. It let our guards off duty. This night drew us closer together.

"Oh, I'm so glad you like it. It's my mother's recipe. She even said it's tastes as good as hers. Eat as much as you like, there's plenty more."

Those words were music to my ears. I didn't eat like a hungry hippo as I'd usually done, but I ate my share. The dinner meal continued with much smacking (I show no shame when it comes to food) and lots of laughter. I really enjoyed myself with Taylor and actually didn't mind if no intimate contact took place tonight. My last thought was wasted.

Taylor and I finished our meal, cleaned the kitchen, and went into the living room to put the first of our three rented movies into the VCR. I don't know what the movie was about and can't tell you anything about the opening previews or credits. Taylor sat next to me, and we began a game of touch football. I don't know if we played by the rules, but his hand was in my blouse, on my breast, and I didn't see a flag thrown anywhere.

I didn't do anything to stop him because you and I know that this is what I wanted. He led me into his bedroom, and both our clothes were off in less than ten seconds. If anyone had seen us, they would've thought they were looking at two wild primal animals that'd been starved for years and let loose on a grape. There was heavy breathing, pawing, groping, and loud pleasure yells from both beasts.

What time the attack started I can't tell you but when I was able to look at the clock by his bedside, it was 12:34

a.m. I didn't want to speak first; I really didn't know what to say. Taylor's breathing began to die down, and I wanted him to say something, anything before he drifted off to sleep. I felt ashamed all of a sudden; stop frowning please? Well yeah, I got what I asked for, but now I don't think I did the right thing. *Oh really?*

"Lynnde? Are you asleep?"

Whew. "No, Taylor. I'm awake."

"Oh, uhm, I hope I didn't take advantage of you. I mean, uh, just because I cooked dinner didn't entitle me to have sex with you."

"No, Taylor. That's not how I feel at all. We're both consenting adults, and I could've stopped at any time if I didn't want this to happen."

A heavy breath came from him, which soothed the darkened room.

"I was worried. I know it didn't look that way, but I was. I've had something on my mind for a while now."

In my mind I began moving out of his bed to get dressed. This was the part I was ready for. He was going to ask me to leave. Another garbage bag would escort me to the dump.

"Uhm, how would you feel about dating me? I know you have other things going on right now, and I won't pressure you, but you're a special lady. I want to see more of you if I can. Is that okay with you?"

Huh? I've endured many changes in the last few years, but I still need to take a few extra credit courses when it comes to relationships with men. Secretly I thought he was showing me attention because he wanted something that he knew a fat girl would give up. Thank you for allowing me to be wrong in my thinking again. Taylor likes me, not because I'm easy, as I'm sure some of you're thinking, but because I'm me. Just Lynnde. I don't want to rush into anything, but I'm tired of being single. It can't be possible for me to make the same dumb, idiotic mistakes I've made before, can it? I hope your answer is the same as mine. I want to give Taylor a chance with the new me.

"Taylor, I didn't know you felt this way about me. I'm still working on getting myself together, but seeing you in the process would make it much easier."

"Thank you, Lynnde. I was so afraid I made a mistake tonight and blew any chance of being with you. It's been so long since I've met anyone who really wanted anything out of life. The way I feel with you is so refreshing. I don't mean to sound corny, but it's the truth."

"There's nothing wrong with the truth. I'm the one who's going to sound corny now. Taylor, as long as we're open and honest with each other, we can't go wrong."

"I knew you were special, Lynnde. I knew it the first time I talked to you."

Taylor began kissing me passionately. Regardless of the fact that he'd shown me how so very well equipped he was, and that he could use his equipment to the best of it's ability, I felt nothing more than friendship for him. I did, however, have a feeling that if I denied myself the chance of getting to know him, I'd miss out on something. I wanted to find out what that something was. If we truly worked together there would be nothing we couldn't build. If it were meant to be, everything else would work itself out in time.

Hearing him say he wanted a relationship was Belgian waffles with strawberries and cream, but I must not forget Lynnde. Please, dear reader. Help me not to forget. We all know where I've been. Would dating the first man since my two year hiatus make my mind revert to one of irrationality when a man said hi to me?

Oh wait, before I continue to go any deeper into my save Lynnde from her past speech, I must tell you that protection was used during my first romp with Taylor. I found out what the pill was and have been using it for a few years now. And yes, I know the pill can't protect me from venereal diseases so a condom was used, as well.

Taylor must be an expert at putting one on. During our assault of each another, he managed to keep up with his plan of action and put his hat on at the same time. This was a man of many talents. Taylor was attractive, smart and had the stuff any bedroom partner would want. These three things by themselves would've made me buy a one-way ticket to the land of dummy-dum. I heard Esta's voice from years ago and it brought me back to my senses. I remembered the time she said Larry was an enhancement of her life. I didn't understand what she meant then, but learning the hard way makes me understand completely now.

I can do this. I can be me and date a man at the same time. My previous relationships were all wrong and I'm not going to carry any pain or bad memories over into this one. My brain will definitely be used this time as I take things nice and slow and do only what feels right to me. No, I don't think I'm starting out with a negative attitude, just some good attitude. Knowing I have some say in what happens to me is something I never saw before. Lord, don't let me go blind now.

# Is He What I Want Or Need?

Usually, when I end up talking positive about a man I always come back with a horror story. It's too bad to be made into a movie, but just right for me. Not this time, though. Did I hear a few hallelujahs?

I'm in a training class at the Fashion Track that teaches the art of ordering accessories for any occasion. I know I just graduated from classes that prepared me, but Esta wants me to be in tiptop shape. We call each other everyday and our last conversation made me wish for days gone by.

"Lynnde, when this boutique opens, up you're going to be in charge of everything. I trust you completely, but I want you to be ready for anything that comes your way. A little extra training isn't going to hurt, girl."

I almost dropped the phone when I waved my hands and shouted, "Oh, please! You'll never hear me complain! I'm going to run this boutique as if it were my own."

Esta laughed for a few seconds. "But it is yours, Lynnde. It is. Whatever I have, you have. This is ours together. And one day if you decide to be my competition, you'll be the best competition I have."

"Thanks, Esta. You always support me and push me along my bumpy trail. I don't know what I'd ever do without you." My eyes watered but I blinked the wetness away.

"Girl, don't even think like that. I'll always be here for you. Your life is really going to move at the speed of light. Are you going to be ready, Lynnde girl?"

"Yes, Esta. More than you'll ever know."

Lowering her voice as if we were on a corner making an exchange she said, "I know your professional life is going to explode, I have no worries about that. Now I want to hear about Taylor. He sounded nice when you spoke of him earlier. Is he still nice?"

This time I laughed. "Yes, girl. He's better than nice."

"Ohhh, Lynnde! Girl, tell me more."

She made me think of our High School days with her excitement. I wish I could hug her. "Well, he respects my thoughts, my feelings and is never, I mean never, too busy for me."

"Ohhh, Lynnde! Is there love in the air?"

"We never told each other we were in love, but I think it's coming. He knows I have to concentrate on my new business venture, but I make time for him. You'd think between his job, classes, and kids he wouldn't have time for anything else, but he stays up way past his bedtime for a spell of me."

Esta's voice changed once again. This time she spoke in her loving wisdom tone. "You know I'm your best friend and would never say anything to hurt you, but this relationship isn't just sexual is it?"

"Oh no. Sometimes we just talk on the phone or spend the night at one of our places falling asleep in each other's arms. I'm not basing anything on sex anymore. I've gotten to know Taylor and he has a lot to offer. Besides his physical appearance and that sexy voice of his, he has a brain he uses. His care for me is real. Taking my time is something I should've done a long time ago."

"Girl, don't bring up the past. Life goes on. Taylor sounds like a good man for you, and I can't wait to meet him." Satisfied, she changed the subject. "Wait until you see the boys. They've gotten so big. Larry wants to enroll them in basketball camp this summer."

"Esta, they're only a year old."

"That's what I said to Larry, and he says the sooner we get them started, the better. You know I'll love that man until the end of time, but there's no way my babies are going to any camp any time soon."

The large lump in my throat prevented me from responding to Esta. Hearing her say my babies brought back the painful memory of my baby I wished away. She has every right to use any combination of words to describe her children, and I love her for doing so. I love her for loving her children so much.

"Lynnde, girl, are you alright? Did I upset you?"

"No. I was just letting your words linger in my mind, that's all. I miss you."

"I miss you, too. But let's not worry about that. We'll be home soon enough. Oh darn, I think Lester is crying. Are you sure you're alright?"

"Yes, Esta. Go see about my godchild and I'll call you tomorrow, okay?"

"Oh, alright girl. I love you. Bye."

"I love you, too."

I hung up and my past filled my thoughts. I didn't let it overwhelm me and go on an eating binge, but instead, I asked God to please forgive me again. When I stood up I didn't feel like there was a heavy weight holding me down. I'd made a mistake when it came to my baby, but felt one day I'd have another chance. I wasn't going to make a mistake and rush to get one either. Whenever I had children would be on time.

My mind came back to present thoughts of how fantastic my life felt. I lived successfully on my own and was striving for a goal I could see. Things with Taylor were also drama-free. I never felt pressured by him, and he always gave me enough space to be me.

There was one incident that caused a minor rift between us. Afterwards it made me look at myself and see exactly how much I haven't grown. It involved his sister, Taylisha. Taylisha was one of those roll out the red carpet women because I'm so fine with no brain. She always made comments about how fat women were disgusting, and any man that had sex with one had to be crazy. Hello, stupid. Look at me. She had the nerve to say that it didn't pertain to me because I was just big boned. Dinosaurs were big boned and they don't exist anymore. I was always right in her face.

I got tired of her comments one night and instead of addressing her in a lady like manner, I waited until Taylor and I were driving home from her room full of bitches gathering and blasted him in the car. Taylor managed to maintain his cool until we were inside my apartment.

"Lynnde, what's wrong? What happened?"

"Your stupid ass sister is what's wrong!"

"Now, wait a minute. You don't have to yell, and please don't call my sister stupid. Tell me, what happened?"

"Taylisha and her stupid ass comments! I'm sick of her fat jokes and her embarrassing me. She's such a prissy bitch!"

Taylor remained peaceful and tried to bring me down to his level. "Look, you need to get off my sister and the name-calling. Yeah, Taylisha is a little superficial, but you know how she is. I hope you didn't say anything to her you'll be sorry for."

His words would have been better heard if he'd spoken to a rock formation. "Sorry! Sorry! I'll tell you who's sorry! Your dumb ass sister! That's who's sorry! She never liked me and never will! I don't like her either! She can go to hell!"

"Okay, Lynnde. Let's calm down. I don't want to argue with you about something Taylisha said. I'm sorry you had to go through this tonight. I don't want to fight with you, okay? Arguing has never been my style and I don't want to start with you. I'll talk to Taylisha, but please, let's not fight anymore, and please don't call her anymore names in my presence."

I stood quiet looking dense, trying to ingest what the man standing before me just said. He should want to argue. What's wrong with him? Arguing is what I did in the past. That's my problem, my past. This wasn't the past and I promised myself I wouldn't treat Taylor as such. He apologized for something he didn't do, and I should apologize for something I did. I was wrong to take my anger out on him, and wrong for treating him like the days gone by.

"I'm sorry, Taylor. My feelings were hurt and I had a childish thought of wanting to hurt someone else. I'm sorry. I don't want to fight with you."

Taylor walked closer and pulled me towards him. We were standing face to face and I felt like the old fool I used to be.

"Lynnde, you're special to me. I never want to hurt anyone as special as you. If you have a problem with something I do, talk to me about it. Don't yell. I know our relationship is still new, but I'm hoping one day it'll be good and old. I really do care about you regardless of what my sister has to say. You don't have to deal with her, and I shouldn't have tried to force her on you. I'll never over step my boundaries again when it comes to you."

"Huh?" I'm so stupid. I didn't mean to say that out loud or mean to have the dumb look on my face when it came out. I didn't mean for any of the previous exchange of words to happen either. I need to learn the exact meaning of the word mean. Did that make any sense? Taylor was special. Instead of treating me the way my actions deserved, he apologized, still wanting the girl who had a flashback and covered his face with another man's.

"You don't have to respond, Lynnde. I know what's in that kind heart of yours. Let's just seal this one away and concentrate on us, okay?"

"Huh?" I'm so stupid.

No more words were spoken after that. Well, no words you'd find in the dictionary. I'm a size sixteen, but that didn't stop Taylor from picking me up and carrying me into my bedroom. I guess I'm not so plus-sized after all. I wanted to tell him to put me down; that he was going to need his back, but a man had never picked me up like that or any other way.

Taylor had a nice muscular build, but I know he wanted to grunt and groan before we made it to the bed. He spared my feelings and held it in until we were in act one of our production of animals in a sauna in a traffic pile-up. It was hot and jammed in that room and I loved it. Our play won't make it to Broadway but many of the better ones never do.

I don't want you to get a visual of our sexual encounters being overly rough, but he makes me understand the statement to bring out the wild in someone. If I keep this behavior up my next physical checkup will be with a veterinarian.

You'd think I'd be glad that the man I'm dating wants me and only me in every way. I know I shouldn't put too much emphasis on a sex life I shouldn't be having before marriage, (here comes the but) but Taylor and I have been dating close to a year. The life I didn't see with him before is starting to show itself clearly now. I trust Taylor, so why am I letting the use of a condom bother me? Using one when you first meet someone is the way it should be, but hey, if you think about it, should you really be having sex with someone if you have to use a condom? If you need to be protected from their past and the spread of disease, keep your legs closed. I'm not the one to try and give advice on anything, we all know better than that. These are my own personal thoughts, and as I've said before, this is my story.

Intimate contact in any form is good, (here comes the but) but when I feel him, I want to feel him. We've talked about not using one and his logic is although he loves his children dearly, he doesn't want to make anymore before he gets married.

"Taylor, I'm on the pill. What's the big deal?"

"Look, the pill isn't one hundred percent safe and extra protection never hurt."

"I can use a cream or get a diaphragm."

"Lynnde, I've tried those methods before and my kids can vouch for their reliability. The answer is no."

Before I can finish saying my thoughts out loud, he cuts me off and says he's heard all that. He's been lied to before, and no, he doesn't think I'm a liar; he just cares for me. If things don't work out he won't be an absent father again.

I know, I know. Wait, Lynnde. Slow down. *After being able to come from the places you've been a condom should be the first thing on your mind.* All right. I had to get my thoughts out and now that I've said them, you're right. I guess for once in my life things have been going well. Why go looking for something to destroy it again? I'm still working on myself and haven't gotten used to a peaceful life yet. Sometimes I still feel like I'm tiptoeing on someone else's eggshells. Walking slowly and lightly, knowing I'm going to crack more than one and the consequences that await me when I do.

These thoughts come to me when I let insecurities and weakness pay me a visit. They never stay long, but the way they make me feel when they're here is enough for three lifetimes. They leave when I remember the only eggshells I have to worry about cracking are mine. If I happen to view a yolk, I'll have no problem cleaning it up.

My weight is something I haven't talked about much lately. I've been sticking to my exercise routine, and I'm down to a size fourteen while tipping the scale at one hundred and sixty-two pounds. I love every inch of me. Getting a grip on my mind's thinking about food is something I wished would've come sooner, but I know all things happen for a reason. I've been exercising three times a week for the last eight months and promised myself I'd stick to it. If I never lose another pound I'll be satisfied, but never gaining one is the goal I'm aiming for.

A few tears graced my face when I threw out my stash boxes. They didn't last for long because they were tears for days gone by, not for them moving out and into their new address on Garbage Can Lane. I ask God everyday to not let me struggle with my weight anymore. My struggle goes away because she knows He hears me, and she isn't very strong on her own. I'm not going to talk down to you, and I don't think I'm super sexy fine, but these next thoughts are ones I have to get out of my system. If you're someone who's been described as a plus size times a few and don't like it, take action. I spoke on weight before, but my problems with it will always be a part of me just like the rest of my episodes that won't show in syndication. I made excuses and blamed everyone else for my over indulgence in food but me.

If you really want to take control of your body, don't focus on the negative and what you can't do. Don't leave it at: I can't afford to join a gym, I don't like those kinds of foods, I don't have time to exercise, diets don't work, I'm not ready to lose weight yet, or the famous excuse of, I'm like this because everyone else in my family is fat so I might as well be, too. You may say you want to lose weight, but excuses like that call you a liar out loud.

I've learned to wait on many things, but waiting for someone to lose weight for me was not one of them. Do you really think someone else is going to sweat to see you reap the benefits? The days of free slavery and "massah" are supposedly gone, so I really can't see what you see.

I'm not the wizard, but look to yourself, dear reader. Don't blame others like I did. There's so much more to life than food. If all you do is eat for whatever reason, enjoyment, comfort, sickness, or because you have nothing else to do, you've already wasted so much time.

I'm talking like this because I'm hoping to stop many dear readers, and if there's only one I'm satisfied, from going down glutton road. I'm going to stop now. I think you understand what I'm telling you and you know it comes with no maliciousness attached. Besides, my parents will be here for dinner soon and I need to get started.

As I cleaned off the kitchen table the doorbell rang. I thought it was a school kid selling something, but I opened the door anyway and was pleasantly surprised.

"Taylor, hey baby. What are you doing here?" He wore all black and had a sexy masculine scent about him.

"So should I assume you're not glad to see me?"

"No, no, come on in. My parents are coming over for dinner tonight. What's up?"

"I was on my way to pick up my boys and saw a flyer posted advertising a circus that's coming to town next week. Since I was only a few blocks away, I thought I'd take a chance at seeing my lady, and asking if she'd like to accompany me and my brood next week when we go? Please say yes?"

"Yes! That sounds like fun. Count me in. Do you have time to stay for dinner?"

"No, but thanks for the offer. I promised Tyler and Tyree that I'd take them to the movies and for pizza afterwards. I don't want to be late so I'd better get going. I'll give you a call later, okay?"

"Okay and thanks for the invite."

We kissed and I watched him walk to his car. He turned to wave and blew a kiss at me before getting in. I blew one back and caught the one he aimed at me. Leave me alone, will you? Things were good with Taylor. We still hadn't said the L word but I knew it was coming.

I'm glad he asked me to go to the circus with him and his kids. Usually when he gets them, it's just the five of them, but lately he's asked me to go on some of their outings. I get along okay with the three boys, but I'd swear his daughter was the omen, part ten. She was the baby and wanted her daddy to herself and didn't stop until her brothers and everyone else knew it.

Taylor gave all his kids' attention, but since she was the baby girl, he spoiled her rotten. It could be my jealousy talking. When I see them together, I'm reminded of times with my father. I long to be a time traveler who's stuck on a day when she's seven years old, sitting on her father's lap. Not being able to be that time traveler is acceptable, but I wonder if sitting on my father's lap today will feel the same as it did when I was seven. Maybe not to his lap but I'm going to do it anyway.

My parent's arrived as Taylor was leaving and they said their hellos and goodbyes. Our dinner was wonderful and was filled with laughter and love. 9:30 came quick, you know they have to be home and in bed by ten, and we made plans to do something the upcoming week. With the way they were acting, I wondered if this "in bed by ten" really meant something else? I can't bear to think of my parents that way, yuck.

"Well, baby girl, we gotta hit the road now. Ten o'clock is coming and your daddy has some business to take care of." He gave me a wink and a kiss before his laughter started and went outside to warm up the car.

"Lynnde, don't you pay your daddy no mind, you hear? He's happy that you're happy. I swear sometimes that man has too much fool in him. Now if you need anything, just call, you hear? Is everything all right? You can tell me if it isn't?" "Everything is fine, Ma. And if I need anything, I'll call." "All right, baby. I'll call you in the morning. I love you. Bye."

"Bye, Ma. I love you."

For the second time on that cold November day, I watched a car carrying people who cared about me pull away. It was excellent knowing they wouldn't be gone for long, and I could count on them anytime I needed them. Before cleaning the kitchen I sat down on my couch and hugged myself. I thanked God for letting me have good thoughts about myself on my own.

# What Did You Say?

The Wilson family came home for the Christmas holiday and returned to California three days after the New Year. Another year has come and I'm grateful that everyone I love is still here on this earth to share it.

While home, Esta was able to finalize the paperwork for the boutique. She bought a stack of fashion catalogues with her, and by the time she left, I had every picture and address memorized. I'm so ready for this. I can't wait until the grand opening on March tenth, which is Esta's birthday. This gives us plenty of time to get everything we need to make the opening spectacular.

I've always loved Esta and always will, but I don't know why I can't make this small feeling of jealousy go away. When I'm having a pity party for myself, I look at her life and pretend it's mine. This birthday will be her thirty-fifth; she's been happily married for over ten years, has two beautiful children, three fashion boutiques in California, and will soon have one in New York.

My thirty-fifth birthday is in July and over the past ten years I've had no husband, three failed relationships, no children, been fired from my job, evicted from two apartments, had my car repossessed, and ran back home to mommy and daddy so I could grow up all over again.

Where did I go wrong, and why must I compare myself to my best friend?

I think I'm supposed to feel sorry for myself, that's why. Am I starting a new business? No. I'm only involved in the process because of my association with my beautiful friend. I wouldn't even be in the position I'm in if it weren't for the charitable works of my extended family. Someone else has always straightened my life out.

Why? Why can't I be the one who's had the prospering life? Where's my husband, my children, my new business venture? And should I even be asking for this or anything at all for that matter? Should I just be grateful that I've been allowed a second, third, fourth, and fifth chance to get myself together?

Should I be grateful that I've had much needed help along the way? Yes. That's what I'm going to focus on. Not the deeds of my past that allowed me to do nothing, but the deeds and generosity of others that make me strive to do better. So jealousy, you need to go away. There's no place here for you. The person you're making me look at will never know you paid me a visit. I cannot take someone else's life and make it belong to me. I'm not upset or angry Esta has taught me another lesson, just grateful she deemed me special enough to do so.

I've been pretty busy readying myself for my new job. I've just about mastered the ordering process, and I go to the boutique everyday after work to clean and re-clean the store. Less than a month remains until the grand opening and I can't remember the last time I felt this energized about anything. Men included. The realization of knowing you can be needed by something other than a man is the cause of it.

Taylor and I still see each other, but he's not contributing to my happiness. With the way things are going, he probably never will. Don't even say you knew it was coming, because hearing put-downs from you, dear reader, is something I'm not accepting this time. I'm in control of this.

He proposed marriage to me on New Year's Day. I know you're wondering why I haven't mentioned it. Before, any man in my life came first, and the fact that marriage is involved should've had me talking about him much sooner. His marriage proposal was something I longed to hear, but it came with conditions. Will someone please tell me what the conditions of love are? I've heard love sometimes has nothing to do with anything. Well, I listened loud and clear when love told me it had nothing to do with this proposal.

Taylor decided to bring in the New Year by having his children over for an all-nighter, which I was invited to but declined. New Years is a holiday I've always spent with my family no matter where I've lived or whom I was involved with. We made a date instead to get together that evening and have a private celebration.

Some celebration. After his proposal that was presented to me in a business like manner, I was given a time limit in which to make up my mind. Is this the love I waited for? Hell no. I declined his proposal. Close your mouths and let me finish.

All my life, all my dreams, all I needed was a man, and all things would be all right. My many disappointments taught me I was so wrong. I never said it before, but listen to me as I say it now. Happiness begins with self, comes from self, and should always walk with self before self can join with another person.

Well, my self was happy and the happiness I felt was not about to be taken away by another. The fact that I had to have a man finally got it's ass in the back seat when my self told me she wouldn't be happy with this one. She said we, meaning she and I, should come first.

Never before in my life had I come first. The self that wanted to have a man to make all things right wouldn't fight with the need for my self-happiness. There was no competition for it here and the want left. My self told it not to come back until it would work in a positive way for us. I told you I was in control.

This proposal taught me to better phrase what you ask for. I constantly asked for a husband, and with Taylor that's all I would receive. No love, no children, and no room to grow. He didn't see things the way I did. He felt when we got married we'd have all the kids we'd ever need.

I know and understand families' come in many shapes, sizes, and forms. I believe you don't have to be related to someone to consider him or her a family member. I had no problem with adopting all four of Taylor's children; I wanted every part of him, especially the part where his children were concerned. I had no problem with not going to work outside of the home either. My problem is with the children he wanted me to give up parts of my life for.

I'll say this next statement many times with this being the third because I just said it in two sentences before this one. The children he wanted me to quit my job to raise were his children. I wanted to quit my job to raise our children.

"Lynnde, I love you, but if you want a marriage to occur between us, there will be no more children. If we get divorced, I don't want to be an absent father. I'm having a hard time dealing with that now."

Huh? Where is the love? Shouldn't a marriage be a beautiful, joyous, everyday celebration of the union between two people? He was walking into it with reservations and a closed and locked mind that would never be open to change.

Taylor didn't know of my miscarriage and how bad I wanted my chance, once again, to make my baby happy. I didn't tell him of my need to feel unconditional love from someone God let belong to me on this earth, someone He gave me the privilege to create. Someone I'd protect with my love, the kind of love only a mother can give until the end of time. I didn't tell him because I knew of no words that would make his closed mind understand. I wouldn't give up my beliefs and easily conform to another's again. I refused. This one thing I could not do.

How dare he create this stupidity for his mind and his mouth to ask me? He loved his children, number four, and told them so everyday. What made him think he should be the one to take that opportunity away from me?

Yes, I was capable of loving Taylor's children, number five, but first and foremost, for the sixth time, that's what they'd always be, Taylor's children.

Yes, I'd help to raise his children, number seven, in the most respectable way possible, take them shopping if the need existed, tell them every bedtime story in print before I tucked them in, and listen to them call him daddy, because for the eighth time, they were Taylor's children.

Yes, I'd attend school functions if they asked me, nurse them when they were sick, bathe them when they were dirty, and never let them go any amount of time knowing what it meant to be hungry. All these things I'd lovingly do, for the ninth time, for Taylor's children.

What words did I need to say to make him understand that only my baby would call me mommy? When did he make the law or be granted a patent that told him he could deny my ears, my life, my self, the pleasure of hearing my child call me mommy? Who was he to deny my child his or her right to want and need me, and know I'd always be there?

No, I wouldn't give up my baby for him. I wouldn't let my baby leave me again because of my feelings for another. Taylor would be the one receiving papers stamped denied. Denying him was my right. He cannot go back and change my past, and I wouldn't allow him to change the future I saw for me.

These were my thoughts during the two-week time period he gave me after making his business proposition. He came over to my apartment on New Year's Day after taking his children, (I'm not counting anymore) home. As I waited for him to arrive, I listened to soft music, sipped on champagne, and wore a sexy New Year sky blue baby doll teddy Esta made especially for him. She called the week before the holidays and asked him what his favorite color was. Three days later a package with my address on it, but Taylor's name as the recipient, arrived at my apartment.

I couldn't wait to wear his new present and begin a new year. My thoughts were, finally, I have a good job that will lead me towards a promising future, I live on my own stress free, and I am in a good, prospering relationship with a man. The man I'd been waiting for my whole life. Yeah I know, I know. Every other man before him was the one I waited for, also. You don't need to say it, but I thank you for wanting to help me along the way.

Taylor arrived at 8:22 p.m. and five minutes after nine he left. After he left, I sat immobile on my couch in his sky blue baby doll teddy, listening to the same soft music and sipping on the same glass of champagne I had before he got there. Why did he even bother to show up if he knew the words he spoke to me would bring me so much pain?

He thought about those words carefully, planning the pitch, the correct order, and the speed at which they would come from his mouth. He knew. The one equation he should've figured into his plan is his insensitive words to me were the same words that gave me gratification when I spoke of their contents to myself. Any words concerning a child that could belong to me brought me pleasure.

If you're tired of hearing it, I'm sorry, but I must say it again. My self's pleasures come first. It's a shame that all I could think of was going to Oz with Taylor, yellow brick road or not. Oz may have been my destination but somehow I ended up sitting next to Humpty Dumpty. You know, I felt bad having to tell him I couldn't help him repair his cracked shell.

"Humpty, this girl is leaving before your appearance starts to look appealing and I begin to crack. I can't let myself be broken again."

When I heard Taylor's knock at the door, I almost fell over my own feet trying to answer it. I wasn't drunk, just overly excited. I didn't put on a robe and swung the door open never bothering to think there might be other people in the hallway. I couldn't see beyond the fine specimen standing before me, so I don't know if anyone else was there or not.

"Hey, baby. Happy New Year," were the words that came from my mouth in a seductive voice.

"Ohh, look a here, look a here. This is a New Year. Girl, you're beautiful. I didn't think you could get any prettier."

We kissed and he came inside. He told me before our year could begin, he had something very important to tell me. I wasn't nervous or scared; this is what I'd been waiting for. This was the something that I couldn't pass on. We sat on the couch and I poured him a glass of now that I think about it, cost too much damn money champagne for the results I received.

"Lynnde, I love you. I may not say it but I do. I'm not going to dress anything up and tell you I can give you all the material things you'll ever need, or that we'll have a bank account or a home that will equal a kings. I can tell you that I will love you and provide everything you'll ever need to be happy. Would you marry me and let me show you all the things we can become together? Marry me."

I didn't start to cry or get emotional. Something walloped me all over my body. It didn't bruise me, though.

"Don't answer me just yet. I have something else to say." *Hello?*

"The only way for me to say this is to say it. I don't want any more kids. I have four kids and that's enough. I pay child support and I have no more money to support anyone else's kids and a wife and that's that."

Someone else's kids? That phrase jumped out at me.

"I want to marry you, but you're going to sign a prenuptial agreement. It'll say you'll get your tubes tied right after we're married. It will also say that if you do become pregnant during our marriage, I'll divorce you and you won't be entitled to any alimony or support for your child."

Your child? I wanted to scream, "It's our child!" but anger doesn't come out right all the time.

"I thought about having a vasectomy, but I heard sometimes it causes problems with a man and I don't want to deprive you of any of me."

*Huh?*

"I hope you can understand how I feel. I'm going to give you two weeks to think this over. Make the right choice. I have nothing else to say. If you say anything now you'll say the wrong thing, so I'm going to go. I'll call you and you can give me your answer. Bye."

He added the other shit I told you about a few pages earlier before he got up and walked out the door. I watched him with my eyes bucked out of my head and my mouth wide open. Hiroshima, let's try Lynnde-shima. I just got bombed, busted, blasted, and blown to pieces by the man that wants to become my husband, and he didn't even realize that he destroyed me.

Am I supposed to want to marry him? Tubes tied? Prenuptial? Alimony? Child Support? Divorce? I asked someone to tell me what the conditions of love are and if these are your answers, I'll show ignorance in hearing them.

I started getting madder and madder wondering who Taylor thought he was. Who was he to come over here and give me his 'take it or leave it, it's my way or no way' stupid ass proposal? I wish you could have seen me sitting there in a sexy outfit waiting to give my body again to a man. A man that would drop me as if I was a walking form of leprosy, the plague, and syphilis, for wanting to share my world and child with him. I looked like a rejected porn movie slut. I felt so damn dumb.

I had a hard time with my anger; thinking of words to say to him to make him understand his wishes cannot be fulfilled. The words will never exist for me to tell a baby not to come to me again and give me one more try. Never. Why should I have to be a play house mommy when I can be a real house mommy?

Taylor said he never told me he loved me but he does. I never told him I loved him because I don't. He's a good man that's excellent with his children for wanting the best for his life and theirs. But his belief of my having no children will never be known as true. He's not the man for me. I won't make another mistake and treat him as if he is.

Yes, we enjoy each other and the sex is wonderful, but Lynnde girl has gotten past her wants for just those things. I started to see Taylor in my future because I wanted my future to hurry up and get here. Then I told myself to slow down girl, slow your roll, and remember your thoughts about being patient. Every time I think the way I should, Taylor disappears, but the happy life I want for myself doesn't. So why bother being with a man you don't love and putting time and energy into something that won't be everlasting? I don't know. I haven't evolved to that point yet.

I said at the beginning of my story that if all a relationship has is sex, and the sex isn't even good, and you know the rest. At this point the sex was good, and I thought we had something else. Maybe knowing I have to continue to wait was the source of my procrastination. I know for my happiness to continue I must play by the rules. I've been in the game this long, and it makes no sense for me to cheat now. *Wait for love, Lynnde. Wait for love*

The next two weeks came and went with me declining Taylor's proposal in between. I told him I cared about him but wasn't ready for marriage yet, said I still needed work. I should've told him the truth, but if I did, I knew I'd receive no more physical contact from him. Look, I'm not there yet, but I'm on my way.

He told me he understood and thanked me for my honesty. Hey, straying from the truth to spare someone's feelings doesn't hurt all the time.

Taylor and I continued to see each other but on a much more scaled down basis. When he picked up his kids for their outings, I never went along, and he never mentioned them saying they missed me. We didn't talk to each other every day anymore, or go out as much as we used to. Sometimes weeks would go by before we'd speak to each other, so we both knew where our relationship was headed. But as the song says, "Neither one of us wants to be the first to say goodbye." We just wanted it to happen. The word goodbye doesn't sound right trying to fit in with all the other noises during sex, and yes, we were still having sex.

When our relationship got to the point of sex without spending the night together, I began feeling used, but not used up. Taylor took the place of food. I had to get to the point where I felt I needed nothing to take the place of anything. I wanted to just be, and be fine with that. For an unknown reason I wasn't quite ready to give up the male counterpart yet. Even though I knew he'd never be more than what he was, I still had an occasional rumble in the jungle with him. I made myself a promise of ending things with him once the boutique opened up, telling myself I'd have no time for him, and I planned to keep it.

When the boutique didn't open up as scheduled, I used that excuse as to why I still saw Taylor. Esta wasn't able to come home for the grand opening because Larry had an unexpected training duty come up, and she didn't really want him to miss it. She told me to open the boutique since it was half mine, but that didn't feel right to me. This was a vision she had with the both of us in it, and that would be the only way I'd see it clearly.

Instead of spending March tenth with my best friend working at my new job as a fashion consultant and saleslady, one-day part owner of Esta's Exquisite Fashions, The New York Connection, and reveling in all the joy it would bring me, I spent the morning on the phone with her giving her the best long distance birthday wish I possibly could.

I wanted to go to California, but Esta told me to save my money, she'd be home on April seventeenth and we'd have our long awaited grand opening then. My mouth told her I'd be satisfied with seeing her and opening the boutique next month, but my heart and stomach didn't agree. Instead of staying true and faithful to the beliefs that our dream would one day be real, I let a little depression visit me. I didn't bother to let it know that I had enough happiness to take its place, but listened as it talked me into turning to three big greasy burgers first, and Taylor second, for comfort. Most of the morning of March eleventh was spent regretting the evening of March tenth, even though the day began on a positive note.

I called in sick on the eleventh, mostly due to the disappointment of not spending the first birthday with Esta's since she got married and moved away. I didn't want to admit it to her, but I was mad at Larry for taking that opportunity away from me. I knew she loved him and he was her husband, but I wanted her to myself just one more time.

My relationship with her may sound strange to you, but I need her, she's my best friend. I'm much closer to Esta than I've ever been to any man. Why couldn't she come home anyway? I know I sound selfish and should respect the fact that she has a husband, but sometimes all I can see is what I want. I hate myself for feeling this way towards her, knowing she's never conjured the same thoughts about me. Damn, I can't stand it when my beliefs go haywire.

When the old thought of 'if only I had a man' comes flying back to talk to me, I run to the first one who'll have me, pretending he feels exactly about me as the one man who'll love me forever does. Of course, he isn't my man. It's Taylor. But Taylor will have to do for now or until this feeling of neglect disappears.

# This Is What Life Is

April seventeenth is here. Whoever said, "There's no such thing as a perfect world," should pay me a visit today. The best thing about it is, my eyes will witness it again. I bought a video camera so I can replay it over and over again, making April seventeenth a new holiday to celebrate in my life.

I feel so stupid for being mad at Esta and Larry last month. He's running around like a broke man in a bank vault full of money. I'm so glad he's here to share this day with us.

Taylor came by earlier with his brood to show support, and to purchase a couple of outfits for his daughter. I was happy to see him even though we haven't talked much lately. When I saw him and Tayleka at the register paying for their items, anger tapped me on my shoulder, sending my thoughts back to New Years Day. Hearing his words once more, solidified for me, that it was a positively known fact that would go down in history, he wouldn't deny me my right to do the same thing. *Now that's the end of that. You know what to do, Lynnde.*

My mother's been in and out of the dressing room three times, trying on "This high fashion stuff" as she calls it. The second time she went in wearing a long gown. The exchange between her and my father was slightly embarrassing, but I plan to hit rewind on the videotape every time that part comes up.

"Lynndon, how does this gown look on me?"

"Hell, Cecelia! If I could see past all of those sequins and glitter, I might be able to tell you what you look like!"

"Lynndon! Why can't you just answer the question that was asked? I'd swear sometimes you just like to give me a hard time."

"I did answer your question. I can't see you."

"Why are you standing there staring at me if you can't see me?"

"I'm looking in the direction of your voice, that's why. Nobody in this store can see you with all the blinding light you're putting out. And just where is it you plan to go with that thing on, and how much do I have to pay to get you there? I hope this boutique has family discounts."

By this time, everyone in the store was laughing, and the more they laughed, the more my father got on my mother's nerves.

"Never mind the cost or the discount. I'll pay for it myself. Sometimes, Lynndon, I don't know why I bother with you. I should've listened to my daddy when he told me not to marry you all those years ago."

"Ahh woman, don't start that mess. You know you love me. Now come on over here and give me some sweet suga'."

My mother giggled and the sight of them smooching was weird. Who would've thought my father would become so compassionate in such a short period of time? Viewing my parent's affection for each other made me glance at Taylor, and I secretly thanked him for showing me his version of love.

I'm not one to judge, so I won't say if it's right or wrong. I'll just say that I'm going to have to pass on it. There's always a new and improved version of the original, so I'll save my love and invest it in that one.

I'm not going to look for any instructor to blame as to why my dances with men always end up with my feet hurting. I'll just sit down and soak them until they hurt no more, without paying any mind about how long it will take either. I'll stay off the dance floor until it's time for me to join with a new dance partner, letting the electric slides, hustles, and chicken dances that come in between pass me by. If I have to soak my feet until they look like pretty brown prunes, that's okay, too. I'm in the fashion business, I'm sure I can find a sexy pair of shoes to cover my feet.

I have finally realized that I must wait. This is the last time I will say it aloud. The best part about it being the last time is the part about it being the first time I truly believe it in my heart, my soul, and my mind. I'll have the love that was created for me, this I know. Trying to play the guessing game as to when it will arrive, and picking the first man I see to try to make him the man love will be with won't happen again. So for my heart's content, I'll say wait, Lynnde. Just wait.

# Why Is She Gone?

Another year has passed. Every mistake I previously made doesn't own me now. The pain I caused myself disappeared after this year was half over. This year, my thirty-sixth, is the worst year of my life. Esta died three weeks ago. I said it. I hate that it's true. Believing it is the part I'm having trouble with. Esta is dead.

I won't see her beautiful self or hear her smiling voice on this earth anymore. Esta Renee Phillips, the daughter of Mr. and Mrs. Phillips, my best friend, Larry's wife, Lester and Chester's mother, is dead.

Her name and the word death should never have met each other so soon. This is something I'll never understand. No amount of prayer, church, bible stories, therapy, or support from friends will help me to understand why she was the one who had to die. Esta is dead.

Esta was beautiful in my eyes. She was five-feet-seven inches just like me, but with a lot less excess baggage. Her hair was always silky bone straight, and that girl could dress. I always told her she was the color of cappuccino, and had the biggest doe shaped eyes in the world. She had sistah hips, and a set of sistah lips to match. Every man I know loved her lips, and she knew it, too. She never went anywhere without them made up to grace a magazine cover and she received compliments every time.

Esta was someone who was my friend no matter what size I chose to be. Her motto was, "Lynnde, girl I don't care how big or small you are. You're still you and I love you." She never knew how good those words made me feel. Thank you Esta. All she ever wanted for me was happiness.

"Lynnde, girl, just hold on. Your turn is coming. Just wait for love. You'll know when it's right. Just wait for love."

She said those words to me at least ten times a week. That girl loved me. Those were the last words she said to me, wait for love.

We talked on the phone one Monday night for three hours. On Tuesday morning, she died. Exactly what is a brain aneurysm, and why did it have to happen to her?

Larry told me she'd gotten up early with him, like she did every morning, to have coffee and their morning chat before he went off to work. She told him she had a slight headache and was going to lie back down before the boys woke up. He kissed her good bye, told her he loved her, and that was the last time he saw her alive. He said she never even made it back to bed. The boys found her on the kitchen floor. The next-door neighbor went over to ask her if she could special order a dress for her, and she found the boys sitting next to her.

I wonder if Esta knew what was happening to her? I wonder if she did know, who did she think about? Did she think about me? Did she know how much I love her, and that I would take her place in heaven and even go to hell if it meant she could live? I pray that she wasn't afraid, and if she was, did she know she wasn't alone? I was there in some way. I'd never abandon Esta if she needed me. I love her more than I love my own pitiful self.

It's hard explaining my mixed emotions. I was angry because Esta was so far away. If she were here this never would've happened. Numbness and helplessness were the only emotions I felt because there wasn't a thing I could do. I felt like garbage dump trash, and begged God to bring Esta back, and take me. He didn't because I wasn't worthy. Who wants trash?

Damn you, Esta! Why did you have to leave me? I'm being selfish, I know, but I always wanted Esta for myself. Who was going to be my best friend now? No one will ever love me like she did. I didn't believe she was gone, and wouldn't believe it until I saw her. She loved me; she loved Larry and the boys. What about her parents? They were planning to take a trip out to California in a few weeks. She wouldn't leave before they got there, that's not like Esta. If she said she's going to do something, she did it. What about her new boutique and all the other children she planned to bring into this world? She can't be gone. Not with all the plans she made. She can't be gone.

I made it through the worst night of my life by following instructions that didn't exist. Up until a couple of weeks after the funeral, I stayed at my parent's house. My father asked me to move back home and I almost said yes to his request. The thought of regressing further was the only reason I declined.

The funeral was long and draining. In no way possible did it seem right. Seeing Esta lying in her coffin made me want to get in and lie next to her, like we used to do at our sleepovers. I stared at her hard; half trying to will her eyes open so she could see me. Larry looked like another man. There was so much sorrow in his eyes, but his love for Esta was prominent.

The little strength I had left me when her boys kept asking, "When is mommy going to wake up?" I started screaming for Esta to wake up, that we were all waiting for her to get up. Why couldn't I be strong?

Esta's funeral was the same size as her wedding. There was the same amount of love there, also. The day was rainy, but I noticed a few bright spots I'm sure Esta told me to look at. She always took care of me. Watching her boys showed me I had to go on. I'd never let another child down in life again.

Desmond and Tori were the other spots. Receiving hugs, and words of comfort from the greatest part of my past untied the knot in my heart I had created concerning them. Knowing they thought of me, along with a special person like Esta, showed they once cared for me. Maybe some of the pain I caused them had subsided.

While standing over her coffin one last time before they closed it, I silently begged her to open her eyes but she didn't. When they closed the coffin, I fell to my knees.

"Just let her be. They were sisters," said her mother on my pathetic behalf. Even her parents were stronger than I was. I would get it together for Esta. I had to. Larry and the boys would need help, and I'd be the one to give it. I was dazed, confused, and just plain bewildered by this. Grief takes you through a maze that has no end. There aren't any set rules on how to grieve you just do it. And then one day, after bumping into walls and slipping on the soaking wet floor your tears have created, your grief decides to loosen the chokehold it has on you. It never, ever, ever, lets go, though.

Every time death interrupts the world we expect everyone to take notice. We expect people to know why we're walking around looking like crap, and why we're sad and angry. At least that's how I feel now. I think the world should stop and grieve with me. Every continent should know that Esta left us, but that's not the case. World adoration only happens with celebrities. Esta is the only celebrity I'll ever know.

I knew she'd never leave us willingly, and I know everyone else misses her, but what is it I'm supposed to do now? Am I supposed to continue to breathe freely after this? I can't stand life. I can't stand myself. The air I breathe has such a strong stench that's due to the funk I'm in. I'm waiting for the day it suffocates me. *Are you going to die, Lynnde? You won't even fight it? Fine then. Just die.*

The boutique's been closed since the day she died, and I haven't been able to reopen it since. I hate myself. Why am I always so weak? I'm the reason she's dead. As soon as she included my fat, bad luck charm ass in her business, her health started to decline. She never had a cold before we started talking about this joint venture.

Sometimes, I ride by the boutique at the strangest hours of the morning with a gas can in my car. I want to burn it down because with this particular boutique gone, Esta will come back. If I'd done this when she was still alive, she'd still be here. I'm so damn dumb.

Maybe she'd want me to continue working at the boutique. After all, this was her dream. Why am I so selfish when it comes to Esta? I can't and won't do this without her. It's not normal for me to live, breathe, and sell clothes she designed without her being on this earth.

The encouraging words of others tell me to continue, and if I need just one reason, the reason should be for Esta. I say I understand with a smile, and that keeping the business open is the best thing to do. What I really want to say is they can all take their rehearsed words of encouragement and go to hell. How can I tell them I had a hard time existing with her here on this earth? How am I supposed to go on now?

It's funny how you can feel so much love for a person and never think the day will come when those feelings collapse. You think your life won't go on without that one person in it. These are the thoughts that tell me I have to go on for Esta. I never thought I could live without Lamar, Otto, Desmond, or Terrance. Too many men in such a short period of time. I don't feel the same type of love for them, but something will always be there, whether it's good or bad.

My feelings of love for Esta will never go away. I must pick myself up and keep going, smelling the funk until it loses its strength. I have to keep the boutique going for her children, husband, mother, and her father. Doing so will help to keep her alive. What will they think of me if I don't?

I have to keep the boutique going for me. Larry plans to sell the ones in California and invest the money in the one here. He told me the boutique was Esta's and my baby, and the way I run it wouldn't matter to him. He'll never know calling the boutique my baby gave me the power I needed. He said Esta wouldn't like him trying to tell me what to do, and he wouldn't like it either. Why do these people love and trust me so much?

Going on without my girl will be hard, but allowing weakness to take over won't be the next mistake I make. I promise. Tomorrow will be the first day of the fourth week that the shop has been closed. The first day of the fourth week will be the day I reopen the shop. I have to do this. I thank God for giving me the people who filled my life with love. This boutique will be a constant reminder of the one I shared my love with the most. The doors will be open before the rooster's crow; I need my reminder to begin as soon as possible.

# I Will Always Love You

The days and nights since Esta's passing have been too long. I spend the day at the boutique and stop by my parent's house every night on my way home from work. They've worried about me for years, and I have to show them everyday that I'm going to be all right. I also go by Esta's parent's house to check in and see the boys.

Larry went back to California to start the process of selling the boutiques and close up their home. Esta's parents offered to go along and help, but he told them he had to do it himself. He has to heal his way, and seeing the boys gives me a chance to get to know them better. I want them to know I'll always be here, there, or anywhere for them.

So many times people say, "If I only knew that was the last time I was going to see them." We often go into the disbelief stage when someone passes. Most of the time you haven't had contact with the deceased in years. Try not to be one of those people. Let your loved ones know they're loved. I'm lucky I didn't go through that with Esta. I'm grateful I had her as my best friend. We always told one another we loved each other. I know this is something she knew on her last day of life. It will be something I'll know on mine, also. Esta taught me to love myself when I didn't think I could. She showed me how to respect myself, and how to get respect from others. Esta taught me so much in her brief lifespan by leading by example. From her I learned to listen, to appreciate, and to live. I learned to wait for love.

Thank you, God, for Esta Renee Phillips, my best friend. One of the women I want to be just like in my journey called life. I will cherish our friendship forever. Esta, I love you.

# It's Alright Now

# We Love Me

As I sit here thinking of all the things I've told you, the next words from my mouth have to be those of thanks. I must thank you for allowing my life to intertwine with yours. Thank you for offering words of encouragement and support and continuing to do so even when you knew I wasn't going to listen.

I guess my fortieth birthday is making me think about how much I have and all the things I should be grateful for. I should've felt this way on all my birthdays and the days in between.

When your birthday comes, you make all these plans, and if they don't work out, you make new plans for your next birthday. How do you know if you're even going to see another birthday?

I'm grateful that I'm allowed to breathe and smile and walk and eat and listen and see, and there are so many more wonderful things to mention. I am grateful that I didn't stump my baby toe this morning when I walked out of the bathroom much too close to the door, but slightly bumped my knee instead. My eyes and mind miss nothing anymore and notice everything. Being grateful will do that to you.

Thinking about the times I wanted to die, and asked for death to come take me away brings tears to my eyes. I looked, watched, and waited for a form of death that didn't need to come from somewhere else. It was with me all along. I was the avenue, the street, the city, and country for my own death.

While I waited for this magnificent act to happen anyway it chose, I should've opened my eyes and saw it was already there. I was killing myself and wouldn't see it until I looked at a gravestone with my name on it.

The only good thing about the death I prayed for is it's the same death that made me feel so alive. I had to die both inside and out before I realized the amount of joy I should have in my life. Death made me realize there is no amount of joy. Joy has no limit. I can have it anytime I want without having to pay a fine or a monthly surcharge.

Thank you. I can't say these two words enough. While reflecting on the years gone by, I think about the things I used to value. What were my reasons, and why in the world were these things so important to me? Why did I have to have a man? Why did I eat so much? Why was I so weak? Where was I? And why was I so worried about what everyone else was thinking?

Some days I ask myself these questions over and over. Yesterday was the first time I came to a conclusion I can live with. All my whys came from my perception of myself. Somewhere, on any day in my short life span, I started believing I was different from everyone. On this any day, I philosophized that I wasn't as good as, or as special as anyone else. How can you think you deserve love, but don't deserve to get it? This was the legacy I made stick with me on any day after one bad experience. On the outside I asked for a good life, but my inside was totally different. Trying to keep secrets from yourself is no way to live. You've already told yourself the truth and know what it's all about, so what's with the secret? What are you trying to hide from your eyes that they can clearly see?

Lying again and again in the past while telling this girl she would be all right, knowing that wouldn't be the case, was my only purpose. Creating a vicious circle of lies about yourself, and telling them to no one but you, is one step away from shopping for a straight jacket that's custom made and fitted for your life. A straight jacket only you know about and can put on and take off when the need exists. Does that seem like strange behavior to you? It didn't seem strange to me at first. I let myself make, sleep, and roll over, and damn near die in the king sized bed I made. I didn't realize what I was doing until my jacket started to get tight, and I was having trouble putting it on. I wouldn't ask for help and started thinking of other ways to get in it. Not being able to think of a better way made me say, "Hey, maybe I don't need this jacket after all."

Today, I don't feel ashamed about my past. I don't feel I was the only one who's ever been a plugged sewage pipe for someone else's feces (I wanted to say shit) to call their final resting place. At times, you don't see how much dirt is on a window until you look at it from the outside. I never wanted to go outside and tried to clean everything up and make it better from where I stood. Being afraid of change will do that to you. Being afraid to ask for help or letting the world know you're not perfect makes it complete. Don't make the same mistake I did and mix all three of them together. That's a combination that'll get your one-way entrance to hell denied because you're not considered worthy enough to burn. Don't ask me where you'd end up because I don't know, and will never, yes I said never, find out.

I'm not going back to the land of the lost again. I've visited that place more than once and it wasn't very entertaining for me. I couldn't fit on any of the rides, lost all the games, and I made myself sick from eating too much food. I've learned to let go of many things that happened to me by accepting the fact that I was a growing person, and the people I shared the times with were growing, also.

Sometimes I feel I should apologize to everyone for making them get to know the sorriest Lynnde to ever exist. I should apologize for asking them to treat me with disrespect and being disappointed when they did it. I had a problem with dwelling in self-pity, and I plan to do that no more either. Learn to forgive yourself and others, dear reader. The weight that'll be lifted makes walking on clouds possible.

This next block of words is directed to my many, lovely female readers, whom I love more dearly today than any other day. If we had problems in the past and meet on the street, please speak to me. If you don't, whose problem is that? I'm not claiming that behavior as mine. It may be my story, but those actions will belong to you.

Yeah, I've had men who slept with other women when I thought they were all mine. I didn't like the fact that they did it and didn't want them to continue cheating on me. This is not the last time I'll say this. Who ever does what is expected of them the first time? It's not me and it wasn't you. It's what they decided to do.

I've never been able to say that out loud. I need to say this to all the pretty fine other women. Let it go. I was hurt, you were hurt, but scrunching your face, sucking your teeth, or whispering to your other pretty fine friend, "There she is," when you see me walking by, isn't the proper procedure for getting over a man that wants nothing to do with you anymore. All these gestures aren't cute or becoming to the person who does it. I'm not saying this because it disrespects me, ladies. I'm saying it because it degrades you.

I'm sure some of you receive enough ugly treatment from others, so there's no need to do it to yourself. I'm not perfect, and no I don't know all there is to know because it's my fortieth birthday. I don't think I'm extra special today because there's no one treating me like a raggedy, rusted pickup truck that can only be used to haul trash with, and when it stalls it gets kicked, cursed, and told the next stop for it will be the junkyard. Whew. I'm saying this because I love me, and I know if we met, we'd love each other.

Loving yourself should come naturally, but I had a hard time treating myself to me. I know there's at least one other person out there that feels the same way, if not worse. People always say life is too short, and you only go around once, so live it up. I say you should respect your life, and the person that gave it to you, and love it up. If you believe your Creator is called God, Jehovah, Messiah, Buddha and the list goes on, opening your heart to thank him first will do your life good.

If you don't believe the Creator concept to be true, well then, this girl really doesn't know of any uplifting words to say to you. I'm not an expert on the good book, but being a rehabilitated fool tells me I should've learned to read it before I was born. I know you're wondering how I'd be able to do that, and I have no answer to give you. I say this because I needed all the help I could get, and getting a jumpstart wouldn't have hurt me.

Don't think since I'm at the end of my story, having told you everything there is and was to know, (telling you was my choice, I know) that I'm in a position where I think I'm the speaker, and teacher of all truths. This isn't some version of a courtroom show that I just happen to be the star of. I'm not talking down or at anyone; I'm just rambling on in my joy. And besides, I've talked to you this long and you never wanted me to shut up before. What's the hurry now? Listening to me for a few more pages won't hurt.

I don't think I've told you where I happen to be doing all of this recollecting. It's on the patio porch of my new home. Yes, I said new and home in the same sentence, and both pertain to me. I spoke about buying a home earlier and closed the deal on this one two months ago.

It's a two-story home, two bedroom, two bathrooms, with one of those being in my bedroom. Two must be my favorite number because it also has a two-car garage. I have a living room, den, dining room and a very spacious eat-in kitchen. There's also a utility room off the kitchen that I use as the laundry room. The front yard is small and fenced in, but the back yard is large enough for the pool, gazebo, and the two sets of lawn furniture. I'm planning a big cookout in two weeks, and I want everything to be perfect. My parents will be here, and it'll be my father's first time over since his stroke.

I remember his facial expression and the tears he cried when I told him I was buying a house. He hugged me, told me he loved me, and put himself in charge of everything. He drove the moving van and made sure everything I needed was taken care of. He hung ceiling fans, ran phone lines, laid carpet, painted again and again, and hung curtains. I love him for all he's done and he knows it.

My mother's invited so many people that trying to give you an exact count at this time is pointless. Check back with me in a couple of years. I should have it by then.

Esta's parents are coming. They gave me a house-warming gift, which brings tears to my eyes every time I look at it. No, it's not an ugly gift. Very funny, dear reader. It's a portrait of Esta and I that hangs in the living room. It was taken from a photograph of us when we were thirteen years old. We went to an amusement park and her father took our picture when we'd just finished riding a roller coaster. There's so much laughter in our smiles. Every time I look at the portrait I can hear Esta saying I screamed much louder than she did, and the laughter filled debate that followed.

I'm not going to tell you again how much I miss her or talk about her not being here, because I know she is. Larry's coming with the boys, so wherever they go, she's always with them. We're all working together, giving each other support, and it's made our family closer.

Crawling into the grave with Esta after she died was all I wanted to do. After my father suffered his stroke, I had thoughts of joining her once again. My thoughts changed when I remembered my family wanted me here, Esta needed me here, and there's no better place for me to be.

The boutiques are outstanding and I'm in the process of expanding. It's wonderful to say I'm the owner of two, and I'm working on number three. I've given credit to Esta for getting me involved in this business, and my parents for pulling me out of the pothole I was in. I'll never forget and will always be thankful for their love and support. Can you see my joy? Can you feel it?

It feels so good now to include myself along with the people I thank. I thank myself for opening up my mind to learn and accept the new changes that were coming, for not wallowing in my own specially made version of self-pity, and for not allowing anyone to judge me in the present by my past, while painting a dreary picture for my future.

Dear reader, we must remember, we are not judges. Your life is not my life. It will never be, so don‘t you dare request me to live it as you prescribe. I wish you could hear my voice as I stress this and see my face as these words come out of my mouth. Never expect another to live the way you do and know that everybody's business is not your own. The talk about walking in someone else's shoes goes here. Sure, I see the looks and hear some of the talk, but you people on the attack are going to lose.

"Isn't that the girl who owns them boutiques?"

"Didn't she date so and so, and so and so, and so and so, and who knows who else in between?"

"Didn't she get cheated on, and beat up, and used to be real fat?"

"Is she the same person who had her car taken away, and got fired from her job?"

"She may think she's doing alright now, but one day her past is going to catch up with her, because you know people never really change."

The walking in the shoes part can go here, too. If you don't know where someone has been, what he or she has accepted, and what they've changed, you need to keep you mouth tightly, tightly closed. Locked would be better.

The past will never catch up with someone who isn't running from it. It's too scared of what may happen to it. It knows the person it used to belong to is no longer afraid of what it holds. The past has nothing to offer, so it stays put and dies from lack of activity. The only way the past can survive is on the energy it receives from the person it belongs to. The past can choke you, but you have to help it. I don't want to choke, don't like to choke, and am not going to choke.

So for all you high horse riders out there, with oh so righteous rules you created for the person you want to emulate you, find a new animal to ride on. Start with something small... oh like...hmmm...let's see, how about a skunk? A skunk is perfect because when we smell you, we'll know you're up to no good. The smell will be a more than powerful signal for us to leave.

I know I may sound a little angry, and maybe I am. I'm talking this way because I don't like ancient Stone Aged Bedrock history, which never made the books, being thrown up in my face. We humans have a way of doing that, you know.

If I have a car accident tomorrow, don't tell me it's because my car was repossessed, and how many years ago it happened. If I get married and somehow manage to get divorced, don't tell me it's because I had too many relationships with men that never worked out, so why should I expect this one to. If I never get married, don't tell me it's because I had too many relationships with men that never worked out, so why should I expect this one to. Did I just say that twice? You know what I mean, though, don't you?

Dear reader, if God forgives me, I've forgiven myself and let it go, would you please tell me why in the world you're still trying to hold on to something that didn't belong to you in the first place?

There's a lesson to be learned in everyone's life, but the lesson to be learned belongs to owner of the life. You may want to live, or not live like a person, and very well may learn something from them. I can guarantee you it's not the lesson that was meant for them, even if the path of your lesson is exactly the same as the person you are trying to emulate.

If I sound repetitive or my joy rambling is getting to you, I apologize. This feeling and moment has been a long time coming, and I want to revel in it as long as it took to get here.

Hey, I just thought about something. You never wished me a Happy Birthday. I know I've been going on in my joy, but you could've said excuse me at any point and said the two words that were created for this occasion. I'm waiting. Hold on, let me shout it with you. "Happy Birthday, Lynnde!"

Thank you, dear reader. You've just made my day even more special. I'm happy that I've been able to talk for more than five pages without going into an, oh no, what has that fool done again story.

I am going to tell you a story, but this one has a happy ending, like a beautiful black princess from New York in a fairy tale. You've never heard of a beautiful black princess from New York in a fairy tale? Well, when you put this book down, Lynnette Donna Lee will be the first because I'm all of the above.

Of course, I'm going to tell about my fiancé. If he weren't in my life, my story's ending would still be beautiful. That's how the power of loving yourself can make you feel. The best part I learned is that I'm so good to love and can love myself all the time. My favorite times are the first thing in the morning when I roll out of bed and thank God for one more day. I love myself when I walk into the bathroom, look at my face in the mirror, and notice how my hair is sticking up all over my head because the scarf I tied it up with the night before came off. I love myself when I decide to run to the store in whatever wrinkled up sweat suit I grab off the floor, thinking no one is going to see me looking busted. It's funny when I end up seeing everyone I know, and they don't notice a thing.

I especially love myself when I go through the day with a smile on my face, and strangers wonder what it is I'm so happy about. I want to tell them I'm happy about me, but shouting words to a stranger in the city may get me arrested. My own original form of true love happens when I try on an outfit that I think is too small for me, but it fits and makes me look slim. I love myself because I've learned how to prioritize my life, and a man, for the first time, was not at the top.

I'm going to tell the truth and say I like my life just a little more with Myles Harper in it. Myles Harper is a man Esta introduced me to after she left this earth. That girl is always taking care of me. Myles was someone Esta associated with through business, and he attended her funeral. I don't remember seeing him there, but Esta definitely brought us together.

She'd been gone a year, and I went to the cemetery, as I'd done everyday that week, to talk to her. As Esta and I were deep into our conversation, I noticed a man walking in my direction with flowers. I figured he was going to pass by me but when he was about fifteen feet away, he stopped and stood as if he were waiting on someone. I didn't know he was waiting on me so I continued my conversation for another half hour or so, not noticing him standing there the entire time. As I stood up to walk away, he continued walking in my direction. He approached me and asked if my name was Lynnde.

"Why, yes. I'm Lynnde. Who are you, and how do you know me?"

"Oh, I'm sorry. I didn't mean to startle you or be impolite. My name is Myles Harper. I worked with Esta, and she talked about you all the time. Her description of you was picture perfect."

I smiled through my not-so-picture-perfect face at the vision I saw of Esta gabbing on about me.

"I'm sorry you had to wait so long for me to finish. You should've come over with your flowers. I wouldn't have mind."

"Oh, no. Esta told me how close you two were. There was no way I'd interrupt. She was a very special person and she loved you."

"Yeah, special she was. I miss her so much sometimes I feel like I can't go on." My eyes started to tear up again, and I turned to face Esta's grave.

"You don't have to be ashamed to cry in front of me, Lynnde. Why do you think I'm here? We were working on our own line of plus sized women's clothing, and I sold a few outfits to a store three days ago. I came here to show my respect and to thank her for helping me achieve my goal. I miss her, too."

His eyes teared up, also. I stepped back and let him put his flowers on her grave. He bent down, bowed his head, and his shoulders shook slightly. Myles stood up after a few minutes, faced me, and sighed.

"Lynnde, would you like to go for coffee? It would be nice to talk to someone who knew Esta so well."

My heart ached to be near anyone who knew Esta. I declined his offer, though. "As much as I'd like to, I'm going to pass. I don't think I'll be good company."

He looked at me in my eyes and studied my face. "I understand. Well, how about some other time? I know you run the boutique and I've never seen it. If you don't mind, I'd like to stop in for a visit and take you to lunch. I'll show you some of my designs. Maybe you'll want to sell them in the store."

"Now there's an offer I can't refuse. Bring whatever you have. If Esta had anything to do with it, I'm sure the clothing is beautiful. It would be an honor to sell them in the boutique."

"How about this coming Tuesday? I have to fly back to California this weekend, but I'm returning on Monday. I'll get some items together and come in around ten o'clock. Is that too early?"

Seeing the excitement in him was the best thing I'd seen all day. "No, ten o'clock is fine."

"All right then. It's a date. Here's my card with my number in case we have to change our plans. I'll call the boutique if anything happens on my end, but expect me to be there with at least twenty designs."

"Twenty designs it is. We have a new display rack and your clothing will fill it right up."

Myles facial expression resembled a mischievous schoolboy for a moment. "You sure I can't change your mind about that coffee?"

"Trust me. I wouldn't be much fun. How about walking me to my car instead?"

"Sure, that'll be fine." Myles started walking away but before I took a step, I turned towards Esta's grave and blew her a kiss. I knew we met because of her, and for the first time that day, a smile made good use of my face. As we walked to our vehicles, Myles told me how he met Esta.

"I was a small fashion designer who was waiting for my turn in the spotlight. I went out shopping ideas to stores in California and stopped in Esta's boutique for directions. I wasn't going to show her any designs because her boutique was more of a specialty shop, and I really didn't think she'd be interested. She asked what was in my design case and a friendship was born."

A vision of Esta's face made me glow at that moment. "That sounds exactly like her. She could make friends with anybody."

Eagerly Myles responded, "Oh, she was such a wonderful person. She put my name out in circles that would take me years to travel in, and treated me as if we'd known each other our entire lives. We talked a few times a week, and when she died, I felt lost. Knowing she'd want me to continue is where my strength comes from."

I didn't reply because he sounded a lot like me. Right then, I knew he'd be a friend of mine. Thank you, Esta.

You know, many of us have a picture in our mind as to what the man of our dreams is going to look like. Is he going to be tall, dark and handsome, or medium, light, and all right? You ask for a pretty boy that comes in your flavor and fits your description to a tee, but of course there's always something that's just not right. Maybe his teeth aren't straight and he wears glasses.

Maybe he's perfect in every way, but his hygiene isn't up to your standards. I guess he wouldn't be perfect then. He could be that special one, but when he takes his clothes off his shape makes Elmer Fudd look like a GQ model. Maybe he's just what you've been looking for until he opens up his mouth, and shows you how he's invested his life savings into the platinum teeth in his mouth. To make matters worse, his conversation belongs to a twenty-year-old who failed the ninth grade twice, the tenth grade once, and you're really not sure if he graduated High School at all. Maybe he has hard feet, hard hands, and a rotten tooth in his mouth, so at certain times of the day, if the air is blowing in your direction, you get a whiff of dead dragon breath.

Mr. Right could be what every other woman wants, and you have him, but you're not satisfied. He doesn't wash dishes like you do, doesn't write letters like you do, and you have different tastes in music. God forbid he washes clothes as a birthday surprise for you and shrinks some of your favorite items that can be replaced. Is it a crime he thought to make dinner reservations and forgot to bring you flowers? So you have different interests, and he doesn't like to go bargain hunting for shoes and would rather stay home and play some stupid video game that you can't understand?

Do you ever wonder if there is a man of our dreams and if there's such a thing as a Prince Charming? I think there is, but he isn't going to be the vision that you have in your mind. No matter how long and hard you look or try to make him be that vision, it just won't happen.

I believe in this world there's a God-created person for all of us. Many of us never meet that person because we're too busy trying to make the wrong one, the right one. If there's nothing special about him or her, don't take the time to make up what it is, or explain why the undetectable quality is so special. If they are that special person and happen to say the wrong words at the wrong time, continue to hold on tight, and don't try to let go. Yes, it's easy to give up, especially when he doesn't look like the man of your dreams. If you were sleeping when you envisioned him, you probably don't even know what he looks like.

Spending the rest of your life looking for your second chance, when you know you've passed that number, and wishing you were still on the first one isn't a good feeling. I'm speaking this way because I'm in a beautiful place and I'm positive this marriage will work. It's not happening because I want to be married, or he knows how to put it down in the bedroom, or he's so fine, or I have to hurry up and have children because time is running out. Nor because I have to have a man on the holidays, or to go to public functions with because that's the way it's supposed to be. My marriage is happening because I took the time to get to know Myles for the man he is, with all of his not so perfect ways. The best reason is because I know I love him, and I know I won't search for someone who looks better, or someone who has more money. My love for him won't allow me to.

I was one of those hurry, hurry, hurry people that had to go through different versions of love to see clearly what the real thing feels and looks like. I truly appreciate Myles Harper and notice everything positive he's brought into my life.

After our first lunch date, we began talking to each other daily and saw each other at least twice a week when he dropped off new creations. I thought about broaching the subject of dating but decided against making the first move. I'd been out of circulation for a much-needed welcomed rest, and didn't want to look like I was throwing myself at the first man I met. I'm glad I didn't say anything when I learned he was involved with someone and had been for the last two and a half years.

Now, don't think of me as Myles's rebound woman or that he's only marrying me because he really wants to be married. He didn't pick the next available woman because his former flame didn't want to take the plunge. That's nowhere near the case. I didn't sit by like a hungry, patient dog waiting to be given a treat that he knew would soon belong to him. That's not the case either. Myles was actually on the tail end of his relationship and did find me very attractive. He wanted to get to know me, but felt it was better to end things with his current interest and take a break, so when he approached me, he'd give me one hundred plus percent of him.

I'm glad he wasn't the hurry up kind of person like I used to be. Myles was the first man whom I took the time to know on a serious friendship level first. I've heard people say the best way to enter a relationship is as friends first, but I never waited long enough to make a new friend. I did wait long enough to have a most-of-the-time sleepover buddy.

The first time we did anything together that didn't involve work was his invitation to me to attend his church. When he first asked me, it caught me by surprise because he told me earlier he was involved with someone. He never mentioned his personal life again so that's where my surprise came from. I didn't think of him as the cheating type, but how many times had I been wrong before? He could've been asking me as a friend, and I shouldn't have jumped to any conclusions about him.

Attending church would be wonderful, but cheating is cheating, and people have been known to attend church and cheat at whatever worldly good makes them happy. Cheating and trying to make yourself look like a Christian at the same time will make you look like a cat at a dog show. The cat knows it's wrong for being there, and so does everyone else. Instead of leaving, it goes through the motions, knowing the things that are said behind it's back will never be told to it's face. Sure, there are dogs that want to chase it away, but the Christian dogs make them leave him alone and join in on the chatter of the day. I think you know what I'm saying.

When he asked me to attend church, the look that said, "What?" on my face didn't let me respond until he told me he was a member of the single life again.

"Lynnde, I can tell my request has surprised you, but it's all on the up and up. Janelle and I aren't dating anymore. We haven't seen each other in months, and things between us ended on a friendly basis. We were going in separate directions and had been doing so for the last year of our relationship. We made it official about eight months ago, but we knew it was over long before that. I wanted to ask you sooner, but I didn't want you to think I was asking because I was lonely. I waited until I thought enough time passed to be acceptable to you. I hope I was right in my decision."

Myles moved his feet around trying to fill the accepting air between us. He continued with a burst of renewed strength.

"Now that the formalities have all been cleared up, how about attending church with me on Sunday? I promise you it won't be a sixteen-hour affair, and you'll really enjoy yourself. If my offer is too much of a surprise, I'll understand. I mean, we never talk much outside of work, but I think this would be a good way to start. So how about it? May I pick you up?"

I know I told you I've changed, but in good olden day Lynnde fashion, I stood still and stared at him for a moment. The moment must've been a long one because he began talking before I could respond.

"Lynnde, are you okay? If you don't want to go to church we can go someplace else, or we can wait until we get to know each other better. Is that what you want?"

"I'm sorry, Myles. I let my mind wander for a moment. Going to church with you would be nice. I know I'll enjoy it. I'm ashamed to say I haven't been in more than a few Sundays, so your offer couldn't come at a better time."

"Oh, good. Service usually starts at eleven a.m. so I'll pick you up at 10:30. I guess I should ask what denomination you are. If we're not the same, I still want you to come, okay?"

"I'm a Republican. Is the invitation still open?"

Myles' facial expression didn't change. The vibrant look on his face remained, and I couldn't hold my laughter in any longer.

"I'm just kidding, Myles. I'm a Baptist. Is it still open?

"It's wide open now. I'm a Baptist, also."

We both laughed, and it was the nicest laughter I shared with a friend since Esta.

"I'd better get going and make the rest of my dress deliveries. I'll give you my usual Wednesday morning call at 9:30."

"Myles, I'll be looking forward to this Sunday more than ever now."

Our conversation paused for a moment while we gave each other a "let's see what else we have in common" look. Myles seemed pleased with whatever thoughts that were on his mind and spoke first.

"Okay, Lynnde. I'll talk to you tomorrow. Bye."

"Bye, Myles. Have a good day."

I watched Myles cool step out of the boutique, and he turned to wave at me before he left my sight. I felt kind of stupid for standing there watching him, but my feet wouldn't move. I couldn't believe a man, a grown man, a man I'd known for almost a year, asked me to attend church with him. What do you mean what's so shocking about that? I've never been asked by anyone to visit their church before, that's all. I guess the first time I received an invite is a shock, and that it came from a man I'm showing interest in makes it a double whammy.

Some of Myles' family members were there on our first church outing. It was wonderful. He has three sisters and one brother. His father is deceased. That Sunday I met his mother, two of his sisters, and five of his seven nieces and nephews. His mother invited us back to her house for Sunday dinner but Myles declined, telling her he'd made reservations for us at the soul food restaurant where we first went to lunch.

Mrs. Harper was a short Brazil nut shell colored heavyset woman with welcoming eyes. She wore a pale pink suit and had matching accessories down to her sequined shoes. The feather in her wide pink hat flapped with every word she said.

"Well, well now, aren't you the big spender? Before you, Lynnde, my Myles was over for Sunday dinner and every day of the week in between. You must be mighty special if he's turning down his momma's cooking."

I felt a little embarrassed at her comment, but when she took my hands and started smiling, the feeling left. His sisters were very cordial to me, but I know I was definitely the topic at their dinner table. Both our mothers know each other from various functions, so I can only imagine the conversations they had about us. Every time his mother sees me, she mentions that she can't wait for Myles to make her a grandmother. She does this while she's yelling at her grandkids that visit her everyday.

Shortly after Myles and I started dating, I was always invited to his sister's homes for dinner and to every womanly function they attended. I've never been to so many baby and bridal showers in my life. I'm not complaining, though. They were always genuine in their invitations and told me what to expect, so when they talked to each other with their eyes, I knew exactly what was said. His family accepted me right from the start, and receiving love from them comes easily. Some people go their entire lives not meeting anyone who shows truly genuine care and concern that comes from the heart. Meeting Myles gave me the chance to receive real love from an entire family. If you could see me, you'd see what gratitude and love look like.

On the second anniversary of Esta's death, Myles and I went to the cemetery together. He paid his respects and told me to take all the time I needed, he'd wait in the car. When I went back to the car, he had the sweetest gift I ever received. It was a dachshund puppy that makes me cry every time I look at him. Giving me the dog is one of the caring things Myles does for me. If I mention I forgot to get a certain item at the store or that I'd like to try something, he makes sure I have it. He says my wish is his command.

Many of the gifts I receive I didn't ask for, but I appreciate all of them. I don't love Myles because he gives me material possessions either if that's what you're thinking. Sometimes, he'll draw me a silly picture that brings a smile to my face on my twentieth time looking at it. He sings songs over the phone or to my answering machine so I can hear his voice anytime during the day. The times he calls me at 3:43 in the morning because he can't sleep until he hears my voice, knowing he talked to me a few hours earlier, are moments I treasure, also. Those are the special things about him I love the most.

Before, I'd go into detail about what the men I meet look like, but not this time. This time when I say looks don't matter, that's what I mean. It's always someone in this world who looks better than you, whether you want to admit it or not. There will always be a woman with bigger breasts, a rounder butt, a sexier look, longer hair, a better complexion, no cellulite, prettier hands and feet, a prettier smile, bright eyes or a size twenty-two waist.

How about sexy lips that can wear any shade of lipstick, a face that can wear any color makeup, and look fine doing so? I'm sure you don't want your man looking at or describing her to you, wondering why you can't wear your hair like hers, and on and on the drama will go. Now, don't go turning up your lips at me. The only woman that needs to care about his physical appearance is I. I used to be so into how tall a man was, how flawless his skin complexion was, or how many blemishes were on his face, and how white and straight his teeth were. I'm not settling for anything, and will never say as long as he's not musty I'll take him.

I will settle for a man who believes in God. A man who believes in himself, believes in me, and loves me, just me. I want him unselfishly, un-judgmentally, unconditionally, and faithfully. This is the kind of love I deserve to get and I am going to give. Who said he must be ugly if she won't tell us what he looks like? Trust me, dear reader. He's not ugly. I'll never use the word ugly to describe another human being again. We all look different, that's all.

If you're thinking Myles is different, he is. He's different from anyone I've ever met, and I'm accepting him just the way he is. Okay, okay, the man is fine, but that's all you're going to get from me. Everyone's perception of beauty is different, and the way I see Myles is beautiful to me, regardless of what anyone else thinks.

Our honeymoon, which is a gift from Myles' siblings, will be a seven-day cruise of the Caribbean. I've always wanted to go on a cruise, or to any exotic place, and going with my husband will make it ideal.

Myles' mother, who I call Miss Sophie, said she heard all women get pregnant on cruises, so she should be a grandma in no time at all. I don't know when or where she listened to that, but if we do manage to make a baby, I'll probably be the first pregnant woman who floats.

Myles and I don't really have a time frame for children but we both want them. He says if we have to try everyday until they come, he won't mind. He's the first person besides Esta that knows about my miscarriage. He comforted me by saying it wasn't my fault and not to let it worry me anymore. Myles eased my mind even further by saying if we aren't able to have a child by the first God given way, we'd go with the second and adopt. It doesn't matter to him. It only matters that we were going to be raising our child together. I told you he's perfect.

Now listen up as I tell you of our beautiful proposals to one another. We'd been seeing each other a little less than two years and things were going marvelously. We always had long discussions on what we wanted out of life and from each other, and knew the most fulfilling way this would happen for us was as a married couple. Myles and I connected on every level, but we didn't know our proposals would come from each other at the same time and day.

My workweek was a very busy one, and Myles invited me over for dinner that Friday. I'd been putting in long hours trying to get things ready for the new boutique, and I thought of him constantly, wishing I had him to come home to every night.

We saw each other everyday, but living together was not an option. He said the only woman he'd ever live with was his wife or his mother. I totally agreed, having tried the living together routine and didn't care to try it again. I felt I was way past the point of playing house, and you can only play a made up game so many times before you start to change the rules.

Deciding to ask Myles to marry me didn't make me feel embarrassed. Love is love, and if both of you are giving and receiving it equally, it shouldn't matter who asks or does anything first, as long as the results are benefiting both of you. Asking him to marry me had been on my mind for the past three months. Being away from him or close to him for that matter made me realize he was truly the man I wanted to marry. He was the one good thing I wouldn't let pass me by.

Someone else showed me that Myles and I were meant for each other. It wasn't either of our family members, a coworker, or a friend. It was someone who I hadn't thought about in years. He wouldn't have crossed my mind if he didn't show up in the boutique looking for something I could never give. Seeing Otto, yes Otto, didn't startle me, annoy me, or make me happy. I don't think I was even surprised by him. I can't quite explain how I felt because I'm not really sure how you explain the feeling of nothing, followed by heart palpitations, and then nothing again. Humph, I guess that's how you explain it.

The one man whom I used to love, the one man who I'd do anything for, and wait any amount of time for him to do nothing for me, walked into the boutique. I did feel dirty and ashamed for a second because I knew I loved another man, but I still looked at him and thought he was fine. For a moment I wondered why we weren't together. I then felt bad, but the thought came so quick I had no time to control it.

The last time I saw Otto was the day of Esta's funeral, and I hadn't spoken to him since the telephone incident. I trembled slightly, wanting him to leave, but not until he told me why he was there, and what it was he wanted. I should never have wanted to talk to him again, but there had to be a reason for my feeling of interest, and I needed to find out what it was.

Otto grew closer to me and I muttered, "Damn he looks good." I might as well get this over with now. "Otto Parker? Is that you? How are you?"

"Hello, Miss Lee. How are you? You're looking very, very, well these days. How about a hug for an old friend?"

I should've given him a handshake, but I didn't think about that until our hug was completed. You'd think a pistol went off with the way I walked from behind the counter and stretched my arms out. Sometimes you don't realize what you'd do until you're in the act.

"Oh, Lynnde, it's so nice to see you. I wanted to come here sooner and congratulate you, but I never knew what would be a good time. Every time I see you is a good time, so here I am. Are you busy?"

*What does he want?* "No, Otto. I'm not busy. Is everything all right? I mean, I haven't seen you in so long. Do you need something special for a lady friend?" Why am I hoping he says no? *What? Have you lost your mind?*

"No, I'm not here to shop. I'd like to talk to you if I can. Can you meet me someplace with a little more privacy?"

Returning to my senses I responded, "Otto, what's this about? It's been quite a while since we've talked. What could you possibly have to say now?" *Thank God.*

Otto crossed his arms behind him and spread his legs slightly, taking on a soldier's stance. "I know this seems strange, but I promise you it's not. I've been thinking about you lately, and I need to tell you some things. I hope your response is positive but if not, I'll keep trying."

*Girl, slap the shit out of this fool and tell him to leave!* "Does this pertain to business because if it doesn't, I don't think there's really anything I should hear from you." I should be ashamed of myself for wanting to hear his voice and what he had to say, but the reason for this has to be coming soon.

"Lynnde, please. I know a lot of time has passed but please, just hear me out this one time. I don't have the right to ask you for anything but please, say you'll listen to me."

I've never witnessed a look of worry on Otto's face before. Maybe it was something of importance to him. I wouldn't betray Myles if I talked to Otto, and I'd surely let Myles know that Otto came to see me.

"Otto, you seem very serious, and I guess it wouldn't hurt to hear you out. The shop closes at nine and I'm usually here until 9:30 or ten. You can come back then if you like."

"Thanks, Lynnde. I'll see you at 9:30, okay?"

"Bye."

Otto walked out of the boutique, and I went and stood behind the counter. What had I just done? *Do you want me to tell you?* I didn't want to talk to him or hear what he had to say. *You know what? I'm not going to get upset. You've come a long way. I trust you.*

What is it about Otto that won't let me say no? I know I don't love him, we all know that. Why didn't I tell him I'm involved with, no, am in love with someone, and I don't think we have anything to say to each other? See, I know the answer to my question and never thought the day would come when I'd have the chance to reveal it to all of you.

All these years, deep down inside, I've wanted Otto to come back to me. I never mentioned it through Desmond, Terrance, or Taylor, but I've secretly wanted one more chance with him. Just one more chance to show him I was the ideal woman, and I could make things right. I wanted him to need and desire me, and to come and tell me. This thought settled in my mind, and I started to believe it was the truth.

I love Myles and am going to ask him to marry me. I've moved on in my life, and this mind made-up truth with Otto shouldn't exist anymore. I've waited so long for this opportunity, and I feel I have to go through with it. It shouldn't have been there when I went through my other relationships, but I made it stay for the duration. I thought if I were with him, I wouldn't have had any heartache. Being with Otto would have made my life all right.

We didn't have a good relationship, but I made it seem that way. Our relationship was better than all the rest that followed, at least that was my pretend thought. I surmised that Otto and I should be together, and it was his fault I had to sleep alone and feel pain from another.

I don't feel that way today, yesterday, or last year, but my made-up truth seemed so real. The reason for Otto's appearance has got to be for me. The time has come for me to confront my made-up truth and tell it it's not real. Just because you've loved someone and still care for them in a mankind way or think about a person from time to time doesn't mean you still love them or want to be with them. These feelings are mistaken and mixed up, and you could end up going through life putting all of your energy and time into someone who's not deserving of what you have to offer.

I did this with my feelings for Otto. I used to love him, so I felt I always should. He didn't love me and never would, but made-up truths cloud your vision of the real ones. I realized this years ago, but the times you feel the loneliest, are the times the feelings are the strongest. If you only had that person in your life, it would be perfect, and you'd be lonely no more.

That's a lie I hope you don't tell yourself. Being with the wrong someone will never take the feeling of being alone away. Doing everything in your human power to please them will never make you or them happy. The hurt that comes from trying and trying, but never getting it right, will always be there. That's when the made-up truth starts to set in. You hold on to nothing, waiting and wishing for it to turn into something that you know in your heart and mind will never happen. But since it's a made-up truth, that only you believe, you keep holding on tightly, making yourself sick from stressing and waiting for one more chance. That chance you really don't want to take to go back and make it right.

Walking backwards will get you hurt. Who knows what you may bump into or fall over. Think about all the things you may step in because you're not looking. No one will tell you if something's coming to hurt you because if you're too stupid to turn around and look, why should anyone else waste their time?

That's the reason for my having to talk to Otto. I'm going to tell him my made-up truth doesn't exist anymore. If he has one for me, it'll never come to pass. In the past I've wanted to tell Otto many things and never could. That won't be the case tonight. I love Myles. I'm not telling myself that to stop me from walking backwards. It's being said because it's the real truth. The only one I believe.

This talk is mostly for Otto. He needs to know the Lynnde he knew moved out of the country, had her passport revoked, and will never make a return trip.

At eight o'clock I wanted to go home but hey, I have nothing to be afraid of, and leaving will give the made-up truth power that it's not privileged to have.

At 9:23 a car pulled up, and I wished it wasn't Otto. The moment I'd waited so long for could wait a little longer. My wish would not come true. It was Otto riding in his new Mercedes that I just happened to hear about from one of our faithful customers, Mrs. Roberts. She was a retired widower who kept up with all the gossip, good, and bad. She knew I used to date him many moons ago and knew I was with Myles, but you know how some people are. They just have to say things to try and get any kind of reaction. I lied and told her I'd heard of his new car, so she'd stop blabbing sooner than she planned.

Otto's talk with me must be important for him to be on time. He was never on time when we were together, and it's much too late to try to make a first impression all over again. You only get that chance once in a lifetime, so you'd better make it right when it happens.

I don't know why I feel butterflies in my stomach. He's not the man I want. Maybe they're here for my excitement in telling him I've moved on, and I don't have room for him in my new place. Yeah, that's it. That's all it is.

I walked to the door, unlocked it, and asked God to help me by giving me extra strength, just in case my made-up truth puts up a fight.

As I opened the door, Otto approached with a bouquet of flowers in his hands and a sexy smile on his face. I swear he looks better than I remembered.

"Hey, Lynnde. I'm glad you didn't change your mind and leave. These are for you."

"Thank you, Otto. They're beautiful, but you didn't have to."

"Yes I did. You're a beautiful woman and beautiful women deserve beautiful things."

Okay, God. Can you give me that extra strength now? I'm just kidding dear reader; I'm better than that, remember?

"Otto, will you please tell me what's on your mind?'

"Let's sit down, okay?'

"Come on. We can sit over here." Over here was in front of a try on room.

"Lynnde, the first thing I have to say is I'm sorry. I'm sorry for all the crazy things I did to you. I should've treated you much better, and I'm sorry that I didn't. Can you find it in your heart to forgive me?"

My mouth wasn't hanging open, and I didn't have a stunned look on my face. "Otto, I haven't thought about anything that happened between us in years. I forgave you a long time ago." *Ha, ha, ha!*

"Thank you. Hearing that makes what I have to say so much easier. Lynnde, I've always loved you. Believe it or not, I loved you the first time I saw you at the party and never stopped."

Now, I'm not stupid and I don't believe him, but I managed a half smile, and let him continue talking.

"I never treated you with respect because I didn't know how to. On the outside I may have looked like a grown man, but I wasn't ready for everything you had to offer. I didn't know how to handle it and instead of running, I should've talked to you. I've matured and grown over the years. The woman I want to settle down with is you. It's not too late for us so let's try one more time for loves sake. Okay?"

*Loves sake? What the hell is that?* Otto's words are running through my mind and leaving, right behind my made-up truth. I sat facing Otto knowing what to say, but waiting to make sure he was finished with his presentation. I didn't want him interrupting me.

"Lynnde, I know we haven't had any contact with each other, but I had to stay away. I had to take some time to get things right. All I needed was to see that there was no other woman for me. I couldn't go on any longer without telling you this. I know you still love me, and you really shouldn't let that love die. I'm here for you and only you, just like you've always wanted. We can make it work. How about it?"

What the hell did this fool just say to me? *I was just going to ask you that.* Laughing in his face will make him think something is wrong with me, so I continued to sit in silence.

"If you need time to think about this, I'll understand. We can go to dinner tomorrow to celebrate if you like. How about six o'clock?"

I think I'd better start talking now.

"Otto Parker. Otto Parker. Please don't speak until I finish taking. Otto Parker. I loved you more than you'll ever know for a very long time. Once I finally realized you'd never love me in return, the one thing that hurt me the most wasn't the cheating or the lying. It was the plain truth that you never knew how much I loved you, and you never would. You never understood the depth of my feelings because if you did, some of the words that came out of your mouth would've never been given a voice."

Otto sat up in his seat and faced me head on.

"I wanted you, needed you, loved you, and waited for you in my mind for so long that telling you this now feels so very sweet. Thank you for the opportunity to release this waste. I've long ago accepted the fact that you're not the man for me. You'll never be capable of accepting the love I give or giving me that love in return."

A puzzled look graced Otto's face and stayed there for the duration of our chat.

"Yes, you are beautiful on the eyes and most likely can spend more money on me than is required, but those aren't the only things I want. I need a man to take care of me and love me. Money is a blessing but love is the seed. Knowing you can never give me unconditional love doesn't make me a better person than you, but instead, makes me the wrong person for you."

Otto added on a stone-face as I continued.

"Otto, I need someone who gives love the way I do and I have him. Trying to make a wrong a right that never existed is something I won't do again. For so long after you left me, with shit on my face, I felt useless. I know you were a different person then, but you came here with something to say and that requires your listening to something, also. You made me feel unattractive, ugly, nasty, stupid, and lost. I know it wasn't all your fault because I allowed it."

Otto began to speak but I cut him off. He was not allowed to interrupt my roll.

"I used to wonder did I ever mean anything to you but now, I don't care. It doesn't matter and it never will. I know I was never anything more than a sometime lay and an all the time cook. We're not the same, and I don't blame you for anything. I won't go back, though. I can't. I don't love you, don't want you, and the needing feelings I had for you so long ago no longer exist. I'm not sorry for saying these words Otto, but sorry you had to hear them."

He hung his head and shook it slowly from side to side as I wrapped up.

"I thank you for coming to talk to me. You've just proven a fact I already knew. I know when something or someone special enters your life; you have to hold onto them tightly. You have to let them know this is the place where the both of you belong. It doesn't matter what the person who came before has to say. The love you have now deserves all that you can give because they appreciate everything they're going to get. So no Otto, I can't be the woman for you because I'm the woman for someone else. I'm in love with Myles Harper. He's the man I deserve and the man who deserves me."

I stood up signaling to Otto that it was time for him to leave and added, "I've said all I have to say and it's late. I really need to get home. You take care of yourself. You'll find the special one for you. Just know that I'm no longer sorry it's not me."

Otto didn't respond. He sat and stared at me the entire time I spoke, probably trying to connect the face with the voice. He couldn't believe the words he heard, but he knew they were true.

"Lynnde, I'll never forget you. I'm glad you're happy. A special lady like you deserves more than her share."

"Goodbye, Otto."

We stood up and he half leaned forward to hug me. When he noticed I wasn't joining in on the gesture, he stopped. I followed him to the door and was glad he didn't say anything else. He didn't face me until he was seated in his car and gave me a quick wave before he pulled off.

It's a liberating feeling when you realize you can let go of hurt and let something superb into your life. You never think you're going to stop hurting or that anyone will ever love you, but trust me, dear reader, that's not true. Giving your love to the right someone makes all the wrong ones obsolete. You can't even remember what the pain used to feel like when the right love comes along. No more made up truths for this girl. No more past practices either. Everything that's in my life right now is for me and asking Myles to marry me will make sure things stay that way.

On my way over to Myles's place, I thought I'd be nervous. I had an engagement ring for him and I was ready. No ladies, the engagement ring wasn't a form of begging, but a show of how real and true my feelings are for him. So what I begged in the past, and what did I tell you about bringing up someone else's history? I'm not going to get into your backside like your behavior calls for; I'm too good for that. Now with that being said, do you mind if I continue on in the present? Thank you.

If you think I'm the first woman who's ever asked a man to marry her, you're so mistaken. No, I can't give you any names of women that I know who've done it, but there's never just one person who does anything. There is just one person who tells it, though, and in this case, I happen to be that lovely number.

I don't mind. I have it all planned out, and wasting time is not part of the plan. No, there's no need to rush, I know. My vibrant love is leading me along, and right now, it doesn't want to slow down. If you've never felt this way I don't expect you to understand what I'm talking about. I've always told you the truth, and trust me; this kind of love is superior.

Seeing Myles as I pulled up to his gated condominium community made my need to ask him to marry me grow stronger. I pulled through the gates slowly and asked Myles if he was going my way.

"I'm going any way you are, gorgeous woman. Is my response correct? May I ride with you?"

"Your response is correct, and yes you may. Now hop your sexy self in so we can get going."

"I'll do anything for you, Miss Lee. I have a nice relaxing night planned for us, and the sooner we get started, the better."

Myles sat in the passenger side and we shared a passionate kiss. My foot pressing down on the gas pedal was the only reason we stopped.

"You see what I made you do, girl. I'm the reason your foot was on the pedal. My kiss sent waves of electricity all the way down to your feet."

We laughed and then proceeded to Myles' condo.

"So, tell me, Myles. Why were you at the gate? We're you waiting on someone special?"

"I couldn't wait any longer to see you. I would've walked down the street if I knew exactly what direction you were coming in."

"Thank you, Myles. Hearing you say that has made more than my day. I couldn't wait to see you either."

"Well, you're here now and I plan to keep you safe and sound in my arms. I know you're worried about the new store, but I want you to forget all about work tonight. For starters, I barbequed ribs and I can't wait to help you lick the sauce from your fingers."

"Umm. I can't wait, either."

"Good then. Let's get out of this car and get started, gorgeous."

I parked the car and Myles hopped out, ran around to my side, and opened the door. He took my hand, and we stayed that way until we reached his condo. Candles were burning all around the room, and Teddy Pendergrass was telling me to 'come on over to his place' and 'turn off the lights.'

"I'm sorry, Teddy, not tonight. I'm at the place where I belong, and the lights are already out, so there's no need for me to leave." I said this out loud and Myles turned to me and laughed.

"Lynnde, I always love to see you smile. Can we dance before we eat? I've been waiting all day to hold you close.

Knowing you'd rather have me instead of Teddy makes me want to hold and squeeze you right now."

"Squeeze me, Myles. Squeeze me."

We met in the center of the den and pulled close to one another. If it were possible to slip inside each other, it would've happened then. Every moment I spent with Myles was beyond lovely, and this was the ideal time to ask him to marry me. He felt the same way because the exact same words that came from my mouth came from his. Talk about being created for one another. Neither one of us were shocked that our words were the same, nor that they were said with the same rhythm. These things happen when you let them come about in their own time, just the way they're supposed to.

We were joined together as one in our dance and would stay that way in every other aspect of our lives. The song that played was another Teddy Pendergrass song called, When Somebody Loves You Back. We may not have been on the same beat as the music, but we were definitely in tune with the lyrics. Teddy was singing how it feels when you have a fifty-fifty love. On a few occasions, Teddy threw down because he really stressed how good it is to give love, and be loved in return. One of those occasions was created for Myles and me, and that's when we spoke our words of marriage to one another.

"Myles?"

"Yes, Lynnde?"

"I have something to ask you."

"Lynnde, I have something to ask you, too."

"Do you want to go first?"

"No, baby. I think we should go together because we both know what it is."

"Myles?

"Lynnde?

"Will you marry me?"

The yeses came out in unison along with everything else we did that night. Teddy hung right in there with us. I guess he felt this was his doing, so he might as well stay around to see how things turned out. I had his engagement ring in my pants pocket, and he had mine in his shirt pocket. The only time that evening we weren't within one centimeter of each other was when we pulled apart to place our rings on our fingers. It doesn't matter what the rings looked like, or how much they cost, but for all of you I just-have-to-know-dear readers out there, I'll tell you. I purchased Myles a solid gold band with diamonds around it. My ring is a four-carat princess cut boulder with baguettes intertwined in it.

Myles and I didn't do much talking that night because neither one of us felt the need for conversation. We knew no goal was unattainable and had just taken the first steps to reach them. Our night continued with dancing, dinner, and a few activities that I'll leave to your imagination.

I may not have made many right decisions in the past, but taking the initiative and asking Myles to marry me has given me immeasurable confidence. I'd still have that confidence if he said no, but I probably wouldn't see it as vivid as I do now. Feeling it was the right thing to do and receiving a proposal from him didn't hurt any, either. I do have a few more words I want to say to you, but right now, I want to stay in the moment of remembering my proposal night. Although I love your company, I've been reminded that a little alone time in your thoughts is always a good thing.

Wait for Love: A Black Girl's Story is the first novel from Wanda D. Hudson. Miss Hudson also has a collection of romantic short stories titled, LuvMe. The next novel from Miss Hudson will be, Dating Wanda, which will be available in the fall of 2009.

Miss Hudson has a story included in the NY Times Bestseller Zane anthology, Succulent - Chocolate Flava ll, which is available now.

Check out Purple Panties, Miss Hudson is in that Zane anthology as well.

Please visit Wanda D. Hudson's website - www.wandadhudson.com - to read excerpts and to stay in the know about this sexy dynamic writer.

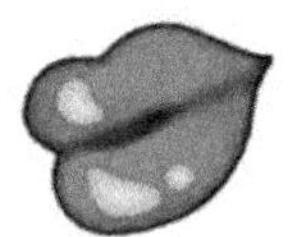

*Miss Luv's Books*

®*Miss Luv's Books*

*Because Everybody Needs A Little Luv!*

www.ingramcontent.com/pod-product-compliance
Lightning Source LLC
LaVergne TN
LVHW020525100826
845148LV00010B/1349
*9780981532516*